INHERITANCE

Colleen Snyder

MONDAY

Glass shattered. Metal screamed as it shredded into a thousand shards. Tires exploded from the force of being violently twisted and dragged along the gravel embankment. The chassis of the Beetle spun wildly, careening through the underbrush, gouging saplings, and finally coming to an abrupt halt at the foot of an unyielding oak tree. All the myriad pieces-parts found a resting place. And finally, silence. A strangled voice whispered brokenly, "Lord Jesus, help me. Please…" The voice trailed off, "Jeff…" In the distance, a siren wailed.

* * *

Buzzzz… Buzzzzz… Jeff Farrell looked at the caller ID on his phone but didn't bother answering. He focused all his attention on his chess tutor, Trey Weller, who prepared his next move. Trey leaned forward in his wheelchair, looked at the chessboard from one side, from the other side, below eye level… The eccentric man had a thoroughness about all he did. Why he did it, Jeff didn't know. But it always worked.

Jeff volunteered at the community center as a "bridge-building" venture for the fire station. A week after Jeff returned from his second job as janitor to Camp Grace in West Virginia, Trey had rolled into the center. Dark hair, fair complected, Trey was only two years younger than Jeff. He vaguely reminded Jeff of Collin, the love of his life and his intended forever wife. The eyes…something about the eyes. Jeff couldn't quite define the resemblance. But he saw it. And while the man's body may have been tied to his wheelchair, his mind proved sharper than most. Even if it did work in strange ways.

Trey talked to the pieces as he set the board. He made sure each piece knew where to stand. He also made sure the pieces knew the opposing team was the enemy, and it was the duty of the white team to eliminate the brown team. Nothing personal, just how the game is played. Only after he had spoken to each piece and scolded the opposition for daring to challenge his superiority did the game begin. Jeff didn't know what all the run-up might be about, but in the two months Trey had been tutoring Jeff at the community center, Jeff had yet to win a game. Their weekly sessions, sometimes more often, typically ended in a lesson in humility for Jeff. But he learned. That's what mattered. He learned.

Jeff's phone buzzed again. He pulled it from his uniform pocket and glanced at it. Not the station. Fine. He ignored it.

Trey moved his bishop. "Check."

The phone buzzed again. Jeff stared at the caller ID. His father this time. Dad would wait. "Show me."

Trey looked at Jeff sideways. "Aren't you going to answer it?"

"No. I'm on call for duty, so the only one I need to worry about is the station." *Buzz…*

Trey seemed unconvinced. "Except for your lady friend."

Jeff reminded him patiently, "Her name is Collin, Trey. And nope. Not even for her. I pay good money for these lessons, and I need all the minutes I can get. When the game is over, or the hour is up, I'll check the phone." The phone buzzed again. Dad again. Maybe…no. It could wait. It would have to.

Trey stared at Jeff a moment and shook his head. He looked back at the board. "I don't know about you, Jeffery, my man."

Jeff studied the board, studied the pieces, moved his queen, and smiled. "There. Now, what have you got?" *Buzz… Buzz…*

Trey reached across the board, moved a harmless-looking pawn. "Checkmate."

Jeff groaned. "Right. Again. Score another one for the Master." Jeff glanced at the phone. "We have time for one more round if you can beat me in five minutes. Or less."

Buzz… Buzz… Buzz…

"I'd hope I've taught you better than to fall for the same trick twice. Not twice in the same day."

Jeff shrugged. "No promises. Okay, I'll check these messages, then I'll take you home." Jeff dialed his voicemail. His father's voice came through level and even but filled with concern. Jeff listened to the message, his heart thumping hard in his chest. When the message finished, Jeff hung up, whispering, "Lord Jesus, help her."

Trey's face reflected immediate concern. "What's wrong, Jeffery, my man?"

Jeff swallowed hard. "It's…my dad. Collin wrecked her car."

Trey's voice trembled. "She's okay, though, right? Right?"

Jeff struggled to get his voice under control. "They…uh…they're still trying to cut her out of the wreck." Jeff's gut screamed he should leave. He should throw the red light on his jeep and race across town. Collin…the love of his life. He had to get there. Now. Now…there might not be a later…go now!

But Trey would have no way home. While the young tutor used MobiMobile to get to the center, getting home the same way proved less sure. There had been times Trey would have been sitting for hours had Jeff not insisted on taking him home. Jeff couldn't leave him stranded, could he?

But Collin needs me. I need to be there for her. She could…

A calm assurance swept over him. *You don't think I can take care of her from here? Or can I only work if you're right there beside her?* The Lord's rebuke, though gentle, remained firm.

Jeff ached against the truth he knew. God held Collin. Jeff chauffeured Trey. Period. No arguments.

It took extreme discipline to say, "I'll take you home…"

Trey's voice cracked. "No. No. I'll get home by myself. You go."

Jeff forced himself to remain calm. "No, Trey. I'll take you home. I can't do anything there any more than I can here." Inwardly, Jeff poured out his anguish at the loss of time it would take. Critical time he could be at the crash scene…the hospital…holding her hand…

God held her hand, right? Whose hands would hold her safest? Whose hands could heal? Whose…

Trey interrupted Jeff's thoughts. "Your God. The one you're always telling me about. The one I don't believe exists. You say he hears you. Talk to him. Now. I want to hear you."

Surprised at the vehemence in Trey's tone, Jeff said aloud what he prayed in his heart. "Lord God in Heaven"—Trey unexpectedly took Jeff's hand—"be with Collin. You know how I feel about her…how much I love her…"

Jeff's voice caught. He forced himself to continue. "But You love her more than I ever could. She belongs to You. I know Your will is perfect, Lord." Jeff swallowed hard.

God wanted honesty. Honesty He would get. "I'm selfish. I want her here…" Jeff's voice cracked again. He angrily brushed back the fear threatening to overwhelm him. "…here to marry, to grow old together. You said to tell You what's on my heart. Let her live, Lord."

He should have followed it with "Not my will, but Yours be done." Except the Lord knew his heart. Jeff wanted to say it. Wanted to but couldn't. Not yet.

So quietly Jeff almost didn't hear, Trey mumbled, "Ditto what he said. Except wanting to marry her. That would be weird."

"Amen." Jeff looked at his friend and tutor. "God hears every prayer, Trey. Even from someone who isn't sure He exists."

Trey dropped his head slightly. "If you say so." He looked up. "Will you call me and let me know how she is? Soon? As soon as you see her?"

Jeff nodded. "I will, Trey. I promise."

"Take me home. And I'll try talking to the God of yours for her."

Jeff walked out beside the young man.

* * *

Collin Walker woke to the sound of a siren wailing mercilessly in her head. If she didn't move…if she stayed still and didn't even breathe, maybe it would stop. She exhaled slowly.

A voice called out, "She's stopped breathing!" Strong hands pushed a mask against her face, forcing oxygen into her lungs. *Brilliant idea. Got any better ones?* She fought against the positive pressure of the ventilator in a vain attempt to keep her lungs from expanding against her possibly crushed ribs. The wailing continued. The throbbing in her brain kept time with the siren. Unable to fight pain on two fronts, Collin let the darkness take her.

"Pain? You don't know pain! I'll give you pain! No crying!

Ever! You don't cry! You want to be strong? To earn my love? Never cry. Never show emotion. You're useless! You're worthless. You soil everything you touch!" Collin's darkness filled with memories. *"Oh, you fell. You broke your foot? Get up! You're not hurt. You pretend your hurt! Get up. Walk. I better not see you trying to limp. I know broken...you're not broken. When I break you, you're broken."*

"Smart mouth! Always with the smart mouth! Disrespect me? Think again. I'll hit you all I want. And you will stand there, and you will take it. You got it? You won't make a sound. You do, I'll beat your brother as well. You love him? Prove it. Take the punishment you deserve. Take it all. Take it to spare your brother. But you won't. You're weak. You're useless. Worthless."

Collin moaned. The darkness continued, but the scene shifted. *"This isn't your rich, fancy home anymore. This is the streets, baby, and you get tough or die. You want to live? No? There's the bridge. Seen a lot of jumpers in my time. Do it. Save the city the cost of burying you. Catfish in there big enough to eat a man whole."*

Pushing past the pain, she whispered, "Live. I want to live."

"Get tough! Be tough. Be the toughest one out there. Don't wait for them to come after you. You go challenge their toughest one, and you beat the snot out of him. Make sure you do it right. Make sure he doesn't get back up. You're either the best, or you're dead. Got it? Never let them know you're hurt. Never let them see you cry. Ever. Makes 'em think they can get to you. No pain. Never show pain. Got it? Never ever never..."

* * *

Consciousness returned. Someone tried moving Collin's extremities. Any time an arm or leg or hand or foot or finger or toe moved, waves of pain cascaded through her body. She groaned inwardly. Collin opened her eyes and saw a female in scrubs attempting to be encouraging while checking Collin's limbs. "Take it easy. You'll be fine."

Collin didn't know the definition of "fine," but it certainly didn't feel like this. At least the wailing had stopped. Her head, however, continued to throb. She seethed, "Tell my brain."

"The CT scan showed no cracks or breaks." She paused. "No

recent cracks or breaks. What sport did you play when you were younger?"

Collin wanted to fire off some quick-witted retort, but thinking hurt too much. "Basketball."

"Ever consider taking up something less violent? Like, hockey? At least they wear helmets."

Collin grunted. "I fell a lot. Clumsy child, they said. Can I get something for my head?"

The woman in scrubs entered notes on a computer. Collin couldn't make out a name tag or embroidered identification. Of course, she could barely make out the person as human. "Which hospital am I at?"

"East. The ambulance brought you in." The woman checked her records. "We'll get you out of pain soon. We're waiting on your medical records to be updated. We don't want to give you something you might be allergic to."

Collin closed her eyes and gritted her teeth. "Collin Walker. Birthdate 1-21-um…twenty-six years ago. Height five-six. Weight one fifteen. No allergies. Multiple surgeries for various and sundry things. No next of kin." Well… Collin added softly, "Almost a fiancé. He can be my emergency contact. Jeff Farrell. 614-555-0296. Are you a doctor?"

The woman nodded. "Doctor Roni."

"How long have I been here?" Maybe talking would take her mind off the roaring headache. Re-direction. Alternative reality. Anything. Right? Right??

"Squad brought you in here about an hour ago."

"What time is it?"

"It's almost three."

"A.M. or P.M?"

"Afternoon."

Collin groaned. "I was on my way to work… How can it be so late?"

"The EMTs said they had a hard time cutting you out of the wreckage. From the pictures I saw, you're in better shape than your car."

Collin let it sink in. After a moment, she said softly, "Thank You, Lord. Thank You." Collin attempted a deep breath. It hurt. A lot. "Beyond the ribs, is anything broken?" Maybe she should ask what had survived intact. Might be a shorter list. Collin winced as the pain in her head escalated. She closed her eyes and whispered, "Please, Lord."

She heard Dr. Roni say, "Your records are here. We can give you morphine. I'll write the order."

"Thank you." Collin took slow, controlled breaths, trying to keep the pain in check. But the roaring dragon in her head ignored her and launched itself to new heights. Darkness took her once again.

* * *

Jeff counted to ten, counted again—and again. When he felt he could speak without owing anyone an apology, he addressed the unfamiliar emergency room registrar. "As I told you before, she has no blood family around here. She had her phone and all the contact information in the car. The paramedics couldn't salvage enough of her car to find a phone." Salvaging Collin had been a miracle in itself. One for which Jeff continued to be thankful. Even as he fought the privacy system. "Collin and I are going to be engaged in two months." Jeff indicated to his father and mother sitting on the bench next to the wall. "We're the closest thing to a family she has right now. So please, if you won't let any of us go in to see her, at least let us know how she is. Is she even alive?" He felt the anger and frustration building again. Maybe he should count to ten in Cantonese. Especially since he didn't know Cantonese.

Dad placed a hand on Jeff's shoulder. "Jeffery, go sit with your mother. I'll see if I can do anything. Go." Jeff nodded silently, turned, and walked to his mother. His mom patted the chair beside her cheerfully. "Here, Jeffery. Sit by me. I'm sure Collin is fine, dear. She'll be walking out of the ER any time now. And we can all go home and have dinner like we planned. She is coming over tonight, isn't she? I thought I remembered you said so. And Leesa is looking forward to her coming over. Your sister loves Collin. We all do. I'll never understand why you haven't asked her to marry you yet. You'll be the sweetest couple, I know."

Jeff let his mother prattle. In times like this, he missed the "old Mom"—the Lacey who had been before the stroke took her personality and fire. The "old Mom" would have busted in the doors and demanded answers. In the years since his mother's stroke, her personality had morphed to "positivity only." Jeff prayed silently, *Lord, I love my mom. But could You restore her mind? Bring back the old Mom? Please?*

The door to the ER bay opened, and to Jeff's ever-mounting frustration, another new staff member came out. Where were all the people who knew him on sight? The normal crew. *Normal might be a poor choice of words. Maybe usual. Never normal.*

The staff member ignored Jeff and his people, going straight to the registrar. The scrubs-clothed man handed the woman behind the desk a notecard. "We've got some preliminary identification on the Jane Doe the EMTs brought in an hour ago. I have her emergency contact number. Call it and see if there is a Jeff Farrell there. Ask him if he knows Collin Walker." He turned to go back to the bay.

Jeff jumped from his chair and all but tackled the man. "Wait! I'm Jeff Farrell. Is Collin alive?"

The man looked at Jeff's uniform with suspicion. "How did you get here when we haven't notified you yet?"

"I'm a paramedic at Station Five. The crew which took the call is…" Jeff swallowed his anger at being questioned. "The guys all know Collin and I are…together." Jeff repeated his question, "Is she alive?"

The man continued to look at Jeff up and down. "Show me some ID." Jeff pulled out both his driver's license and his paramedic ID. The nurse looked at it, looked at Jeff, said, "Yes. She's alive." Relief flooded through Jeff, and his knees went weak. He barely heard the man say, "Doctor Roni is checking her out. I'll inform her Ms. Walker has someone out here waiting."

Jeff closed his eyes and prayed out loud, "Thank You, God. Thank You. Thank You." Nothing else came.

His father came alongside him, placed his hand on his shoulder, and joined Jeff. "Thank You, Father, for the way You take care of Your children. Thank You for Your mercy. Give us the strength we need for whatever You have next for us. But thank You for giving us this glimpse of hope. In Jesus' Name, Amen."

Mom looked up from the magazine she'd been thumbing through. "Did I hear Collin is alright? I told you, Jeffery, you didn't need to be upset. She's fine, dear. You worry so much. I know you love her, but you can't let these little things bother you." The woman looked back at her magazine. She looked at Jeff, a quizzical look in her eyes. She cocked her head a moment as if she sought to remember something. A light of recognition, of depth, of clarity flashed on his mom's face. But it only lasted a moment. Then the light faded. Lacey shrugged and went back to her magazine.

Jeff bent over and kissed his mother. "You're right, Mom. Thank you. I'll try." Jeff turned to his father. Father and son embraced in relief.

Another hour passed before Dr. Roni came out to talk to the family. She introduced herself and leaned against the wall. "Your friend is a very lucky woman."

Jeff nodded. "Yeah, I've been told. How is she?"

"She has four cracked ribs. No other broken bones, no internal injuries beyond the bruising you might expect from a less serious crash." The doctor eyed him and asked, "Have you known her long? Do you know any of her history?"

Three months, two days, thirty-six hours... Jeff dissembled slightly, "Awhile. And some of it. Why?"

"Her skull shows a pattern of fractures we don't see except in children who have had…let's say, multiple blunt force traumas to their head. She also has a surprising number of previous breaks in her extremities she says happened in childhood. Some broken more than once."

Jeff let the information rattle around his head. He would need time to properly digest all it might mean, but it did explain some of Collin's quirks. And intensity. Maybe a few other things Jeff had seen in her behavior. He nodded slightly. "Thank you, Dr. Roni. I appreciate all you've done for her. When can we see her?"

"We will keep her at least overnight so we can check on her and make sure there's nothing we missed or nothing develops later. Until she's in a room, I can only allow one person at a time in there."

His dad said softly, "I'll take your mother home, Jeffery. Spend as much time as you need with Collin. Give her our love and prayers." The elder Farrell turned to his wife. "Let's go home, Lacey, my love. Jeffery will let us know how Collin is later."

"Oh, she's not coming home now? Is she not coming to dinner tonight?"

"No, dear, and I'll explain on the way to the house."

The "almost there" look returned to Lacey's face. But the

moment and the memory passed, and she shrugged it off. "Well, if you say so. Kiss her for us, Jeffery, and tell her how disappointed Leesa will be not to see her."

"I will, Mom." Jeff kissed his mother lightly on the cheek, hugged his father one last time, and followed Dr. Roni into the empty ER bay.

His first sight of Collin brought flashbacks of multiple car crashes he had worked. Crashes where no one survived. Or survived, but barely. Her face had bruised almost beyond recognition: torn and puffy and red and still covered in dried blood. But her eyes were as bright and sharp as they had ever been, albeit swollen almost shut. He approached the bed carefully, feeling the raw emotion of the day threatening to overwhelm him once again. He bent over and very, very gingerly kissed Collin on top of her head. "I love you, lady."

Collin looked at him. "Your aim is lousy."

Jeff ignored the comment and hugged her as carefully as he could, trying to find someplace he wouldn't hurt her. "There are so many people praying for you right now. You don't have any idea."

Collin said, her voice unsteady, "I think I do. Doctor Roni tells me I shouldn't be here." She swallowed hard. "I told her I shouldn't be here, either. I should be home watching football. Or basketball. Or anything other than the heart monitor."

Dr. Roni shook her head. "No, and no. With your injuries, we're keeping you for twenty-four hours, minimum."

"If I promise I won't sue? I'll find someone's first-born male child to give you." She tried to smile at Jeff and added, "He doesn't qualify."

"Give it up, lady." Jeff squeezed her hand gently. "Let the doctors do what they do. Let your body catch up to itself. Your brain may be all in one piece, but I'm sure other parts will protest by tomorrow."

"Oh, they're protesting now. I'm not listening." Collin paused. "Much."

Jeff knew even the smallest of admission she could be in pain equaled most other people's screaming. They had yet to have the heart-to-heart discussion—the one where she shared why she refused to admit pain. Or ask for help. Or admit defeat.

The two had met at Camp Grace, an extreme sports challenge camp in the mountains of West Virginia. Collin had been there with forty-some other campers and counselors to give the inner-city children a chance to see life from a different perspective. Jeff worked at the camp as the janitor. Their paths crossed over and over—and over and over—until they struck a friendship, which became more. She had shared a little—very little—about her past. How her mother had died when she was five. How her father abused her. She had a twin brother who died at fourteen, playing football. She had accepted the Lord after a street preacher took her in. All bare-bone facts, but not the whos and hows and whys. With conflicting work schedules, finding the time for the conversation had been hard. But it needed to happen. And soon.

Jeff pulled out of the memories. "Take the meds they offer you, let your body adjust and heal, and stay safe. Okay? This one time, do it their way."

"This time. On one condition."

"What?"

"You go home after they get me in a room of my own. I don't need you hanging around this place, ogling the nurses." Collin looked at Dr. Roni. "Or the doctors."

Jeff smiled. "No ogling. I only have eyes for…"

Collin groaned. "Do not sing. I know you can. But don't."

Jeff nodded. "Yes, ma'am. No singing." He dropped the military bearing. "I love you, milady."

Collin sank back in the bed. "I love you, Jeff." She closed her eyes and whispered, "One month, twenty-eight days, and I have no clue how many hours." She opened her eyes and warned, "No, I do not want to know, either."

Jeff stroked her brow. "Sleep, Collin. Sleep and rest and let yourself heal. I'll be here when you wake up." Collin closed her eyes again. Jeff kissed the top of her head tenderly.

Without opening her eyes, Collin whispered, "Aim." Jeff kissed her lips even more gently. She whispered, "G'nite."

Jeff straightened, looked to Dr. Roni. "When will they move her to a room?"

"Probably in the next hour or so. We weren't sure if we needed a bed for her in ICU or not. Apparently not." She motioned to the chair beside the bed. "You can stay with her. I gave her a dose of morphine about an hour ago, so she should sleep. We'll be in and out—"

Jeff interrupted her. "It's a hospital. I know the drill. Thank you for all you've done for Collin, Doctor. You ER doctors are miracle workers."

Dr. Roni accepted the praise. "Thank you." She turned and left the room.

Jeff settled back with a deep sigh. He squeezed Collin's hand and whispered, "I love you."

A thought popped in his head: Trey. He needed to call Trey. As he saw no "No Cell Phones Allowed" signs around, he pulled out his phone and punched in the number.

Trey answered it before the first ring finished. "Is she alive?"

"Yes, she is. And the only things broken are some ribs. She's going to be fine. The doctors can't explain it other than to say she's lucky."

The silence on the other end of the connection told Jeff plenty. Jeff could hear Trey muttering. Finally, the younger man said, "But you can. Right?" It sounded like a challenge. Or a plea.

"God spared her life. He's got work for her here, and so He protected her."

Trey sounded bitter. "So, she's a tool to be used. Otherwise, He lets her die? How is that loving?"

Jeff interrupted quickly. "No. Not like a tool. Next time we get together, I'll try to explain it. If I get caught talking on the phone in here, they might throw me out."

Trey sounded curious. "Where are you?"

"In the ER bay, sitting with Collin. She's asleep, and we're waiting for them to get a room ready."

The younger man's voice grew incredulous. "You're in the ER, and you're calling me? You're with her, and you're talking to me? What is wrong with you? Are you insane?"

"I'm not insane. I promised I'd call as soon as I found out anything. I didn't want you hanging on waiting longer than you had to."

Again, mutters punctuated the silence. "I don't know about you, Jeffery, my man. I don't. But thanks. Thanks for letting me know. Give your lady friend a…um…tell her I'm glad she's not dead. It won't matter to her but tell her anyhow."

"I'll tell her. She wants to meet you when you can get free for lunch or dinner or something. You keep canceling on us."

"I know. I know. I told you my schedule changes from hour to hour. We'll get together, I promise. Hang up and pay attention to your lady friend."

"Collin, Trey. Her name is Collin." The call dropped. Jeff slipped his phone into his pocket. As no monitors or alarms had gone off, he figured the transgression would go unnoticed this time. He said softly, "I'm sorry. I should have gone outside, I know. Next time." Jeff settled back again and began praying silently for anyone he knew. It would be a long list.

WEDNESDAY

Collin gritted her teeth as the transport volunteer wheeled her into the late morning sunshine. No lingering pain would keep her in the hospital. And the headaches would subside. So said the doctors. Give them time. No matter each new one felt more severe than the last, no matter the last one had almost dropped her to her knees with its intensity. Post-concussion headaches, period. They'll get better. Trust the doctor.

Adding to her frustration: no one she called could take her home. Coworkers worked, married friends had children, even the hands and feet and vehicles of Christ had a conflict of schedule. No one but Jeff could help her. Collin groused inwardly. *Not fair, Lord. I planned to tell him. I did. But today? Really?*

Her answer arrived in the form of Jeff's black jeep pulling into the patient pick-up area. Collin could make out a figure in the shotgun seat, but not who it might be. The attendant wheeled Collin to the back door and reminded her, "Remember, no lifting anything heavier than a spoon for four days. Call your primary physician for a follow-up appointment tomorrow. If the headaches get worse, or if you develop any other symptoms—"

"I call my doctor. I know the drill." Collin swallowed her frustration, forced a smile instead. "Thank you for all your help. I appreciate all you've done."

Collin stood, aware each strained and bruised and over-stretched muscle in her body protested all at once. All of them wanted to stay in a reclined, immobile position for a much longer time—like, forever. Collin ignored the cacophony of voices in her head, yelling at the horrendous decision. She should go back to the hospital. Being a total idiot and trying to impress someone never worked, and didn't she still have at least two days of sick time left on the books? Jeff hovered outside the driver's side door, watching, but not getting in the way of the transfer. Collin slid into the back seat of the jeep, let the attendant tighten her seatbelt securely—a little too securely for Collin's comfort—and forced a final smile. "Thank you."

Lacey Farrell turned from her seat in the front. "Oh, Collin! I'm so glad you're finally going home. Jeff asked me to come along to chaperone you two. I think it's silly you two would be worried people might think you two were slipping off to be alone. No one who knows Jeffery would ever imagine such a thing. But he insists it would make you feel better about him taking you home. I'm so happy I could help. You have no idea…"

His mom. He brought his mom. Lord, this is beyond not funny. Taking Lacey to the 'hood? What is he going to think when we get close to my place?

The attendant patted the top of the car to let Jeff know Collin had been safely tucked in the back. Jeff slipped into the driver's seat and looked back at Collin. "You sure about this?"

"Drive, Farrell, before I change my mind." She closed her eyes. She sensed Jeff put the jeep in gear, pull out of the parking lot, and into the city traffic.

Lacey continued prattling. "You look so much better than you did when we saw you yesterday, dear. I'm sure a day or two of rest will get you back to normal. They always take such wonderful care of you at this hospital."

"Mom, I think—"

Lacey continued as if Jeff hadn't interrupted. "The nurses are so kind and look after everything you need. I don't think I ever had to ask for anything while I stayed here, did I, Jeffery?"

Jeff tried to break into his mother's monologue. "Mom, Collin—"

But no dice. Lacey continued, "Doctor McMannon is the best doctor. Jeff says you've been having headaches. You should see him if your headaches don't get better. But I'm sure they will. I had the worst headaches before my stroke, but Dr. Rich took wonderful care of me." She smiled and added, "We call him Dr. Rich because he and Harmon have been friends since they were boys. He's the only one Harmon would trust for our family."

The woman seemed to falter. Collin looked to see an almost puzzled look on Mrs. Farrell's face. Lacey lost the starry-eyed gaze for a few moments…cocked her head as if trying to remember something. She sat for several seconds, then moved on. "I can't exactly remember all the things he did for me. He's my neurologist. He's helped us with Leesa, too. She is our special child, you know. She has Down Syndrome. No one expected her to live as long as she has, but Dr. Rich has taken excellent care of her."

Collin let the words cascade over her, not trying to make sense of them, but letting the singsong rhythm of the woman's voice lull her to sleep. Home. Finally, home…

Jeff's voice broke her nap. "Collin? Can these directions be right?"

Collin didn't have to open her eyes to know the location Jeff saw on his map app. "Yes. 107 Lincoln Way. It's a trailer court."

The silence spoke volumes. Collin opened her eyes. "If I don't live near the children I work with, how can I say, 'I understand'? How do my words have any credibility if I don't share their reality?"

Collin watched Jeff's face in the rearview mirror. She could see him struggling to resolve the conflict in his head, but she couldn't tell which side had the advantage. Collin started to speak, but a silent nudge whispered, *Don't.* So, she didn't.

After several lifetimes, Jeff nodded. Collin could tell from the look on his face there would be more discussion to come. Fine. Later worked. Sometimes later meant never. Which also worked.

As they drove, the neighborhoods declined from uptown class to downtown decay to outright "you don't want to be here after dark…" and maybe not after sunrise, either. Jeff finally turned into the entrance to the trailer court. Collin directed him to the visitor's parking area in front of the office. "You'll need to go in and tell Danita you're bringing me home. She's the manager, and she'll let you drive to my place."

Jeff looked a little surprised but nodded. "Do I need to show her ID or something?"

Collin could feel her cheeks warm. A little. "No. Tell her you're Jeff Farrell. She'll know you."

Jeff turned around and looked at Collin, question in his eyes. Collin tried to shrug it off, but shrugging hurt. "She's a friend. We talk."

The man's eyes sparkled. "You talk, huh? About me?"

"Among other things." Collin refused to incriminate herself any further. Jeff chuckled, got out of the jeep, and walked to the office.

Lacey looked around. "Oh, how lovely."

Collin always thought so. The trailer court presented as clean and neat: yards mowed and trimmed, no piles of trash, no junked cars, no couches on the lawns. This late into October, the flowers were all spent, but even the stems had been trimmed to the ground. Danita ran a tight ship. *"You abide by the rules, or you abide somewhere else. We may be low rent, but we don't have to look like it."* Danita at her finest.

Jeff came back a few minutes later, a woman in her mid-fifties in tow. Danita looked in the back of the jeep. "Child, you late on your rent. Supposed to be in on Monday. Your Jeffery here tells me you crashed your car." Danita raised one eyebrow slightly. "Nobody's used a dodge quite so creative to get out of being behind before. You could have paid the late fee, you know."

Collin tried to laugh without exerting undue pressure on her ribs. She said, "I'll get it to you today, I promise. If you can come by and collect it. I'm not walking too fast right now."

"Humph. Poor excuse for being late on your rent. This better not happen too often, girl." The smile belied the strictness in Danita's tone.

"No, ma'am. It won't happen again."

Danita directed Jeff, "Last trailer on the left before the turn. The one with the dead bush." She glared in mock anger. "You supposed to have it cut back last week. *Before* you crashed your car."

Collin ducked her head. "Yes, ma'am. I'll get to it this weekend. I'll be home for a few days."

Jeff scowled at Collin. "I'll come over and take care of it. You don't need to be playing lumberjack after all you've been through."

Collin scowled back. "I can manage my own landscaping, thank you."

Danita snorted. "Don't look like it to me. You killed all the flowers we gave you to beautify your place. If I hadn't watered the shrubs, you'd a killed them too. Take the help." Danita dropped her official manager role. "If there's anything you need, you call me. You know I'll be there to help." She looked at Jeff. "I expect I'll be seeing more of you now she's spilled her deep, dark secret of where she lives, right?"

Jeff nodded. "Yes, ma'am, you will. If she lets me."

Danita said, "She's a fool if she don't." She looked pointedly at Collin. "Got it?"

Collin repeated for the third time, "Yes, ma'am."

Danita turned to Lacey. "You must be Mrs. Farrell. It's a pleasure to meet you. Collin has told me all about you."

Lacey smiled broadly. "Why, thank you. She's such a lovely girl. And so right for our Jeffery. I will never understand why he hasn't asked her to marry him. He talks about her all the time."

Jeff climbed in the jeep. "I'll explain it to you at home, Mom. Let's get Collin in her house." He looked at the trailers and added, "Or whatever."

Collin let the comment go. The exchange with Danita had been taxing. More taxing than Collin had expected. Maybe she should go back.

Never! She'd had enough of hospitals and doctors and the entire medical profession. They pushed pills, told you they could find nothing wrong, you were over-stressed and needed to change your diet or your job or your…

An internal nudge caught her short. Collin quit grumbling to herself. Doctors did the best they could with the knowledge they had. *Yes, sir.*

They arrived at the trailer, and Jeff helped his mom and Collin out of the jeep. He helped Collin up the three steps to the landing in front of the door. Collin motioned to a pile of dead leaves under the trailer. "There's a spare key in the strut above the leaves. Would you get it for me? My keys got lost in the wreck." Along with a great many other things, including her phone, her wallet, her ID, her license…it would be a long process of getting back to normal.

Jeff's jaundiced look showed his obvious disapproval of the location of her spare. But he had to do some serious feeling around and looking before he located the back-up key. He grumbled something under his breath and handed the key to Collin. She smiled at him as sweetly and innocently as she could. "Thank you, Jeffery."

The glare she got in return said they would discuss her use of his proper name at a later date as well. Like so many other things they hadn't talked about yet. Time. They needed time.

Collin unlocked the door, motioned for Jeff to step off the

landing, and swung the door open over the landing. Jeff stepped back, but Collin stopped him. "I can get myself in the rest of the way. No men allowed." *Not until I see any mess I left behind. Did I leave my unmentionables where they could be mentioned? Left the milk on the counter?*

Lacey laughed, "Oh, Collin, don't be silly. He's not any man. He's Jeffery. You know him well enough to know he would never do anything—"

"I know, Mrs. Farrell. I have a rule not to let men in when I'm the only one here." To Jeff's puzzled look, she explained, "Repair people have to go through Danita first, and she always follows them into any single woman's place if the woman asks. It's safer."

She watched Jeff mull it over. "Makes sense. I'm glad she does it."

"She's a good manager and a good woman." She stretched ever so slightly. "Even though your mom is here, I think we should say goodbye here. I appreciate you bringing me home. I do." Collin offered, "I do love you, Jeff."

Jeff kissed her lightly on the forehead. "I love you, milady."

"When I'm back on my feet, I promise, we'll have dinner again. Between your schedule and mine, we never have a night off at the same time." She touched his cheek. "You're not available when you're at the station, and I'm not when I'm out with my kids. We will get it together, Jeff. I promise." She had so much to tell him yet. Family dinner night at the Farrell's never seemed to provide the opportunity she wanted. Or needed.

Lacey teased, "Jeffery, give her a real kiss."

"Mom!" He looked at Collin. "I can't. When I do, I want to grab the nearest ordained anything and marry you on the spot. So, we either keep it simple, or one of us has to move. Monastery or convent, you pick."

Collin touched his lips tenderly. "Neither. We'll keep it simple. Love you." Collin walked into the trailer, shut the door, and sagged against it.

Why are you waiting? Say, "Yes, you can ask." You think you're going to change your mind?

Collin sat gingerly in the wooden rocking chair. *No, I'm afraid he will.* Jeff could shrug off her having a past because he didn't know it. "We all need forgiveness," he said. "We all have a past."

Whatever her background, it didn't matter to him.

But it does matter. It always matters. He'll hear you out, and he'll leave. Like all the others. They always do. Why should he be any different?

Because he is Jeff, not all the others. He—

If you believed him, you wouldn't be afraid to tell him all the things you were. The things you did. You'd come out and tell the whole sordid truth about the lying and the stealing and the selling your—

Collin cut the accusations off angrily. "I know who I am. I know what I did. The Lord forgave me. I made restitution where I could. I settled it. All of it."

So, call him. Now. Right now. Call him and tell him straight out. You won't. You're a coward. And you're lying to yourself thinking the Lord forgives you. Other people, yes. But not you. You're special. Different. You're required to do more, to be more. You know it. You've always known it. Forgiveness is for those who deserve it. You haven't earned it. You never will. You...

Collin felt the weight of the condemnation reaching into her soul, pulling her back into the past, into the darkness which had been her world for so long. She whispered, "Help me, Jesus. Please. Help me."

Scripture flooded her mind. *"I won't ever leave you or reject you." "I love you with My eternal love." "I am always with you, forever and ever." "There is no judgment against anyone in Christ..."*

Collin let the verses roll over her. Light and life and peace and love swept to her, over her, through her. The darkness receded, beaten again, but never really defeated. Ready to raise its head at a moment of weakness.

Collin picked up the cell phone Jeff had given her. She calculated how long it had been since he'd left, how long it would take him to get home, how long before he got his mom into the house and gave her an explanation—again—of why he needed to wait to ask her to marry him. The call could hold off for a few minutes. Not because she didn't want to tell him. But because he needed time to take care of his own business. She rocked slowly in the chair and let the tension slip from her body...

Only to have a lightning bolt of pain slash through her brain. The shock radiated so fast she felt her head snap forward then back against the chair.

And left as quickly as it came. Well, most of it. Like echoes of thunder continue to rumble away in canyons, so echoes of the pain faded slowly through her head, leaving her shaken.

Post-concussion headache. Expect them. Ignore them. If they get worse, call your primary physician. Right. Ignore it. It will go away. Sure, it will…

Collin gritted her teeth and continued rocking.

THURSDAY MORNING

A strong knock on the door interrupted Collin's morning. She looked through the curtains and saw Danita standing with two men in, of all things, trench coats. *Cops. Could you be any more obvious? Father, what now?* Collin opened the door and tried to look bright and cheerful. She failed, but at least she tried. "Can I help you?"

Danita said, "These two say they need to talk to you about the accident." The skeptical look on the woman's face matched her tone. "I told them I would see if you was up and around. And wanting visitors." The set of Danita's mouth said she would be perfectly happy to escort the men off the premises if Collin said so.

Collin sighed. "It's fine, Danita. I'll talk to them."

The office manager stepped back to let the men past her. She held Collin's eye for a moment. Collin nodded slightly. If the men weren't gone in an hour, Danita would return. Protective. Always watching out for her tenants.

Both men flashed detective IDs. Collin motioned for them to sit at the small kitchen table. She took a chair across from them. Both were tall, Caucasian, mid-fifties, and wore no-nonsense looks. A memory flashed in Collin's mind. She'd seen these two before. Where?

As she tried to remember, the one identified as Jim Russo said, "We're here to ask you some questions about your accident."

The memory clicked. Collin asked, "Since when does Homicide's finest investigate a traffic accident?"

Detective Russo's eyebrow lifted slightly. "You know me from where?"

"My job lets me hang around the precincts. Trying to find my clients' parents, mostly. I've seen your commendations on the wall."

Russo shrugged. "Eh, I got lucky."

Russo's partner, Nick O'Conner, asked, " What do you remember about the crash?"

"You mean before the crash, right? What happened before is as fuzzy as the crash itself. I…" Collin trailed off. She let her mind go back to Monday. "I left for work."

"Time?" Russo asked.

"Six-thirty? Maybe a little earlier."

Detective O'Conner said, "Social Service office doesn't open until nine. Why leave then?"

"I like to be early. It's my normal routine. I get there first so I can make the coffee. It's the only way I know I'll have at least one good cup for the day. Makes the rest of the day go smoother. For me, at least."

O'Conner asked, "So you didn't go in earlier than normal? You left at your regular time."

"Right."

"And you drove your regular route?"

"Of course."

"So anyone who knew you would know where you would be and when you would be there." The detective seemed to be confirming his hypothesis.

Collin looked to Russo. "Why is Homicide interested in my car crash?"

Detective Russo pulled a file folder out and showed Collin a photograph. Its graininess suggested it had come from a security camera. "Do you know this man?"

Collin studied the picture a moment. She started to hand it back, hesitated, and took a second look. *Patrick? Maybe? No. Yes? No.* Finally, she passed it back to him. "No."

Russo asked, "But you looked twice. Why?"

"It looked like someone I might have known a long time ago."

Detective O'Conner asked, "Name?"

Collin refused to answer. "No. I haven't seen him in twelve years, and there is no reason to think he would be anywhere around here. I'm not going to throw his name around on a 'might look like' chance." Her eyes narrowed as she added, "Especially since I don't know what any of this is about."

Russo slid Collin another photo. "What about this truck?"

Collin looked at it, and bells went off in her head. A white truck. A big white truck. A big white truck with a black pipe grille, the kind used for pushing other vehicles around. Collin studied the truck for several moments. "It followed me. Monday morning. I saw it go past me twice. Thought it strange, it would go by two times. Like, did he get off the freeway and back on again?" She stared at the picture. "He got behind me again. But he didn't go past me. Didn't go around me, either."

Bits and pieces of memory flowed together to form one consolidated scene. "We came to the Rogers fly-over. He bumped the back of my car, playing tag. I slowed, sped up, changed lanes. Nothing worked. He stayed right on my bumper." Collin let the final memory chip fall into place. "He accelerated and smashed into me. I remember leaving the roadway." Collin came out of the memory and stared at Detective Russo. "He did it deliberately. He pushed me over the edge." *Why? Who would…Patrick?*

Do not implicate him in this. He hated you before. Dragging him into an attempted murder investigation on a "could look like" would only make it worse. If it were possible. It would make you look like the vengeful vermin he always accused you of being.

Detective Russo slid out one more picture to Collin. "Know him?"

This one, Collin knew for certain. "No. I've never seen him before." She looked from Russo to O'Conner back to Russo, and something clicked. "His truck ran me off the road. But you don't think he drove it. You think the first man did. Because this man reported his truck stolen. By this man?" Collin pointed to the figure in the grainy photo. "But it still doesn't explain why Homicide is investigating…" Collin trailed off as another possibility waved its hand for recognition.

Detective Russo said matter-of-factly, "His wife called him in missing. We tracked his last known location to the bar where"— Russo touched the grainy shot—"we lifted this picture. People there remembered the truck owner drinking a little too much with this guy. They left together when the bar closed. No one has seen either of them since. But someone abandoned the truck near your crash site with minor damage to the front end."

Collin snorted. "Right. Like my beetle had any chance against such a behemoth." She hesitated before asking, "Did you match any paint samples from the grille?"

"Forensics is still working on it. Getting a sample large enough to test from the remains of your car has been the toughest part."

"Tell me about it." Collin thought it over. And over. And over. "I'm sorry. I can't give you any reason why someone would try to kill me, much less murder someone else to get it done. I'm nobody." She motioned around her mobile home. "There's nothing here anyone would want." *There's not much here I even want. Need, yes. But want? Yeah, no.*

An Interceding thought nudged her. Collin corrected herself. *I am grateful, Lord. I wouldn't reach the parents and guardians I have if You hadn't put me here. So, yes, I am grateful for all You've given me. Except the mice.* Collin shrugged. "I can't help you."

Detective Russo handed Collin the requisite card, with the requisite, "If you think of anything, give me a call. We appreciate your time." As Collin struggled to stand, the detective added, "Don't bother. We can see ourselves out." The two men left without taking the photos.

Calculated. Leave these where I have to look at them again and again. Maybe develop sympathy for the missing man. Change my mind about giving you the name. I'm not stupid.

Collin shoved the photo of the truck owner under a stack of old reports. The grainy photo she left out and looked at again. She whispered, "I'm not stupid. But are you? You used to be. Tell me you've learned something in all these years. Haven't you?"

* * *

The phone rang at noon. Collin looked at the ID. Lacey Farrell. Collin picked it up. "Good morning, Mrs. Farrell."

"Collin, dear, you sound good today. How are you feeling? Jeffery asked me to be sure to call and check on you. He's at the station, you know, and can't call from there. But he wanted me to check on you. I told him there was no need, you were probably fine and needed rest, but he insisted. How are you, dear?"

"I'm much better, Mrs. Farrell. Thank you for calling. I—"

"I knew you would be. But you know how Jeffery is. He worries about you all the time."

"Tell him I'm fine, Mrs. Farrell. I—"

"And please, don't call me Mrs. Farrell. It makes me feel so old. Call me Mom Lacey, please. If your own Mom won't mind, of course. I'm not trying to take her place. That would be silly. You have a mom—"

The phone went silent. Collin looked to see if they were still connected. As far as she could tell, nothing had happened to the connection. "Mrs. Farrell?"

A different voice—still Lacey Farrell, but deeper, more lucid, maybe—said, "But your mother is gone, isn't she? You told Jeff…you said…"

Collin held her breath. What happened?

The phone went silent again. After a moment, the Lacey Farrell Collin knew came back on the line. "I'm sorry, dear. I lost track of what I was saying. Seems to be happening a lot these days." She laughed, her voice lilting.

Collin sighed. "I understand. When you see him, you can tell Jeff I'm doing fine, better than yesterday, and rest is all I need." *No way am I going to pass the message about the police along through his mom.*

Wise move.

Lacey finished with, "I will, dear. Now you rest, and I'm sure Jeff will call you when he can. He always does, you know. He loves you so very much. I wish you two would hurry and get married. I'll never understand why he hasn't asked you to marry him, yet. You'll make the sweetest couple."

"Thank you, M…Mom Lacey. I'll talk to you later."

Collin hung up. And sighed.

* * *

At close to three in the afternoon, Collin heard a knock on her door again. She hoped whoever it might be had something good to tell her. The pain medication she had taken in the morning had worn off three hours ago. Yes, she should have taken more. Yes, she knew the adage about not "chasing pain." Yes, she would be much more pleasant if she weren't hurting so much. But Collin wanted off the pain pills. She never liked taking them, and never wanted to like taking them. *You conquer pain with force of will. If you are strong enough, if you want it bad enough, you can do anything. You have to want it. You have to be…*

Collin muttered, "Oh, shut up. I'll take the pills after whoever this is leaves." She pulled herself out of her rocking chair and opened the door.

Robbie Sider stood there. He looked surprised and concerned at her bruises and bandages. "What did you do to yourself this time, caseworker lady?"

Collin started to speak, shut her mouth, waited a moment, and said, "I had a car crash. Where is your phone?"

Rob left the door open when he came in. He also opened the curtains over the picture window as wide as possible. Propriety. Protection against recrimination. By now, he knew the drill. He threw his book bag and books on the kitchen table, went to the refrigerator, and took out a power drink. "My 'mother'"—Rob stopped, looked for a word—"confiscated it. Again."

Collin nodded approval of the wording but asked, "Why?"

Rob took a long swig of the drink, sat, and pulled out some papers. "She took… exception to my essay on parenting."

Collin joined him at the table. "Nice use of vocabulary. She looked at your homework?"

"Yeah. She ain't looked at my papers since I left kindergarten. But she got to read this one." Rob flipped the offending essay over to Collin for her perusal.

Collin read the one-page paper quickly. It deserved the "A" it received. The essay sounded clear, concise, informative, persuasive. All the things an essay should be. Unfortunately, the parenting style and skills the essay championed opposed the manner his mom practiced. To say he had no parents would be closer to the truth. Collin served as the only constant in his life, the one stable adult he could count on being present.

Rob griped, "I know you an' Jeff talked about dying for Christ. I think it'd be easier than trying to live for Him. He got to be all in my 'biz-ness.' How I talk to people. How I treat people. How I live every minute of every day. He say I'm becoming all new."

Collin could sense the young man's frustration. *Been there. Done that. Have the T-shirt. Coffee cup and keyring, too.*

Rob continued venting. "Except nothing around me change. I

still gotta live with my mom and all her 'boyfriends.' I still gotta live with all the bad choices she make in a day. Like choosing cigarettes and booze 'stead of feeding the little kids she got."

Rob swallowed more of the drink. "Her current man told her he needed a phone. My phone. So she took it, sayin' I'd dissed her at school." Rob's voice broke in anguish. "I don't know what to do, Collin. She and him running some kinda scam on Worford. Ain't gonna end well, I know."

Worford was the neighborhood dealer. *Excuse me, "medicinal marijuana distributor."* Rob spoke the truth. Worford would know whatever scam his mother and her current live-in had planned. He always knew. Retribution would be swift and inclusive. Shelby would not be the only one he targeted. All members of the household would share equally in the penalty for crossing Worford.

Collin fingered the card Detective Russo had left behind. *Maybe…*

Are you out of your mind? You can't interfere with this. Client confidentiality and all.

He's not my client. I gave him up when we got back from camp. His friendship means more to me than anything.

Yeah, well, Rob will never talk to you about anything again if you rat his mom out.

If you don't do something, Rob may never have the chance to talk to anyone again.

Don't rescue. He hasn't asked you to solve this.

Let him figure it out on his own. He's almost a man. He has to learn he can't count on you to pull him out of his messes. He can't count on anyone but himself. He better learn it now.

Collin shut down as many of the voices in her head as she could. They continued to echo, but she ignored them. "Have you prayed about it?'

Rob looked skeptical. "Pray? How prayer gonna help?" Collin fixed him with a raised eyebrow. After several moments, Rob admitted. "Yeah. I need to."

Collin bowed her head. *In her mind, she crawled into her "Abba Father's"—Daddy's—lap. She put her arms around His waist, or as far around Him as she could get her stubby little girl arms and hugged Him tightly.* Out loud, she said, "Father…Daddy…We have a problem. It's not a problem for You, but we're still on *this* side of it. Rob is hurting, Father. He's hurting and needs to know what to do. Help him, please."

Rob prayed, "God, I'm still new at this praying stuff. I know following You ain't supposed to be easy. I didn't think it would get this hard this fast." The young man hesitated. "I don't know what to do about Mom. Lord, I don't want her to get hurt."

Collin heard Rob shifting in his chair. He continued, "I don't want anyone to get hurt. I'm afraid, God. Afraid for Mom and for me and everyone else she got living with us right now."

Collin heard Rob take a long breath. "Lord…I need…I want…" Rob faltered, and his voice broke. "God, I don't know what I want. I don't know what I need. 'Cept I need You. I need Your help. Please."

Collin finished, "In Jesus' name, amen." She put her arm around Rob's shoulders. "He hears, Rob. He knows."

Tears stained Rob's face, but he nodded. "Yeah. I'm learning, Collin. I am. I'm trying to, anyhow."

"And He knows you're trying." *And how trying you can be.*
Unfair. Rob's not trying. He's—
You said he's trying. Now you say he's not. Which is it?

Collin growled the chorus into silence. "Okay, do you have homework I can help you with?" Collin chuckled. "Other than chemistry."

Rob grinned. "I'm never gonna ask you for help with chemistry, caseworker lady. My 'magniary dog know more about chemistry than you do."

Collin huffed. "At least I admit the things I don't know."

A whiplash of pain rocketed through her brain. Collin froze, unable to do anything more except let it tear through her. She could hear Rob's worried, "Collin? Collin? What's wrong?" but couldn't answer. Not and keep from screaming.

Only when she figured she could speak in a semi-normal voice did she answer, "Post-concussion headache. Old data. Pay it no mind."

Rob didn't buy it. "Yeah? You sure?"

"Yeah, bro. I'm sure. They said so at the hospital. It'll get better."

"Is it?"

Collin hesitated and admitted, "Not yet. But it will. I have faith in the doctors."

Liar! Collin shrugged it off.

A voice called through the open door. "I have a letter for Collin Walker, and I need a signature."

Rob stood and went to the door. "You have what?"

"A registered letter for Collin Walker. Are you him?"

Collin said wearily, "I'm him. Her. I'm Collin Walker."

She motioned for Rob to let the man in. The letter carrier said, "I'm sorry, ma'am. These names…"

Collin waved it off. "It's fine. Where do I need to sign?"

He indicated two lines. Collin signed both places as she looked at the envelope to see the return address. Blood sank from her face and heart as she read, *"Aster, Terra, and Mudd, Esquires. Fort Newton, Indiana."* She sensed Rob showing the letter carrier out, sensed him asking her who sent it (and asking and asking and asking) but couldn't answer. She closed her eyes and whispered, "Oh, Grandfather. I'm sorry."

Rob's prodding broke through her shell. She looked at him in surprise. "Sorry. I…I made a promise I didn't keep." *I promised I'd see him before he died. I'm so sorry.*

"Who is it from?"

Collin steadied herself. "My grandfather's law firm. My father's mother's second husband. She married Fenton Mudd when my father was twenty-two. I never knew any other grandfather but Fenton."

Rob's brows went up. "I thought you didn't have no family. Aside from your father. 'Cept he didn't act like one."

Collin nodded. Her hands shook slightly as she looked at the notice again. And again. And again. Endings. So many endings now. She whispered, "Oh, Grandfather. Did you find a way?"

She slit the letter open, careful not to damage the pages. She could feel Rob's eyes on her, waiting for her reaction to tell him something, anything, about what the letter might contain.

Collin scanned the first page:

"We regret to inform you of the passing of your grandfather, and our partner, Fenton Mudd. Per his instructions, you are the closest next of kin and executrix of his estate."

Collin could feel herself pale even further. Executrix? How hard could this get? She scanned the remainder of the first page, turned it over to look at the second. All hope her grandfather had resolved the family issues over the estate vanished. Collin shut her eyes, lowered her head onto the table, and sat there. For the first time she could remember, the voices in her head went silent. Even they didn't know what to say.

Rob took hold of her shoulder, trying to get her attention. "Caseworker lady! Collin! What's wrong? What is it?"

Collin sat finally, swallowed hard, nodded. "I'm fine, Rob. I'm fine. My grandfather passed. I have…have a…a few…legal matters to take care of for him."

Since when is an estate valued at over three hundred million dollars 'a few legal matters?' How you gonna defer this *kind of paycheck, hmmm?*

The shaking in Collin's hands threatened to spread to her whole body. She took several deep breaths to steady herself. "Rob, bro, I need some time to work through all this." She looked him carefully in the eyes. "I'm going to need your help. Lots and lots of help. But right now, I need it to be me and the Lord, okay?"

Rob's eyes searched hers back and forth. Finally, he said, "'Kay, Collin. I'll go." He stood and added, "'Sides, me and the Lord got some things to discuss, too."

Collin started to say, "I'll call you," but stopped. No phone. Rob had no phone. How… She said, "I'll leave you a message at school. Which class is best?" Meaning, which teacher would be trusted to give him the message without losing it or badgering him to know what it meant. "Chemistry. Mr. Shepherd. He cool."

"Mr. Shepherd." Collin smiled slightly. "He always liked me. Couldn't teach me a thing, but he always liked me."

Rob chuckled. "Yeah, he have some stories 'bout you in chemistry class. Some of your 'experiments' nearly blowed the school down."

Collin huffed in mock offense. "Not the whole school. Maybe the science wing. But not the whole school."

Rob hugged Collin carefully around the shoulders. "Love you, Collin."

"Love you too, Rob. You can close the door on the way out. I'll get the curtains."

Collin waited until the door closed and looked at the letter again. She glanced at the postmark: three days before her accident. How in the world did it take six days to get from Ft. Newton? You could drive there in two hours! Six days?

Collin picked up the cell phone, picked up the detective's card, and dialed. At the "leave a message" tone, Collin said, "Detective Russo. Collin Walker. The name you wanted? Patrick Winger. I'm sure of it." She hung up. "Now."

THURSDAY AFTERNOON

Collin rocked back and forth, almost violently in her frustration. No use asking why. Didn't matter. Only 'what' mattered. Collin voiced it out loud. "What now? What am I expected to do with this? I can't deal with this, Lord. I can't. You have got to help me. Give me direction. A sign. Something. But tell me what to do."

Call Jeff.

Collin snarled, "I am not running to Jeff with my problems. This is my mess. My trial."

You're supposed to be a couple. Solving things together. Working for the common good.

Collin answered her accuser out loud. "We are. And we will. But this has been my responsibility since the moment I came into this world." She dropped her head. "I hoped it would go away before I had to deal with it."

Bury your head in the sand, much? How's that working out for you? Collin stood. "I need to clear my head." She put on her sneakers, grabbed her basketball, and limped outside. The light faded early these days. Collin left her porch light on but refused to grab a flashlight. She knew her way to the courts blindfolded. And the dark didn't bother her at all. *Hello, darkness, my old friend…*

Oh, shut up.

You're falling into old patterns. There are better ways to deal with—

I know there are better ways. But this way works. And I'm doing it.

Call Jeff.

I don't want to add to his problems. This relationship has already caused him headaches. Trying to find time with both our schedules to be together. Trying to find time to sit and do nothing but talk. There's so much I need to tell him, so much he needs to know. But there's never time. Never the right time.

Waiting for the right time is a dodge. Call him.

He's at the station. I don't want to bother him there. I make it a point not to. He needs to keep his mind focused.

He's been a fireman long enough to be quite capable of separating his concerns. You trust him? Call him.

Collin responded by walking to the court. All the wounded pieces of her body protested against the new abuse being visited upon them. Walking? Walking farther than the bedroom? How dare she? How could she? Collin ignored the pain and ache. *The will rules the body, not the other way around. Mind over matter. If you don't mind, it doesn't matter. No pain, no gain.*

No pain, no brain. You know better than this. You should know better. You're falling into old habits.

Force of will. Collin ignored all the voices. She reached the basketball court. The lights were on, the court empty. No one would see her pitiful attempts to dribble, much less shoot, the ball with her ribs screaming. She silenced the internal clamor, dribbled the ball as she walked around the court. Two laps. Three laps. Four…

By the fifth lap, Collin felt sufficiently loose to attempt a shot. She stood at the free-throw line and launched the ball.

Pathetic. Not even an airball. More like a ground ball. Collin retrieved the ball, returned to the line, and shot again.

Better. At least it had some lift to it. Try again.

And again. And again. And again. Only after Collin knew she could hit from the line did she move to another spot. Hit. Hit. Hit. Move. Hit. Miss. Hit. Hit. Hit. Move. She backed out to the three-point range. As she launched the ball, her ribs caught. Collin grabbed her side; the ball sailed half the distance and rolled the rest of the way to the pole.

"Hey, lady! Let some real men have the court."

"Yeah! We show you how it's done."

Collin ignored the catcalls. Didn't matter. She walked to the backstop, picked up the ball, and walked back to her previous launching pad. Collin looked at the group of young men, late teens, early twenties maybe, sprawled on the benches, waiting to use the court. She thought she recognized a face or two. She called out, "Five more minutes, and you can have it."

The ring leader sneered. "How much you gonna learn in five minutes, huh? Clear off and let real players play."

Collin dribbled the ball slowly. *Take 'em. You know you can.* Collin eyed the men, deliberating. Nah, not tonight. She didn't have the energy.

But Mouthy continued his tirade against her and females in general. Only when he switched to regaling his crew with the things women were good for did Collin change her mind.

She dribbled slowly, debating. *Teaching moment?* She studied her opponent, weighed the options. "Why don't you show me?"

The ring leader swaggered out, snickering. Collin asked, "Name?"

"So you can tell people who beat you? Mano."

Collin nodded. "Mano. You good at free throws, Mano?"

Mano sneered. "Free throws? I can make free throws all day and never miss."

"Fine. You make ten in a row, and I'll concede the court. But since you're a man, and no woman is ever half as good as a man, I'll shoot five."

Mano snorted. "Yeah. Watch and learn, lady." Collin tossed him the ball.

Mano caught it, rolled it around in his hands, stepped to the line, dribbled, and fired. The shot caught the edge of the rim and bounced off to the side. Mano retrieved the rock and threw it to Collin with some speed on it. "Your turn."

"You want to warm up a little first?"

Mano snarled, "Give it your best shot and get off the court."

Collin shrugged. "Up to you." She stepped up, bounced the ball, and…

…nothing but net. If there had been a net. Which there wasn't. Collin limped forward to get the ball, retrieved it, returned to the line, launched, and got the same result. Splash city.

Mano's crowd cheered and jeered at the same time. *Catcalls and boos, but which one for whos?*

Oh, stuff it, okay? This is serious.

It's basketball. Can't you even spell?

Collin tossed it again. And again. She stepped to the line for the fifth time and, with the right amount of pressure, managed to hit the front of the rim and let the ball bounce off.

"Your turn."

Mano's eyes narrowed dangerously. He walked to the line, threw a shot, and banked it off the backboard. "One."

The perverse side of her urged, *oo, he can count.* Collin held her tongue. Teaching, not taunting.

Mano shot again. "Two." And again. "Three."

But four went off-line and fell to the side. Collin accepted the ball. "Your form's good. You could use a little less pressure, though." She didn't wait for a response—positive or negative—but stepped and threw. *One.* No one counted her shots.

Two.

Three.

Four.

Miss.

The youth designated to retrieve the orb growled at Mano. "You realize we could've had the court by now if you had waited, right? This'll take all night."

"Shut up. I'm playing with her. I can shoot them all right now."

"Good," Collin said. "Do it. I need to get home." *Yeah, it's past your bedtime. You'll turn into a pumpkin any minute now.*

Mano's eyes told a story Collin happily did not have to read out loud. He strode to the line and fired. "One."

"Two."

"Three." Mano swaggered around the court, bowing to the four corners.

"Four."

"Five." He raised his hand high in salute to his own prowess, no doubt.

"Six."

Collin could see the young man's confidence—and cockiness—returning with each completed throw. So much so, on the seventh throw, he turned to showboat for his crew...and missed. Mano chased the ball himself and fired it to Collin with as much heat as he could put on it.

Collin caught it without comment. She stepped up again.

One.

Two.

Three.

Four.

Before the fifth shot, she called out, "Anyone know the best NBA free throw percentage? All-time high?"

Mano seethed, "Like you know, right?"

Collin said, "I know your foot has been across the line on all your shots. None of them should count. But I figure you could use a second chance."

"I don't need no chances from nobody."

Collin threw her fifth shot wide and watched while Mano carefully placed his shoe behind the line and shot. When he again missed on the sixth shot, Collin said quietly, "We all need chances, Mano." She took her place at the top of the key. "Ain't none of us perfect, and ain't none of us get it right the first time."

She sank her shot.

"Or the second.

"Or the third.

"Or the fourth."

She punctuated her words with sinking free throws. Collin held the ball a moment, studying Mano. Was he listening? "Best free throw percentage ever is ninety percent. Ninety. Which means the best free-throw shooter of all times consistently missed one in ten throws."

Collin dribbled slowly. "I also know the number one thing all coaches teach is respect. For yourself, for your teammates, and especially your opponents."

Collin studied Mano's eyes. Maybe… "Every person out here is someone special. They deserve to be treated like they matter." She fired.

Five.

Before anyone could move, Collin retrieved the ball and threw it again.

Six. "You're gonna meet people with more skill than you. Or less. Doesn't make them better or worse."

Seven. Collin continued to hold Mano's gaze. "Means they're still learning and need you to help them like someone helped you."

Eight. "Or it means you can learn from them. Either way, you both win."

Nine.

Anticipation—or maybe dread so thick you could cut it with a spork—fell on the court. Collin never let her eyes leave Mano's as she asked, "So, what kind of man are you gonna be, Mano? Someone people respect because he learns from others?"

She pointed to his crew, sitting in stunned silence. "Or the kind people try to beat over and over and over until someone finally sticks a knife in your back because he can't beat you any other way? Your choice, man." Collin focused entirely on Mano as she blindly fired at the hoop for the last time.

Ten.

Mano's crew began to jeer and catcall at Collin, but Mano silenced them with a rude gesture. His glare continued to be narrow and focused. He stepped forward, his face against hers. "You a hustler, ain't you?"

"No. But would it matter? You still got outshot. I'm a nobody. Just a woman in love with hoops. And who knows how to learn from others. Who are you, Mano?"

Mano stepped back. Collin could see him thinking it over. She dare not turn her back until Mano had resolved the question. She waited. And waited. And waited.

"I ain't afraid to learn. You a teacher?"

Inwardly, Collin breathed a huge sigh of relief. Outwardly, she said, "Of hoops? Yeah." *No science, though.*

"You teach me how to make ten shots in a row?"

"I promise I'll teach you all I know about the game of basketball. After I get my ribs healed. This is killing me." For the first time since the challenge started, Collin wrapped her arm across her ribs.

"What wrong with your ribs, huh?"

"Busted a couple on Monday."

"And you out here shooting hoops? You ain't right in the head, lady."

"Funny thing about that...." Collin silenced the inner chorus before it could even begin. "I know, Mano. Some things I still need to learn."

Like not being stupid and thinking you can save the world?

Collin mounted her only defense. *Not the whole world. One kid at a time, okay? One kid at a time. Like someone saved me. I owe Him.*

Mano turned to his now silent crew and ordered, "Go home. We meet tomorrow." He looked at Collin. "You get home okay?"

"Yeah. Thanks, Mano." She wanted to say more but figured it could wait for another night. *When you're not in martyr mode.*

Shut up. This once, shut up.

Collin limped home.

Now will you call Jeff?

In the morning. I promise. I'll call him.

Tonight. Call him tonight. He can take the call. Call him.

Fine. I'll call...

THURSDAY EVENING

"Farrell!" The loudspeaker blared.

Jeff looked from the fender of the squad truck he shined for the third time. Boredom. Paramedic life: extreme adrenalin or extreme boredom. Today had been boredom. Keeping the captain happy involved looking busy. Okay, so shining the same fender three times pushed the limit. But it would be the cleanest fender in the station.

"Here."

"Visitor at the front."

Jeff didn't get visitors at the station. He threw his polishing cloth and walked to the reception area. As Jeff rounded the corner, a familiar voice called out, "Jeffery, my man!" Trey sat in a motorized wheelchair looking smug, a portable chess set on his lap. "I figured since you missed our session today, I'd bring the lesson to you." Trey looked around the station. "You don't look too busy."

Trey's appearance at the station caught Jeff by surprise. "How did you get here?"

Trey motioned to his wheels. "I drove myself. Like the treads?"

"Nice. But coming here? Trey, it's five—"

"Five miles, yeah, I know. I wanted to give this thing a proper road test. So far, so good. The real question will be does it have the juice to get me home again?"

Jeff frowned. "Don't know about you, man. Do not know."

Captain Franklin, the station chief, walked out of his office. "New recruit, Farrell?"

Jeff introduced the two men. "Trey's my chess tutor."

Franklin let out a knowing, "Ahhh…so you're the one giving Farrell lessons. I knew he couldn't be getting better on his own.

Someone had to be teaching him."

Trey said, "I try. I do try."

Jeff decided to cut this conversation short before the Captain and Trey could amuse themselves rehearsing Jeff's inadequacies. "Trey came here by himself. Can I take an early dinner hour and let him beat me around the board a few times?" Jeff looked pointedly at the younger man. "And make sure he gets home? He's not sure about the gas mileage. You know how dealers always exaggerate."

Captain Franklin intoned, "Your mileage may 'vary.' I've heard it. Okay, Farrell. Take the time now. But after you see him home, I want to see the rest of the squad's fenders shine like the one you've been polishing all afternoon."

"Yes, sir. Thank you, sir. I'll get right on it, sir." Jeff saluted. The captain scowled at him in mock displeasure and walked back into his office. Jeff motioned to Trey. "The breakroom is in there. I'll be right with you." Trey followed Jeff's direction. Jeff ducked into the captain's office. "Thanks, Cap. I've never known Trey to show like this. But he's a bit…eccentric."

Captain Franklin said pointedly, "Make sure he gets home, or we'll have a real call on our hands. It's been a quiet day so far. Let's not mess it up."

"Right." Jeff walked to the rec room. Trey had the chess set on the table, circling the pieces in the air one by one before placing them in their designated spot. Jeff asked, "What does circling the board do?"

"Why does it have to do anything?"

"Because you always win, and anything you do could be the key to finally beating you. I'm covering all the bases."

Trey smirked. "I like to get the feel of the pieces. They talk to me and tell me how they're feeling today. Which one wants to go first, which one wants to be a sacrificial piece, which one refuses to stand next to the others. All those pre-game rituals, you know? You have to be in tune with the players."

"Uh-huh." Jeff sat across from Trey. "Anyone telling you he wants to defect to the other side?"

Trey shrugged. "The queen is always suspect. She can be evil if you don't stay on your guard." Trey stared at the board. "Most women are. Tell you anything you want to hear but stab you in the back when you're not looking."

"You've been hanging around the wrong kind of women, my friend."

Trey's voice came back sharp. "You think so? Your lady friend won't be any different. You'll see."

Jeff studied Trey a long time. "What got under your skin today? Three days ago, you prayed with me for her to live. Now?"

"Sorry. Been someone yammering in my ear the past couple days. Guess I let them get to me."

"Apology accepted. You want to tell me who's filling your head with garbage?"

Trey set the game in motion. He moved his knight out over the line of pawns. "Tell me about your lady friend. Collin. Why is she special? How do you know she's special? What makes you so sure the two of you are 'right' for each other? Does she have a sister I can date? Or maybe I can try to steal her away from you. You think she would ever look twice at a guy in a chair?"

The fact Trey would motor five miles through highly trafficked areas—trafficked in more ways than one—told Jeff the man needed something more than giving Jeff a chess lesson. And needed it desperately. "I was sitting in a chair when I met her, so yeah, she would look twice at a man in a chair." Trey sneered. "No, she doesn't have a sister. She had a twin brother die when they were fourteen." Jeff countered by moving his king's pawn two spaces.

Trey looked startled. "A twin brother died? How?"

"She said he broke his neck playing football."

Trey scoffed. "It doesn't have to mean he died. Lots of people break their necks and live." He motioned to his own body. "I know." The knight jumped sideways away from the threat of capture.

"I do too, Trey. But her brother didn't. She told me when he died, she thought her world ended. She wanted to die, too. She admits she still misses him." Jeff said quietly, "When we talk about our wedding, the thing she regrets the most is he won't be there to walk her down the aisle." Jeff advanced the queen's pawn a space behind the king's.

Trey looked confused. "Wait…you two talk about your wedding, but you haven't even asked her to marry you yet?"

Jeff chuckled. "Yeah, it's a bit of a technicality, I admit. We agreed…well, Collin made me agree to wait five months before I asked her to marry me. She knows I'm counting hours."

"You mean she could change her mind? I might have a shot at stealing her away?"

"No. She's already said the answer is yes. But I have to wait the time out in case God has an objection He hasn't shown us yet. As there hasn't been anything so far, I'm pretty sure we're safe. You'll have to take it up with Him about stealing her away from me."

Trey cocked his head. "I thought fathers walked their daughters down the aisle. Why not hers?" Trey's second knight made its move out from behind the wall of pawns.

Jeff tread lightly, sensitive to Collin's feelings about sharing too much with too many. He knew how easily the thought of the abuse Collin had suffered could turn his thoughts from light to darkness. "Collin and her father didn't have the best relationship. She hasn't seen him in twelve years. She tries not to talk about him."

"Why not? Can't she blame her failures in her life on him, like other people do? It's always someone else's fault."

Jeff remained patient. "Not Collin. She accepts she makes her own choices and has to live with them." Jeff eyed the board, trying to anticipate Trey's possible gambit. *What to do, what to do?*

"Humph. I hear people say it, but they don't mean it."

"I understand. I agree. Collin is different." Jeff grinned. "In a lot of ways."

Trey looked at Jeff as if catching the inflection in Jeff's voice. "Such as?"

"She talks to herself."

"So? Your move."

"I know. She argues with herself."

"Again, so?"

"She loses arguments with herself."

Trey clucked his tongue. "How?"

"I have no idea. She didn't bat an eye taking down a kidnapper at Camp Grace three months ago. Last week she almost jumped out of her skin when a mouse ran out from under a hutch at my parents' house.

"Collin lives where the kids she serves are. Downtown. Way downtown. Tough crowd, you know? She not only embraced the culture; she made it her own. Street smart and tough."

Jeff moved his queen. "But she sat—patiently sat, no less—through a three-hour sales pitch for cleaning products because my mom got promised a free lunch at an upscale restaurant if she came and invited a family member."

Trey looked aghast. "Why? Why would anyone sit through a three-hour spiel?" Trey countered Jeff's queen by moving his queen's pawn.

"Collin felt bad about someone taking advantage of Mom. She went so my dad didn't have to." Jeff studied the board. *Maybe...* he moved his bishop to take the pawn. "But on the basketball court? No quarter given. None. No mercy at all."

Trey's brows went up. "She plays basketball?" The tutor moved his king's pawn to take Jeff's bishop.

Jeff groaned. "Oh, she plays. Plays for keeps, too. She told me her brother taught her. They had a private challenge, a one-on-one game where the first man to reach a hundred won. No time outs, no excuses. You walk off the court, you lose."

Jeff brought his queen's knight into play. "She says the last game she and her brother played, they were tied at ninety-eight apiece when they had to quit. They never got back to finish it, and she's never forgotten it."

Trey's voice sounded reflective. "Tied at ninety-eight. Sad, Jeffery, my man. So sad."

"She's had a lot of hurt in her life. I want to make it better for her. The Lord's worked on a lot of it, but I want to help her with anything that's left."

Jeff's knight met the same fate as his bishop. Trey asked, "Did she grow up around here? Go to school here? Does she have any family at all?"

Trey's questions weren't unusual, except for the object of the questions. The young man normally plied his questions about Jeff's routines, likes, dislikes, history, family... Jeff answered slowly, "She graduated high school and college here. She told me she 'relocated here' at fourteen. No, I don't know what 'relocate' means. She hasn't told me, and I haven't asked. I'm waiting for her to bring it up. When she's ready." Jeff studied his remaining pieces. He advanced his king's rook.

"But you like her. Not just love her. You like her. She's someone people can like?" Trey moved his bishop's pawn to face Jeff's rook.

"People like her. She goes out of her way to help anyone who needs it. She volunteers at recreation centers, working with the kids." He chuckled. "I watched her let an eight-year-old run circles around her on the basketball court...and follow it by juking a teenager out of his socks ten minutes later."

Trey cocked his head in interest. "Really? How?"

"She had been working with the little kids, and some older teens started making trouble. Collin called out their best man and proceeded to demolish him. He never even got off a shot. They've respected her ever since."

Jeff grinned at the memory. "She made it a condition of the challenge the guys had to come back each week during the summer and volunteer to teach the younger ones. Most of them followed through on it too."

Trey chuckled. "I would have liked to have been there to see it. Your move."

Jeff looked up from the table. "I know. I'm delaying the inevitable." Jeff moved his rook out of harm's way. "People underestimate her abilities—and her passion—because she's quiet about it. They don't do it twice."

Jeff's phone buzzed. Trey said quickly, "I'm on your time. Answer it. And hope it's not another emergency you missed."

Jeff looked at the number. "It's Collin. How much trouble can a woman get into confined to her home?"

Trey snorted. "You'd be surprised."

Jeff accepted the call. "Speak for your servant...yes, ma'am." Jeff listened. "I understand. I'm sorry, Collin. Yeah, we'll meet tomorrow night. I get done at six. I can pick you up after." He listened again. "No. It won't be too late. You need us; we're there. Yeah. Oh, I got a call from Morris at accident clean-up. Someone found your backpack. Yeah. Your stuff is still in it. Phone, wallet, tissues, lip balm. It's in there. I'll swing by and get it before I get you. Right. I love you, milady. Bye."

Trey looked at Jeff with a slight grin on his face. "'Milady?' You call her milady?" Trey's king moved a pace to the side.

Did moving the king signify something? "She's queen of my heart. What else do you call a queen?"

"Are things alright with her?"

"She got a notice her grandfather died. She wants to talk to my folks and me about...things." Jeff's queen moved to intercept Trey's king. "Check."

"Her grandfather died? When?" The king moved away.

"I don't know, Trey. I'm sure it will be one of the things we talk about." Jeff advanced again. "Check."

"What other things?" The king moved again.

"Things, Trey. If she says they're okay to share, I'll share them with you. I don't tell her all you and I talk about, and I hope you would share the same respect with her." Jeff pursued the king one space further.

Trey nodded. "Of course. Of course, I do. You're a man of discretion, Jeffery, my man. It's something I appreciate about you." Trey advanced his rook parallel to his queen, trapping Jeff's king.

Jeff hid his relief at not having to tell Trey "none of your business" by groaning at the loss of yet another match. "I appreciate you too, Trey. I'll appreciate you more when you teach me how to beat you at chess."

"Not gonna happen. But I'll teach you how to beat someone. Someday. Maybe." Trey grinned.

FRIDAY EVENING

Jeff pulled the jeep into the city maintenance garage and told Lacey, "I'll only be a minute, Mom. I want to get Collin's backpack. Morris said I could pick it up for her."

Lacey seemed confused. "Aren't we going to pick her up? I thought we were going to get Collin."

Jeff stayed patient. "We are. After we stop and get the backpack."

"Why would Collin leave her backpack here? It seems like a strange place to—"

"She didn't, Mom. She had the car accident on Monday. The crew which did the cleanup around the crash site found her bag. Morris called me; I called Collin. I told her I would stop and get it on the way to pick her up. It's why we're stopping." *And if I didn't need to explain this to you, I would have been back in the car by now.*

Jeff swallowed his frustration. He should be happy his mom lived, not angry with her for not being able to keep up. *I'm sorry, Lord. I am. Keep me straight, okay, God?*

A prayer Jeff knew God delighted in answering. Even if it took a two by four. He exited the jeep and went to locate either Morris or the missing backpack.

It took longer than Jeff expected to find both. But ten minutes out of his schedule wouldn't compare to the time it would take Collin to replace all the missing documents. Right now, she needed all the help she could get. Even if it cost him ten minutes. Jeff walked back to the jeep—

To find it empty. Now what? Where had Mom gone? Jeff looked

around the vicinity of the parking area but didn't see her. He retraced his steps into the garage; no Mom. He started to call out when he heard a slight "Oh." It came from over by a flatbed truck. On the trailer sat the remains of Collin's light blue beetle. Jeff walked over and saw his mom standing there.

Lacey's hand touched a mangled lump of metal. It might have been a fender. The steering wheel beside it looked like a tortured figure eight. A tire rim held shards of shredded and melted rubber. Jeff said carefully, "Mom?"

Lacey turned toward him, her face pale, her eyes horrified. She whispered, "Collin…your Collin…she…in this…this…"

Jeff continued to speak carefully, not sure about his mother's confusion. "Yes, Mom. She had an accident."

Lacey looked back at the wreckage. "Collin drove this?"

Jeff took his mom's arm and steered her away from the flatbed. "Yes, Mom. On Monday. She's okay. She's at home."

Lacey's mouth fell open. "Monday? And you let her go home? And left her there by herself?"

The woman came unglued. "Are you out of your loving mind? Why would you ever let someone out of the hospital so soon after a wreck like this? Do you see the chassis? The undercarriage? No! Of course not, because they're both gone! Jeffery Farrell, I am…I am…"

Jeff's eyes widened in amazement and surprise and unadulterated joy as his mom—his *mom*—made her full return. He hugged her close, burying his head in her shoulder. "Mom. Welcome back, Mom." His tears came freely.

Lacey caught her breath. Her eyes widened. She stopped ranting, took in a deep, calming breath, and laughed. "I guess I am." She hugged Jeff in return, holding him and matching her tears to his.

They stood unmoving for several more moments. Jeff finally said, "I guess we should go get Collin." He couldn't stop smiling. "She's going to love the real Mom."

As they climbed into the jeep and left the parking lot, Lacey said, "I was in there, you know. Or you don't. I could see you. All of you. But the air-headed ditz wouldn't let me speak. All of life had to be fine and rosy and delightful. I couldn't make her pay attention to me. I am so sorry for how—"

"Don't. Don't apologize." Jeff touched his mom's arm. "We

loved you before, and we loved the air-headed ditz. We were happy to have you alive."

Lacey snorted. "Uh-huh." A light sparked in her eyes.

Jeff noticed the light had a touch of something mischievous in it. "Mom?"

Lacey chortled. "When we get home, I get to tell your father I'm back. My way. You hear me? No letting on."

"What are you thinking, Mom?"

"Never you mind. I want your word. I get to tell him."

Jeff had an uneasy feeling about it but nodded. "Okay. You tell him."

They drove to the trailer court, and Jeff parked in front of Collin's trailer. "Are you going to tell Collin, or can I?"

"I'll tell her. I think she and I have a great deal to discuss, woman to woman. Up to now, we've been one woman short."

Lacey swung out of the jeep and walked the steps with her son. As Collin opened the door, Lacey stepped inside and carefully hugged Collin. "Oh, Collin. You wonderful, dear, sweet thing. I am so looking forward to getting to know you."

Collin looked at Jeff in confusion; Jeff said, his voice tight, "Mom's back. The real Mom's back."

Surprise turned to joy and flooded Collin's face. It spilled over her eyes, and the three of them had a good cry to baptize the moment.

Lacey laughed. "Come on, you two. We need to get this show moving. I have a husband at home I haven't seen in years." She fixed Jeff and Collin with a mock fierce look. "But no telling him until I do. Got it?"

The two nodded obediently. "Yes, ma'am." All three climbed into the jeep and headed for the Farrell household.

* * *

Thirty minutes later, the group arrived at the house on the south side of the river. The river marked the division between old money and new. South had vintage houses; the kind you worked hard to heat in the winter—or keep cool in the summer—but with tons of character. North had planned developments where all the houses looked alike, and you could shake hands with your neighbor through the bathroom windows.

Collin's apprehension grew as they neared the Farrell house. Having Lacey back in her right mind might make explaining Collin's past easier. It could also be another hurdle to cross. Suppose the "real" Lacey didn't think Collin good enough for her son? Suppose Harmon and Lacey both objected to her shady background?

Shady? How about criminal? The prosecutor dropped the charges on a technicality. The judge felt sorry for you. You, with your poor, poor misguided upbringing. You should have gone to prison. Life without parole. Instead of on the streets preaching sanctimonious hypocrisy to truly innocent young people you pretend to —

Collin savagely shut the accuser down. *Shut up!* She prayed, *Father, please. Help me, please.*

Oblivious to Collin's inner turmoil, Lacey winked at Jeff and Collin and walked in the door first. Harmon sat in his leather wing-backed chair facing the window. He rose as the trio entered the room. "Hello, dear. Jeff. Collin, so good to have you here again. I'm sorry it is under these trying conditions."

Collin ducked her head to Harmon's recognition of the passing of her grandfather. "Thank you, sir."

Lacey walked over to Harmon and said, in her most sugary voice, "Hello, dear." Then she planted a lip-lock on him to make a Hollywood romance producer proud. The look on Harmon's face went from surprise to confusion. Finally, realization hit him. He wrapped his arms around his wife and kissed her properly for the first time in years.

Collin felt her tears leak out again. Jeff's voice choked. "Yep, Mom's back."

Harmon and Lacey broke for air. Harmon did not let her go. He lifted his head in wonder and amazement as his tears fell. "Thank You, Lord. Thank You, Lord. Oh, Father, thank You."

Lacey's joy covered her face in tears as well. "Harmon. Harmon, I have missed you so much."

As Collin watched the reunion continue, she had an overwhelming feeling she should leave.

Go. You're trouble. No one needs your problems. Make your own decisions.

Sure. I'll walk home. I'm not going to pull Jeff away from this and insist he take me home.

Leesa came in from the kitchen. "What's wrong with Mom and Dad? Why are they crying?" She took a good look at Jeff and Collin. "Why are you crying?" Her face screwed up in an attempt not to join the others without reason.

Lacey pulled Leesa to her side and hugged her. "I'm back, Leesa." She smiled. "I left, but now I'm back."

"Where did you go?"

Lacey stroked her daughter's hair lovingly. "A long way away, Lees. A very long way away."

Leesa cocked her head. "You went to get Collin. It's not so far."

Lacey laughed. "You're right, honey. Why don't I help you bring out some tea for your father? And Jeff, you can make the coffee." She and Leesa headed for the kitchen.

Harmon waited until Lacey walked out of the room. He looked at Jeff. "I think the party is over. I may need your help getting to all those projects I've put off."

Jeff nodded. "Yeah. And I'll have to start washing my own clothes. And making my bed."

Collin glared at the two men. "You are so bad!"

Harmon nodded. "Guilty. Thank you, young woman, for helping make this happen. I don't know what you did, but thank you."

"I didn't do anything, Mr. Farrell. Jeff…"

Jeff said swiftly, "Mom saw Collin's car. It somehow jarred her into reality."

"I thank you for your lack of driving skills, Ms. Walker."

Collin sighed. "Please, it's Collin. I'd appreciate it if you'd call me Collin."

"If you will return the favor and call me Harmon."

Collin said slowly, "I feel disrespectful, sir. Even if you ask, it feels wrong."

Harmon suggested, "Pop Harmon? It's what the boys at the station call me."

Collin let it rattle around in her brain a few times. Since no one in the choir automatically jumped to object, she nodded. "I'll try. With reminders."

Jeff led Collin to the overstuffed couch opposite Harmon's chair and left to make coffee. A second wing-backed chair—this one upholstered—faced the couch as well. A third chair, comfortably outdated and unmatched to anything else in the room, completed the family setting.

Lacey and Leesa came back into the room, followed by Jeff. Lacey gave Harmon his iced tea; Jeff set down a mug of steaming coffee for Collin and one for himself. Leesa plopped in the third chair, content to sit.

Lacey fixed Harmon with a fierce glare. "Enjoy it. It's the last sweet tea you drink in this house, my dear. I tried it." Lacey grimaced. "It tastes like syrup! Who's been making it for you? I'll bet your blood sugar is through the roof."

Harmon put as innocent a look on his face as he could muster. "Why, you've been making it, dear. Making it as sweet as your personality."

Lacey's face held a no-nonsense scowl. "Uh-huh. Change is coming. Trust me."

Harmon wisely nodded. "Yes, Lacey, my love. And I am looking forward to every change you want to make." His eyes shone with love and gratitude.

Lacey looked to Collin. "Jeff said you had things you needed to discuss with us tonight. About your grandfather's passing?"

You're on. Make it good. Collin nodded. "But I'm not sure tonight is the best time—"

Jeff and Lacey both interrupted. Jeff said, "Collin—"

Lacey said, "Now is the best time. 'Later' can be too late. Or it can mean never. Talk, young woman."

Jeff took Collin's hand. Collin drew in a deep breath; let it out slowly. "I have to give you the dreaded background first. My paternal grandfather was Jeremiah Winger."

Harmon asked, "The Fort Newton munitions Winger?"

"The same. Jeremiah took over the company from his father. He married Joy, my grandmother. They were married for twenty years and had three sons."

Collin resisted the urge to spit, cough, or otherwise display her distaste. "Robert is the oldest and my biological father. Richard is next and finally Rupert. Robert turned twenty when Jeremiah died. Joy took control of a rather healthy estate." Collin paused. "A very healthy estate."

Harmon nodded. Jeff squeezed Collin's hand. She continued, "Two years later, Joy married Fenton Mudd. Her sons believed

Fenton married her for the money—*their* money."

Collin grimaced. She stood, unable to ignore the tension in her body. Maybe if she moved around… "Naturally, all three sons wanted control of the family estate. Grandmother Joy decided to revive an old family tradition of willing the lion's share to the firstborn child of the firstborn child. If Robert had no children, Richard's firstborn child would get control. You get the idea."

Harmon frowned. "Interesting tradition. I can see where it could go bad rather swiftly."

"It did. Robert had…"

Collin looked over to Leesa. Jeff's sister seemed to be listening carefully. Collin looked to Jeff and motioned slightly to him about Leesa. Jeff said softly, "She can hear it. Go ahead."

Collin sat on the hearth to continue. "Robert had a child out of wedlock, a son, Patrick. Robert presented Patrick to Grandmother Joy as heir-apparent, but Grandmother refused to recognize him as such."

Collin shifted her hips on the unyielding stone. "Oh, she welcomed Patrick as a true grandchild and doted on him as any good grandmother would. But the 'heir' had to be legitimate. Robert dumped Patrick's mother, then found and married my mother, Felicity."

Collin yearned for memories of her mother, but few existed. One did, but she refused to recall it. Willingly. The hearth remained as unfeeling as her memories. "A year after they were married, Felicity had twins. My brother and me. Aaron and Caitlin Winger."

Collin closed her eyes and dropped her head. "Except I came out first. Robert's plan of a son he could groom in his image shattered. Girls marry; they give everything to their husbands. Girls are useless." Collin looked. "Or so he told me. Everyday. Out loud."

She fell silent, working hard to quell the surge of emotions accompanying the memories. "Put bluntly, he hated me." Jeff got up, moved to the hearth, and sat beside her. He put an arm around her shoulder.

Collin said, "I won't go into all the details of how life went." She snorted lightly. "Erin didn't get off easy, either. Robert deliberately changed the spelling of his name from Aaron to Erin. Said if he couldn't be man enough to beat a girl out of the womb, he didn't deserve a man's name."

Lacey said, "This makes my heart hurt, Collin. I can't fathom anyone being so hard-hearted toward their children. I can't."

Collin reached across the distance to touch the woman's hand lightly. "Thanks. Mom died before we turned six." Collin could feel the emotions swell as she came to the next part of her retelling. "When we were fourteen is when it all came apart." She closed her eyes. She saw the past replaying in her mind's eye. All of it. Again and again.

* * *

Erin slammed the football into his twin sister's stomach and yelled angrily, "You throw like a girl!! I'll never make JV if you don't throw like a real quarterback!"

Caitlin seethed back, "I am a girl. I'll always be a girl. It's why he hates me. I'm useless, remember? Useless and dirty; I soil everything I touch and destroy everyone who tries to love me."

Erin's anger disappeared. "You're not useless, Cane. Girls aren't useless, no matter what he says. I love you. That'll never change. Forget what he says, you got it?"

Caitlin nodded slowly. Erin took the ball back. He placed Caitlin's hand around the ball. "Like this. Throw it like this. Throw it as far and as hard as you can, and I'll run under it. Don't wait for me to run; throw it."

Caitlin nodded. "Got it, A-One."

"Ready?"

Caitlin nodded, hefted the football as far as she could. Surprisingly, it went farther than either she or Erin expected. Erin missed it by a mile. Caitlin grinned. "You missed."

Erin looked amazingly pleased with himself. "I knew you had it in you. Do it again. Farther this time." He pointed to the sloping field opposite the yard. "Over there. Gives me more room to run."

Caitlin nodded for Erin to start running. She hesitated, launched the ball into the air. She watched as Erin ran under the ball, leaped for it, and landed hard on his back. The boy slammed his head into the hard turf and lay still.

Caitlin waited for her brother to get up, but he didn't move. After a moment, she called, "Erin? You okay?" No answer. "Erin?" No answer. Caitlin screamed, "Erin!" She ran down the slope frantically. She dropped to her knees beside him and screamed again, "Erin!"

The fourteen-year-old remained amazingly calm. "I can't move, Cane. I can't move. I can't feel anything at all."

Caitlin jumped to her feet and ran toward the house. She screamed the entire way, "Call 911. Call 911!!" Her mind began to chant, Don't die, A-One. Don't die, A-One. Don't die…

* * *

Collin came out of the memory. Silence filled the room. Collin felt the tears on her face. Saw the tears on the other's faces and realized she had spoken the memory, not simply relived it in her mind. She whispered, "I'm sorry."

Harmon directed, "Go on, Collin. What happened?"

"The ambulance came." So did the replay.

* * *

Chaos and confusion and uniforms and voices followed. The EMTs shuffled Caitlin to the side of the crowd of grown-ups, left out of whatever they were doing to her brother. She could only chant silently, Don't die, A-One. Don't die. *Finally, the paramedics loaded Erin onto a stretcher and moved to take him away. Caitlin stood by, numb. Erin must have said something, for one of the medics grabbed her arm. "He wants you. Make it fast."*

Caitlin crawled beside the stretcher and looked with fear into her brother's face. Erin looked pale. He said, "Swear on our pact."

Caitlin shouted violently, "Don't. Don't say it."

Erin repeated sharply, "Swear. Swear it now."

Caitlin couldn't keep the tremor out of her voice, nor from her hands, but she placed them both on her brother's shoulders, right on his left; left on his right. She said roughly, "I swear I will fulfill my vow to my brother Erin before I die."

The paramedic said brusquely, "We don't have time for kids' games. We have to go now." He moved Caitlin out of the ambulance; the door closed, and the van roared away.

* * *

"I never saw Erin again." Collin dropped her gaze. She took

several moments to pull herself together. "I sat in the house for hours waiting for someone to come and tell me if he made it. Not one phone call. Nothing. Until Patrick showed up about midnight." Collin refused to allow the memory to play. "Patrick told me Erin died. He said Erin blamed me for his accident and said to tell me he hated me.

"Patrick told me to get in the car. I thought he would take me to the hospital in Fort Newton. But he drove me to Oakton."

Collin raised her head in anger. "Three in the morning, he dropped me off under the downtown overpass and told me to do the world a favor and kill myself. If I didn't have the guts, I should show my face at the house, and he would do it for me. Then he drove off."

Jeff hugged Collin. She shrugged. "I tried. I did. But the Lord had other plans for me." Collin closed her eyes a moment. Finally, she opened them and looked at Harmon and Lacey. "After two failed attempts, I got the feeling I had to live. Didn't want to but had to. If only to fulfill my pact with Erin."

Collin admitted, "I did all I needed to survive. I stole food, I stole electronics to sell to pawn shops, I stole money from unlocked cars." She shrugged and added, "Until I learned to unlock them myself. Nothing like a street education." Collin fell silent. She faltered but pushed through. "I sold myself. Anything. Two years I lived on the streets. I got hard, and I got bitter."

Collin stood again. She motioned for Jeff to follow her. Together they went back to the couch. She took a long swallow from her now less-than-hot coffee. "Eventually, I heard about a soup kitchen with a place to shower, get clean clothes, maybe even a place to sleep. Someone warned me about a guy there preaching about Jesus, but you could ignore him and still get the food and stuff. So I went." She looked at her hands, unable to lift her eyes.

"Brother Golding didn't preach about Jesus. He lived Jesus. He breathed Jesus." Collin's voice quavered. "He didn't care what I'd been, or what I'd done. He simply loved me, like he loved all the other street rats brave enough—or desperate enough—to go to him."

Collin waited until she thought her voice could be steady. Another pull on the coffee, and she said, "He broke through all my walls of hate and anger and bitterness…it took him a long time, but Brother Golding introduced me to Jesus. I accepted Him as Lord. And I've never looked back."

Collin let out a deep sigh. "Brother Golding went to bat for me with the courts. He has connections. Lawyers and advocates and the like. They convinced the judge that going back to my father would put me in jeopardy. They investigated and Robert Winger happily surrendered all his parental rights. Then Brother Golding got me into the foster care program. He had me work to make restitution where I could. He insisted I go to school, stay in school, and made sure I got my diploma. Brother Golding even helped me apply for a scholarship to college. I legally changed my name as soon as I could."

Harmon asked, "Why Collin Walker? If you don't mind me asking."

"Being Winger at birth, and having been abandoned, I decided to call myself Walker. No first name, simply Walker. Eventually, I got tired of people 'calling' me Walker. So I added the Collin." She shrugged, a little embarrassed. "Worked for me. Anyhow, I graduated, got my Social Worker's certificate, went to work, heard about Camp Grace, went there, and met Jeff. The rest, you know."

Harmon took Lacey's hand. She nodded at him. He looked at Collin. "Nothing you said changes how we feel about you, Collin. If you weren't already spoken for, we'd adopt you ourselves."

Jeff said quickly, "You can't! I can't marry my sister!"

Leesa interrupted, "I will not marry you! You have stinky feet!"

The tension in the room broke. Everyone chuckled, including Leesa. She smiled at Jeff. "I love you, brother."

Jeff smiled back. "I love you too, Lees."

Harmon waited until the merriment ran its course. "Collin, you told us all this as background to your grandfather's death and why you wanted our help. I'm guessing there's a will?"

"Worse. Grandmother's will, which the whole family knew about, had distributed it all semi-evenly between the brothers but gave the heir a fifty-five percent share of the corporation. She wanted to make sure the brothers couldn't gang up and outvote the heir's control." Collin scowled. "She knew her sons."

Again, Collin rose to pace the floor. "Grandmother left the estate to Fenton, with the understanding her will would come into effect only after Fenton died.

"But once things passed to Grandfather Fenton, he changed it. He made a new will." Collin steeled herself. "Grandfather knew how

I'd been treated by my father. He, of all the family, tried to find me after Patrick dumped me in Oakton." Collin stared at the ceiling to let her emotions settle. She closed her eyes. "He's the only one in the family I contacted after I graduated high school. We kept in touch through his law firm."

Collin continued to keep her eyes closed. "I found out yesterday he made me sole owner of the whole estate." She gritted her teeth. "The whole blasted three hundred million dollars."

Collin gathered her strength. "I can distribute it however I want. I can keep it all myself. It's my decision who and how much anyone gets. And no one can do anything about it."

Frustration mixed with her anger and helplessness. "I'm a social worker. I defer my paychecks so that I'm living barely above minimum wage, the way my kids' families do. I do it so I can help others. But this…this changes…this ruins it." Her voice trembled. "I don't want to have to move, or quit, or be someone I'm not. But I can't hide this kind of money. No one can."

Collin stopped. "Okay, some people can. But not me." She looked pointedly at Jeff, and her voice quavered. "I don't want anything to change between us because of it." She looked back at Harmon and Lacey. "And I frankly don't want to face anyone in the family. I thought I'd worked past all the garbage, but I haven't had to face them."

Collin grimaced. "I'm not getting answers from the Lord, either." *Except call Jeff. Which I did.* "If He's waiting for me to figure it out on my own, it's going to be a long wait."

Lacey got up, walked to Collin, and hugged her tightly. "I love you, Collin. We're here to help. Any way, any how."

Harmon said slowly, "It's getting late." He looked at the clock. "It's after nine. In my experience, no good decisions happen after eight." He looked to Lacey and added, "Except your decision to marry me. That happened after eight. Nine-thirty, Lacey?"

Lacey's eyes shone. "On the nose." She looked back at Collin. "But Harmon is right. There's nothing to be done tonight." She fixed Collin with a stern glare. "Not even worry about it."

Collin ducked her head. "Yes, ma'am."

Jeff said, "I'm off the next two days. Dad, you don't have anything on your calendar over the weekend, right? Can we make it a family breakfast?"

Leesa said brightly, "Waffles. Dad makes waffles. I make bacon. Mom makes eggs. Jeff cleans up." She laughed at her brother.

Collin swallowed hard. A family circling the wagons when one member hurt. *Lord, I want this. I want this for my family. Make it so, please.*

Jeff tossed a pillow at Leesa, careful not to hit anywhere near her. "For that, you can stay here while I take Collin home." He looked to Collin. "You and me tonight, okay? I want to show you something."

Collin nodded, unsure what he might be referring to. Another revelation. Could she handle one more? *Live a little. What's one more secret between friends, huh?* The woman shuddered.

FRIDAY NIGHT

Collin and Jeff left the Farrell's house a little after ten. Jeff drove the jeep past the freeway entrance, turning left instead of right. He held Collin's hand as he drove. "You remember I told you at camp how Dad owned and managed some properties. And how I worked for and with him as his advisor." Collin nodded but said nothing. Jeff would move this show at his own pace.

Jeff said, "After all you shared, I figured now—tonight—would be a good time to show you where some of those properties are. It might take one worry off your overloaded brain."

Collin said without mirth, "One thing would be welcome." *But which one, aye, matey?*

They cruised and let the silence speak. Jeff drove past the downtown mall, circled it once, circled it a second time, headed uptown. Collin looked behind her at the mall. *Okay, what happened?*

Maybe he needed a place to turn around. Probably got lost. No U-turns in this town, remember? He wanted to see the lights. Go with it.

Jeff slowed as he entered the parking lot of the university's latest and greatest medical facility. He didn't stop but weaved his way in and out of the rows until he reached the end of the lot. He drove around behind the hospital, circled the back twice, exited, and turned back onto the expressway. Jeff drove north to the Arena, built to house concerts and entertainment otherwise too populous for the antiquated mid-town centers.

A chill ran up Collin's back. Jeff made one loop around the arena. He pulled back out onto the freeway, headed back toward downtown. Collin couldn't keep the disbelief from her voice. "Your dad owns those? All of them?"

Jeff nodded. "Every last parking lot."

Collin's eyes narrowed. She saw the catbird-eating grin on his face. "Not funny, Farrell. What are you trying to tell me?"

Jeff drove toward Collin's trailer court. "I'm saying Dad owns a great deal of property in this town. Owns a lot, manages more. I work with him. I inherit the business when the time comes. Dad offered my brothers the same deal, but neither wanted it. They're both doing well enough on their own."

Jeff steered around two slow-moving tractor-trailers playing tag in front of him. "Which means it's mine. The only stipulation is I take care of Leesa after my folks are gone or can't take care of her anymore." He looked at Collin. "It's something my wife will have to agree to as well. I won't abandon Leesa."

Collin said sharply, "Nor should you. You don't throw someone away because they can't care for themselves." She squeezed his hand. "If we marry, Leesa will always have a place with us. And with me, if something happens."

She sat back and let the thoughts roll around. "So what do you really do? Is being a paramedic a cover for your dad?"

"No. Never. It gets a bit tricky, but I'm not actually on the payroll at the fire station."

"Why?"

Jeff frowned. "It's a long story, having to do with staffing and budget cuts and city councils and elections. Council told the city to reduce funding for the stations by ten percent."

His voice became a tad sarcastic. Unusual. But human. "In their infinite wisdom, they figured each station could lose one man and service wouldn't suffer."

Jeff grimaced. "Those of us on the firing line—okay, bad choice of words—knew different. But the council wouldn't listen. It being an election year and all, cutting expenses would be the magic bullet to get elected, or reelected."

Jeff left the freeway, turned onto Grant. "Some of the stations had 'fat' they could cut. But not all of them, and not ours. We worked around it by cutting my position and me working as a volunteer. I work the same shifts the others do, but I don't get paid."

"How is that different from any other volunteer?

"Others get some renumeration for uniforms, mileage, meals and the like. The city has to pay worker's comp, insurance, and a few other technicalities. I pay my expenses, my insurance, and will cover any liability if something happens, and the station or I am at fault."

Jeff turned on Williams. "I feel about my community the way you do about yours. I'll do anything in my power to see they don't suffer if they don't have to."

They rode in silence for a few minutes. Collin said, "Since we're breaking protocol tonight, can we break it a little further and stop and get ice cream? I feel the need for a hot fudge sundae. Two scoops. Lots of whipped cream. No nuts."

Jeff saluted. "The lady wants ice cream, the lady gets ice cream. Any place in particular, or does it matter?"

"Whoever gives the most hot fudge without having to be prompted. Or paid for."

"Ice Cream Palace. They're open 'til eleven on Fridays. We still have time."

"Sounds great." Collin rested her head on the neck support and felt some of the tension drain from her body. Not all of it. But some of it. Any of it would be a good thing. She even closed her eyes for a few moments…

To be shaken—gently—awake by Jeff. "Collin. We're here, milady. You sure you want to do this? Or should I take you home instead? You're wiped out, I know."

Collin cleared the buzzards from her head. "I want ice cream. I'm not going home without it."

"Suit yourself."

Jeff climbed out of the jeep, ran around, and opened the door for Collin. Collin smiled. "Thank you, kind sir."

"You are most welcome, madam. Welcome to my favorite establishment." Jeff waved toward the entrance.

Collin asked, "Not 'your' establishment, right? Or is it?"

He laughed. "No. Neither Dad nor I own anything as fun as an ice cream parlor. Might be a good investment."

"Especially if you're married to me. You should buy stock."

"I'll look into it."

The girl at the counter took the order for two large hot fudge sundaes with whipped cream and cherries, one with nuts, one without. Collin got a table near the back, away from most of the customers. Jeff carried the ice creams.

Only after the first two mouthfuls had been properly tested and met with approval did Collin begin to chuckle. Jeff looked at her with question in his eyes. Collin covered her mouth. "Between our two inheritances, you'd think we could spring for an extra ladle of fudge, right?"

Jeff chortled. "Next time."

Collin lifted her spoon and toasted him. "Next time." After another spoonful or two, she said, "I talked a lot tonight. Dumped a lot on you. I'm sure you have questions." She steeled herself for the onslaught. "Ask."

"No. No questions." Collin eyed him closely. Jeff shrugged. "Okay, two questions." His voice took on a serious tone as he added, "But only two. You have no reason to make apologies or feel ashamed of anything you did. You survived, Collin."

Jeff reached across the table and touched her hand protectively. "What matters is you survived. Whatever happened, God used it to bring you to be the person you are today. If He hadn't, I wouldn't have met you, and I'd die a lonely old man."

Jeff held her gaze. She searched his eyes for the censure she knew he must be feeling. Like all the others had. But she saw only truth and love. No hint of condemnation. No hint of self-righteousness. Nothing. Only love and acceptance.

Collin dropped her eyes, stirred her sundae around. "So, first question."

"What was the pact between you and your brother? If you can tell me. Or want to."

Collin lowered her head. "That one of us would dance on Father's grave. Stupid. And wrong I know now." She looked up. "Second question?"

"You called your brother 'A-One.' And he called you 'Cane.' Did you use those as code names for each other?"

"You want to know about the names? Only the names?" Flabbergasted, Collin stared at him in disbelief.

Jeff said, "Love of my life, I want to ask you about all of it. I want to know where you lived, how you lived. Who helped you? Who didn't. I want to know all of it."

He took her hand. "When and if you ever want to tell me details, I'm ready to listen. Not judge, not try to fix it. Just listen. But only when you want to tell me. All of it can wait for eternity if it has to. But I do want to know about the names you called each other. Where in the world did they come from?"

Collin admitted, "Until we were three—maybe four—we had trouble pronouncing words. I couldn't say the 'r' in his name, so it always came out 'awon.' Erin couldn't get the 'tl' in mine, so he called me 'kayun.'"

She smiled, a little embarrassed. "We kept using them, albeit a little modified: A-One and Cane. No one else ever used them. Robert hated baby talk and would discipline us if he heard. We made it a point not to use the names in his hearing. So, yeah, I guess you could say yes, we had secret names for each other."

Collin scraped the bottom of her bowl, licked the last of the chocolate off her spoon, but resisted the urge to lick the edges of the dessert cup. "I guess you should take me home. It's been an exhausting day."

"Emotional, too. I'll pick you up in the morning around…eight? Nine?"

"Eight. I'd like to get a jump on the day." *Because no one knows how long it will take to find a solution to this mess.*

God knows.

And He isn't telling. So we muddle through on our own.

Jeff bussed the table. They walked out together, climbed in the jeep, and headed to the heart of downtown. Several blocks away from Collin's trailer court, two fire trucks raced past them. Jeff pulled over to let them go. He looked in his mirror. "Here comes another one."

Collin quipped, "I heard they always travel in packs." The look in Jeff's eyes said the joke had fallen flat. "What's wrong?"

"The trucks are from different stations. It means whoever responded to the original call couldn't handle it alone and requested backup."

Collin got serious fast. "Meaning it's something big?"

Jeff nodded. "Yeah." He closed his eyes and prayed, "Lord, watch over my brothers and sisters in arms. Protect them. Please."

Collin added, "Amen." She hesitated a moment. "You want to drive over and see where it is? See if they need help you can give?"

"No. Too many bodies get in the way and make it more of a hazard. Besides, I don't have my gear. Which makes me more of a hazard."

Collin breathed a silent, *Thank You.* She needed to accept the reality of Jeff being a fireman. And what it meant. All of it. The uncertainty. The worry. The injuries. The death...

You aren't married yet, and you're already freaking out about his work?

I am not freaking out. I am facing reality. I am. For once.

Jeff turned off the thoroughfare into the back streets of the bottoms of Oakton. Collin noted the sirens getting louder. A chill ran through her. Not her place. Couldn't be. *Trailers burn fast. Kids are in bed. Adults are sleeping. Even if they hear the smoke detectors, there's not time... Please, Lord. Not my court. Not my people. Please.*

Collin felt the sense of calm sweep over her.

It's going to be fine. Hard, but fine. I am with you. His promised assurance would be all she would get. She hoped it would be all she needed.

They approached Lincoln Way. A uniformed officer waved them down with a "Road's closed. Turn around."

Collin leaned across Jeff. "I live in the trailer court at 107. Is it burning?"

"Sorry, ma'am. Yes. You'll have to turn around and go back."

Jeff flashed his fireman's ID and asked quietly, "How bad is it?"

"Two trailers are gutted. Three more are burning, and the rest of the court is threatened. Fire crews are trying to keep it contained."

Collin demanded, "Did they all get out? Are they safe?"

The officer looked at Jeff first before admitting, "There are casualties. How many I don't know."

Collin felt the blood drain from her face and heart. She closed her eyes, drawing into her shell. *Breathe. Breathe. Calm. Controlled. No panic. No emotion. Controlled. Emotions cloud your thinking. Breathe.*

Jeff turned the jeep around and headed back toward the house. Collin directed sharply, "No. Go right at the alley."

Jeff's look had suspicion in his eyes. "Why?"

"Do it." Collin tempered the demand. "Please."

Jeff complied. At the dead-end, Collin pointed. "There. Go through there. It's an access road."

"Access for who?" The potholes looked big enough to swallow

a small car.

"Is this a jeep? Does it have four-wheel drive? Do it. Please."

Jeff warily and reluctantly navigated the cavernous pits to come out in an open field. Collin pointed again. "Across the field, between the trees."

Jeff idled the jeep. "No. Not until you tell me where we're going."

Collin made the one appeal she knew Jeff would understand and not turn down. "If those were your people, your neighborhood on fire, wouldn't you go back to help?"

Jeff held Collin's gaze. "If they were my people, I'd go charging in there with my ax ready to mow down anything in my way." He paused. "Which is why I'm a paramedic. I'm not to be trusted with an ax. Collin, I understand you feel helpless."

Collin cut him off sharply. "But I'm not helpless. I can go in there, and I can make sure people get out. I can give them a chance."

"Which the fire crews are doing."

"You don't understand. They'll go in and look for people where they should be. Not where they *will* be. I know where the kids hide. I know why they hide, and I know where. Your crews will check off a trailer as empty and decide not to risk saving it…and people will die. Please, Jeff. At least get me to where I can see what's going on. Please."

Jeff held Collin's eyes a moment longer. He silently turned and drove the jeep across the field and between the two trees. Someone had forced an opening between the fences. Beyond the fence, an abandoned lot backed to the south side of the trailer court.

Collin jumped out before Jeff came to a complete stop. She pressed her way to the opening in the fence and squeezed through.

Jeff caught her on the other side of the barrier and grabbed her hand. "Wait. Do not run in there. We need to check which way the fire is moving. Which way the wind is blowing. What's closest. Firefighters are trained, Collin. We know how to stay alive and how to keep others alive. You follow my lead, or I throw you in the jeep and take you home."

This is my home! And it's burning! Voices screamed in her head, urging full-on fight and flight, complete panic, total urgency to act. Guilt mounted its attack. *You're safe. You're out here, you coward. You should be in there, dragging people out. Ignore Jeff. Go! Go!*

Collin appealed to Higher Headquarters. *Father, help me.*

Do as Jeff says. Wait. Watch. Obey him.

Obey? Obey? You're out of your mind! You don't obey anyone…

Collin nodded. "Okay. I'll wait." And pray the others stayed safe.

Collin scanned the area. This side of the trailer court had, up to now, not been affected by the flames. Families milled around a safe distance—or what the firemen had deemed safe—away. Calls went across groups of names, theories, who saw anything, who didn't see nothing, who to blame…in short, the usual crowd noise. Collin turned away. A glint of light caught her eye. She looked again. A trickle of some unsteady glow wound its way from the field toward the gathered families. Collin motioned for Jeff. "Is—"

The trickle touched a dark puddle of something and exploded into a fireball of destruction. Jeff shoved Collin back toward the trees and yelled, "Call 911. Tell them there's fire coming in from the south. The crews won't see it 'til it's too late." He broke into a run and yelled at the onlookers. "Get out! Get Out! Go!"

Collin wanted to run after him and see if he got to the people in time. Wanted to grab as many children as she could and haul them to safety. Wanted to do anything but stand there and make a phone call. Even trying to decide what to do would take too long. Instinct kicked in. She punched the number on her phone and waited for the infuriatingly calm voice on the other end to say, "Nine-one-one. What is your emergency?"

"I'm at the empty lot between Jefferson and Lincoln. The fire at 107 Lincoln Way is building from the south of the field. Something exploded. There are people trapped between the trailers and the field. The fire crews are going to be fighting two fronts any minute. Hurry."

The operator went silent. *Come on, come on. Believe me. This is not a prank.*

The line opened again. "Are you in a safe place?"

"Yes, but no one else is. We need help. Now."

"The message has been passed through to the commander in charge at the scene. Stay clear of the area and do not attempt to approach the fire."

Collin stared at the phone. Why did people automatically assume she would run back into the flames?

They know you.

The operator doesn't know me from Eve. I said I would obey Jeff, and I will. This time.

Collin turned back to the horror which had been her home only hours ago. She couldn't see Jeff, but groups of people now mingled behind the fire, on her side of it and safe. Many were crying. Some choked on the smoke, some stomped on errant flames.

The edict to stay out of the fire didn't include helping those no longer being threatened. Collin stripped her jacket off and rushed to cover a small child wearing nothing but a diaper. She picked the struggling toddler up, getting a knee to the ribs for her trouble. She ignored the pain and looked for the child's mother. She proved easy to find: she would be the frantic-looking woman screaming for her baby. Collin gladly surrendered the equally screaming child back to her mother's arms.

A muffled explosion sounded to the west, maybe two blocks from the conflagration in front of Collin. She looked to see a roof blown into chunks of flaming tar and asphalt raining on the empty buildings, which burst into more flames and chain-reacted up and down the street. Collin whispered, "Dear God, make it stop! Help us!"

The wall of flame seemed determined to join ends and encircle the neighborhood. The firefighters would be trapped inside, along with residents from the trailer park who hadn't gotten clear in the first rush. Collin's heart hammered in time to the voices in her head: *Go! Go! Grab someone and go!*

No! No! Stay safe and away! Do not be a martyr!

Jeff is in there. Jeff is in there. He needs you.

He needs you not to be stupid and do what you're told for once.

No one needs you. You're useless!

Collin did the only thing she could do: she stayed put and prayed. Collin poured out her fear, her anguish, her anticipation of loss, her frustration…if an emotion could be felt, she offered it to the Lord. In defiance of the voices telling her to fight, to run, to jump between the flames, to grab a hose and do *something*, Collin stood and prayed. And prayed. And prayed.

And continued to pray as the second battalion of firefighters arrived on the scene. Prayed as civilians were brought out alive and whole. Prayed as ambulances arrived to take away those less so.

Prayed as police cordoned off the area. Prayed until Jeff came choking out of the smoke, singed but not burned, to take her in his arms and hold her close.

Collin hugged Jeff. She held him as if she would never let him go. Ever, ever, ever. And no words were needed.

They walked to a safe place across the way from the bedlam and sat on a concrete retaining wall. Jeff shrugged out of his coat and draped it around Collin's shoulders. Collin leaned her head against Jeff's shoulder. Silently they watched until the fire finally gave up its life, smoldering and spitting but no longer spreading.

They watched while body bags were carried in empty. Watched the bags being carried out full. Watched as one by one, neighbors, friends, acquaintances, strangers were counted and tallied and recorded and checked off to determine who lived and who didn't.

They watched as the Red Cross came to offer blankets and clothing and assistance with temporary housing to the now homeless. Collin made no motion to join the queue of the displaced. She sat. Jeff sat. And they watched.

SATURDAY MORNING

They didn't move until the last crew of firefighters rolled its hoses and pulled away. Only when the police surrounding the area motioned for them to leave did Collin and Jeff get up and walk the long way around to get back to the jeep.

Daylight lifted its head. As they climbed into the vehicle, Collin asked, "When will people be allowed to go back in and look for anything that's left?"

Jeff put the jeep in motion. "You saw it. There's nothing left, Collin."

"There could be lockboxes. Fireproof safes. Something." Collin didn't know why it mattered, but being let in to look through the debris mattered. It did.

"After the fire inspectors make their determination of the cause, if they can, people will be let back in."

"How long will it take?'

"As long as it takes. Some fires are pretty easy to tell where and how they started. Others take more time to investigate." Jeff paused. "Because there were…casualties, it may take longer. The police will have to be involved."

Collin knew the question would go unanswered. Knew it but asked it anyhow. "Were any of the…casualties…children?"

"I don't know, milady. I don't."

Collin nodded. They rode in silence back to Jeff's house, as if it had been predetermined. Collin could not think beyond the now to what next? No next came to mind. Only here, now. Here, now, with Jeff. Here, now, she could get coffee and maybe clean clothes. And beyond? Did life go beyond?

Numb. She felt numb.

A now-familiar flash of pain lightninged through her brain. For once, it didn't knock her back. Even pain couldn't touch her right now. Numb.

Jeff led the way through the front door into the kitchen. She let him settle her in a chair and move off to fix coffee.

Coffee. She needed coffee. Did she drink coffee?

You breathe coffee. If you can't get it liquid, you eat the grounds straight from the can.

Beans, maybe. But not the grounds.

Collin shut down the internal debate. *Overload. Critical mass. Nuclear meltdown.* She muttered angrily, "There will be no meltdown. None. We will make it through this. God, Jeff, and I will make it through." In case the voices were unclear as to the identity of 'we.' Jeff returned with two mugs of coffee. Collin accepted hers. "Thanks. Any idea what time it is?"

"Seven?" Jeff turned to look at the anniversary clock. "Stupid thing. Never tells you the actual hour. Not until it dings."

Collin nodded. "I get it. I'd check my phone if I had the energy."

Jeff pulled his phone from his pocket. "Six forty-five." He squeezed Collin's shoulder. "Leesa is a little bigger than you, but I'm sure she has some clothes you can make work."

"What time do your folks get up?"

A female voice from the hallway said, "About ten minutes ago." Lacey walked into the kitchen, took a long look at Collin and Jeff, held up a hand to indicate, "Wait a minute," went to the coffee pot, and poured herself a cup. She carried it to the table, sat beside Collin, took a sip of the steaming liquid, said, "Okay, now you can start. What happened?"

Jeff asked, "Is Dad up? I'd like to not have to go through this more than once. I'm beat. Collin is beat. We both need showers and clean clothes and long naps." He gave Collin a semi-smile. "I'll take mine at the station. You can take yours here. We have a guest bedroom."

Collin objected, "I don't want to chase you out of your home. I can…" She trailed off as she realized she had no idea what she could or couldn't do.

Lacey said, "I'll get Harmon. He's awake. Probably waiting for the old me to bring him his coffee in bed." She winked at Jeff.

"Administration change. This morning I'll bring it to him. Tomorrow, he can bring it to me."

Jeff shook his head. "Mom, Dad did not take advantage of you all this time. He never asked you to do all the things—"

Lacey laughed. "I know, son. I will be exceptionally gentle with your father and our restructuring of the rules of engagement."

Lacey kissed the top of Jeff's head, touched Collin on the shoulder, poured a cup of coffee for Harmon, and went down the hallway toward the back of the house.

Collin turned back to Jeff. "I don't want to disrupt things here, Jeff. I don't. You don't need to move out. It's your home. I'll find somewhere else to go. I will."

Jeff nodded. "I know you can. You've probably got a dozen friends wanting you to stay with them, and there will be a feeding frenzy over the privilege."

Collin scowled. "I'll find another place to settle."

"Not today. We're still having a waffle breakfast, and we're still going to talk about your situation with your grandfather's passing."

"Oh, right."

"Right. Nothing from last night changes the decisions you need to make. Except maybe helps put them in perspective."

Collin nodded. "I understand."

Her phone rang. She checked the caller ID. Rob. She tried to keep the fear out of her voice. "Tell me you're okay. Tell me your family is safe."

"Yeah, they safe." A long pause followed. "I don't know how to feel about this, caseworker lady. We lost the trailer. Lost everything in it." Silence. "Ain't enough of it left for Worford to find out Mom scammed him. 'Course, she lost the money she tried to scam him out of in the first place. But now neither one of 'em got it. Guess God took care of the problem, huh."

Collin thought long. "Um…okay." *I need time to think that one through.* Collin hesitated. "Do you know how many didn't make it?"

Rob's voice remained even. "They had four at last count. Hard to be sure as they's always coming and going in some of the trailers. 'Bout ten taken to the hospital. Heard some was critical; some not so much. Bad, but not critical."

Collin hated the next question. "Do you know the names of any who didn't make it?"

"No. Don't know names, but don't know any of my friends be missing."

Collin breathed a sigh of relief and a *Thank You.* "I'm at Jeff's parents' house. Jeff is staying at the fire station while I'm here. Until I can figure out where to go. Where are you staying?"

"With Mano."

Collin looked at the phone as if not hearing it correctly. "Excuse me?"

"Yeah. This dude, Mano—you know Mano, right? He says he knows you. Anyhow, Mano came out last night and said anyone needing a place to go could go to his house. He live over the other side of the empty lot. He's good people, you know?"

I didn't. I do now. "Stay safe, Rob. We'll figure it all out. Somehow. Sooner or later."

Rob said, "I asked God to help about Mom. Didn't expect Him to burn the place down to make it happen."

Collin started to object. Could she say what God did or didn't do? He may not have started the fire, but He could certainly use it.

Why didn't He save the ones who got burned? Why didn't He burn Rob's trailer and not the whole neighborhood? Hmm? Answer that...

Collin couldn't. She didn't try. "I'll talk to you later, Rob. I love you, my man."

Harmon and Lacey came into the kitchen. Harmon's eyes moved from Collin to Jeff, eyeing them both. "First, are you both unhurt?" Harmon took a seat next to Collin. Lacey remained standing at the door, leaning against the frame.

Jeff answered for himself and Collin. "We're fine, Dad. A fire started in Collin's neighborhood. It got out of control faster than a natural fire would. I think someone deliberately set a backfire to try to trap people inside."

Collin's eyes flared. Deliberately set? "Why deliberate? You didn't say so last night."

"I've had time to think about it. Remember the stream of fire you pointed out? Remember how it exploded when it hit the puddle? Nothing does that naturally."

Collin accepted the information with a *Let us get back to you on that one* message from her brain. She still had to reconcile being homeless. Again. Having nothing but the clothes on her back. Again.

Being penniless…

Three hundred million isn't exactly penniless, you know. You could buy a nice chunk of real estate. And a car. And a boat. Maybe even a lake to put it on. You could—

Collin pulled out of her thoughts to hear Jeff telling his mom and dad the sequence of events the night before. The heartrending reality of the situation vanquished all the base-natured selfishness. Grace beat greed soundly about the head and shoulders, stomped it, and danced on its head for good measure. Collin said softly, "I want to help them. All of them."

Jeff squeezed Collin's hand. "I know you do. I know you will."

Collin felt the bottom drop out of her stomach. She looked at Jeff, and her voice became cold with conviction. "The fire. You say it could have been deliberately set. To kill someone? Me? Because of the estate?"

Harmon looked Collin in the eyes. "How many residents are there in the area? We'll discount children under the age of twelve. How many?"

Collin did a fast tally. "Possibly 100-120. Somedays more."

"Your odds of being the one the fire intended to kill are—"

Collin recognized the point Harmon wanted her to reach. "One percent."

"Or less. I understand it's a short leap to conclude we're the base cause for everything happening around us. But—"

"But of those hundred people, I'm guessing I'm the only one who has already had one attempt on my life this week."

Jeff's head jerked to look at her in surprise. "Excuse me?"

"I haven't had time to tell you about the visit from the homicide detectives on Thursday morning, have I?"

Jeff's voice reflected some irritation. "No, you haven't mentioned it. Would have been nice to know before now."

Collin ducked her head slightly. "My mind isn't running on all eight cylinders."

Eight? You've never had eight. Four, max, and three of them have a serious miss.

She defended herself. "There's been so much going on. I honestly forgot about it. Two detectives came Thursday morning to ask about the accident."

Collin had to dig deep to remember the discussion. "The owner of the truck which hit me went missing the night before I got hit. They believe whoever drove the truck deliberately ran me off the road." Conviction flooded through her again. "If they are after me, I'm putting you all in danger." She stood. "I should go."

Harmon, Lacey, and Jeff all started to object at once. Harmon waved both Jeff and Lacey to silence. "Please, Collin. Sit. Nothing touches this family except what comes through the Lord's hands first. You're as safe here as you will be anywhere else."

Collin could feel her body beginning to shake as the emotional control, physical exertions, and general stresses she had demanded from her body all began to post 'payment due' notices at the same time. She would not crack. She would not crack. She would not…

Collin sat again. She took several moments to get herself back under control. "As you say, sir. What would you have me do?"

"We'll call the police and tell them you're here, in case they need to find you. We will wait for the fire investigators to determine if the blaze was deliberately set. We will not panic; we will not overreact, nor will we allow you to put yourself in danger to 'protect' us."

Lacey said quietly, "Collin, I think it would do you a world of good to take a long hot shower, get into some clean clothes, eat if you can, and take an extended nap. You're exhausted."

Collin couldn't argue. Wanted to for pride's sake but couldn't. "Thank you, Mom Lacey." Finally, the epithet sounded natural. And more than a little comforting.

Lacey rose from the table with Collin and led her to the guest suite. She pointed out the particulars: "Body wash, shampoo, conditioner. Towels, washcloths, robes." She looked reflective. "We used to have quite the collection of guests staying here." She paused. "Now I'm back in the world of the sane and sensible, maybe we can start having them come again."

More to make conversation than anything, Collin said, "I'll bet your neurologist will be surprised next time he sees you."

Lacey's eyes lit. Collin noted the same mischievous glint in them as had been there when Lacey planned her surprise for Harmon. The older woman nodded. "Oh, I'm sure he will be." Lacey straightened. "I probably should have him confirm my brain is functioning as it's supposed to."

Lacey pointed out a few other essentials. "There are new

toothbrushes, unused combs, and hairbrushes, a blow dryer, curling iron if you're so inclined…"

"I'm a wash and wear kinda gal. Anything else takes too much time."

Lacey gave Collin a high five. "My kinda person. If you need anything I haven't mentioned, I'm sure you'll find it in the linen closet." She frowned. "I doubt if anyone has been in there since the stroke." Lacey fell silent a moment. "I'll have Leesa round up a few outfits for you to try on." Lacey chuckled. "As the only girl, she will be ecstatic at having a sister to share clothes with. Brothers are so boring."

"One outfit is fine. I'm not fussy about my wardrobe."

"No, but Lees isn't going to miss this opportunity to drag out all the clothes she has in hopes you might wear some of them. She is a fashionista."

Lacey left the bedroom, pulling the door closed behind her. Collin decided against locking it. What if she fell asleep in the shower? What if she passed out? What if she decided to use all the hot water? What if…

Collin grabbed a towel and washcloth, shucked her dirty clothes, stepped into the shower, and set about removing the evening's smoke and grime from her body and hair. She wished she could remove it as easily from her brain. The image of the body bags being carted away haunted her. Who were they? Did she know any of them? Were they her fault? Harmon might discount the probability of her being the catalyst for the fire, but Collin couldn't let it drop easily. Regardless of the senior Farrell's assurances, she should leave. Immediately. If not sooner.

Sooner? You're in your birthday suit. Maybe some clothes would make you less obvious on the streets, hmm?

Can you not trust someone else for a change? Can you not believe there may be people who have your best interests at heart? And they might care about you enough to—gasp—sacrifice for you?

Collin rinsed the conditioner out of her hair. "I don't want anyone to sacrifice for me."

Too late. Already done. Be grateful and allow Me to be God and Savior—even for the Farrells. I do love them as well, you might remember.

Collin wrapped a towel around herself, stepped out of the

shower. On the bed lay two calf-length skirts, a small collection of tunic tops, several belts, scarves, and an assortment of shoes. Leesa definitely wanted to share her closet. Collin picked a skirt, a soft long-sleeve tunic, and a belt to tie it all together. She dressed, then sat to look at the shoes.

Pain slashed through her as the dragon in her head roared back to life. Just to remind her it still existed…and still needed to be dealt with. Collin dropped to the floor, put her head on her knees, wrapped her arms around her legs, and let the darkness take her.

* * *

Jeff waited to see if Collin would wake; when she didn't, he packed a few necessities, called the captain for permission, and drove across town to Station Five. He pulled into the parking area, grabbed his duffle bag, and, as he rounded the corner to the sleeping quarters, nearly tripped over Trey in his motorized chair. "What are you doing here?"

Trey repeated the query. "What are you doing here? This isn't your regular shift."

"I asked you first. And what's with the black eye?"

The area around Trey's right eye looked red, puffy, and swollen. Jeff could see blood had filled the eyeball itself. A jagged tear reached from the temple to the bridge of the younger man's nose.

Trey shrugged. "Lost a fight with a dresser. It's nothing."

Jeff's eyes narrowed. "Has anyone looked at your eye?"

"Why? It's nothing. Ignore it. I'm trying to."

Jeff took out his ever-present penlight. "You sound like Collin. Look up." He reached toward Trey's face.

Trey twisted his head away. "It's nothing, Jeff. Let it go." So quietly Jeff almost missed it, Trey added, "For now."

Jeff studied him a moment. Trey barely nodded. Jeff put his light away. "Why are you here?"

Trey harumphed. "You're not the only man I tutor, you know. Though I could make my living teaching you alone. The perpetual student."

Jeff let the jibe go. "Come on, Trey. Let me put my stuff away, and we'll play a few rounds."

Trey followed Jeff into the bay where the crews slept. Jeff

stowed his duffle in his locker. He flinched as the strap rubbed across the recent singes on the back of his hands. Trey eyed him with his good eye. "What'd you do?"

Jeff snorted. "I'm a fireman. I got burned. Well, singed. They'll heal. Reminder to myself not to fight fires without my gloves."

Trey rolled into the recreation area with Jeff. He continued his queries as Jeff sank into a comfortable chair at an empty table. "When were you fighting fires? You said you were off for three days."

"I am. Or I was. Still am, I guess." Trey's eye narrowed in frustration. Jeff grimaced. "The trailer court where Collin lives—or lived—caught fire last night. I got burned trying to get people away from a backdraft."

Trey's face drained of all color. His mouth fell open in shock. "Is she…she's not… No, you wouldn't be this calm if something had happened to your…to Collin. She's fine, I know it. Right?"

Jeff had stopped being surprised by Trey's on-again, off-again, opinion of Collin. He assured the man, "She's fine. She's staying with my folks. It's why I'm staying here. Until she can find a place. Or we get married."

Trey eyed him sideways, which considering he only had one good eye, proved tough. "A little old-fashioned, isn't it? No one cares about that stuff anymore."

"We care. We don't want to deliberately put ourselves in a bad position. It's better for us this way."

Trey shrugged. He asked, "How bad was the fire?"

"Bad. Four people died. The neighborhood is gone. Maybe a hundred or more people with no place to live."

Trey nodded. He looked at Jeff a moment, his jaw tightening. "Did someone set it? To kill her? Jeff, you need to protect her. Someone may be trying—"

"Trey, she's safe. Honest. No one is going to get to her." He cocked his head. "Fires happen all the time. Why would you think that?"

Trey dropped his eyes. "Too many cop shows, I guess. Everyone is always out to kill someone."

"Uh-huh." Jeff straightened a kink in his back. "Collin jumped to the same conclusion until my dad pointed out statistically, she had only a one in a hundred chance of being the target."

"Did she buy it?"

"Not if I know her. But she didn't run off to save my parents and me from some crazed killer." Jeff shifted in his seat again. "I'm sure she wanted to. But she didn't. I have hope she's learning."

"Learning what?"

"To trust other people. To realize she doesn't have to do everything herself."

Trey mused, "It's hard to break those patterns if it's what you grew up with."

Jeff eyed Trey. "Why would you say that?"

"No reason. Ignore it. Ignore me. I'm babbling. A babbling idiot. I should leave before I say anything else stupid."

"You've never been an idiot, and you're not now. Maybe the blow to your head rattled a few brain cells." Jeff hesitated, then decided to go for it. "Whoever clocked you didn't have your best interests at heart."

Trey looked sideways at Jeff. "Your turn to explain. What makes you think so?"

"In my line of work, I've had to clean more than a few eyes. There's not a dresser made can leave a mark like you have."

Trey looked around the empty-of-people room, looked around again, looked around a third time. "Aliens. Tried to spirit me away in the middle of the night. I had to fight them off. Nearly had me."

Jeff chuckled. "Okay, Trey. I gotcha. I'll leave it alone." He dropped his voice. "For now." Trey ducked his head.

Jeff asked, "Where's the set?"

Trey waved him off. "All the fire stations have their own sets. I'm giving you home court advantage tonight."

Jeff hauled himself out of the chair, dug out the chess set— inelegantly disguised as a checker-chess-backgammon combination—and set the pieces on the table. "Okay, tutor of mine. Tutor." Jeff sat across from Trey.

Trey looked at the board in mock disgust. "You expect me to play with these pieces? This…this… Never. How am I supposed to teach you anything with bone knives and bearskins like these?"

Jeff pointed to the board. "Lower yourself. We're on a budget here."

"Since you leave me no other choice, I shall make each game as swift as I can. The less time I have to subject myself to these primitive elements, the happier I will be."

Jeff pointed to the board. "Play the game, dude."

Trey circled the first piece in the air, grimaced. "Ah, Jeffery, my man. It pains me to see you reduced to playing with these humble implements. No wonder you can't mount a single defense worthy of someone I've taught for two months and fifteen days, now."

Jeff gave an exaggerated sigh. "I know. We all must suffer for our craft. I have a mind to donate my father's ivory set…except he'd kill me."

Trey looked impressed. "I'd kill you, too. Must be a sweet set."

"Mom gave it to him as an anniversary present. Right after she beat him on it, of course."

"She sounds like my kind of people."

"You need to stop ducking me and come over and meet my family." Jeff smiled. "You'd fit right in."

"Why? Are they brilliant and sophisticated and refined?"

"No. Exactly why you'd fit in."

Trey set the pieces in place, studied the board, turned it left, right, left again… "This is impossible. But let's make it look good, shall we?"

Jeff wondered if there might be a double meaning to Trey's words. It didn't take long to find out. The younger man's moves lacked any cohesive pattern of attack, any system, any logic. He made random moves not even a novice would make. All the while, he asked, "So, did you find out about Collin's grandfather?"

Jeff debated, threw up a prayer. "She didn't get the notice until six days after he passed. Either the law firm didn't mail the letter right away, or the letter got lost."

Trey lowered his voice. "Her accident happened after he died? And before she knew it?"

Jeff matched his tone to Trey's. "Right. Two cops came to ask her about it. Said they thought it might have been deliberate. I'm beginning to have the same feeling about the fire."

Trey quickly looked up, then down. He resumed his low tones. "So whoever set it wanted Collin to be in it? She was the target?"

"Yeah." Jeff chuckled. Trey raised his hands, palms up. Jeff said, "She wanted to stop for ice cream. If we hadn't, she would have been there when the fire started."

"Ice cream saved her life? Is that what you're saying?" Trey's face reflected the absurdity of the suggestion.

"Yep. God's grace and ice cream."

Trey studied Jeff a long moment. He leaned forward and lowered his voice. "Did she see a copy of the will?"

Jeff considered his answer long and hard. He looked at the board. "Trey, I trust you. I do. I don't know exactly why, but I have the gut feeling you're on Collin's side." He paused. "But I can't answer your question. I'll say the things she read were not what she expected to see. It threw her enough to make her reach out to Dad and me for help. I can't tell you anything else, my friend."

Trey nodded. "Good man." Trey looked sideways both directions, over Jeff's head, under the table, across the ceiling… In his normal voice, he said, "Your head isn't in this game, Jeffery, my man. I'm going to extend my mercy to you and call it a day. Besides, I have a boat, awaiting me in the moat." Trey gave the line his most theatrical rendering.

Jeff laughed. "Fine. You want I should take you home?"

"Thank you, sir. But no. My faithful steed and I must traverse the blighted streets of this delightful town on our own." Trey's eyes twinkled. He dropped his voice. "Keep her safe, Jeffery, my man. I'll…"

Trey trailed off as five of the current shift's firefighters came noisily into the room. Jeff knew three of them; two others were recruits in training. Not training for his station, of course, but training, nonetheless. Jeff noticed Trey drop his eyes away from the newcomers. The chess tutor began lifting the individual pieces between his thumb and middle finger as if fearing contamination. "And please, before I come again, will you have these disinfected? Who knows what manner of contagion might have touched them?"

Jeff bowed in mock obeisance. "Of course, your highness. Absolutely. Is there anything else you will require?"

"Wine, women, and possibly a song. But I'll settle for a water to go."

"You got it. Careful getting home, Trey."

"Always."

SATURDAY EVENING

Collin woke, groggy and disoriented. She lay on the floor, a pillow under her head and a blanket over the rest of her. How? Where? It took several reboots of her brain to drag out the pertinent memories of being at Jeff's house, being in the guest room, having showered and changed, and fallen asleep. The pillow and blanket were nowhere in her memory banks, however. *Must have been a later modification. System upgrade?*

Collin sat cautiously. She remembered the last headache and wanted no return engagement. *Move slow. Maybe it won't know your alive. Or awake, anyhow.*

She climbed to her feet, still moving with deliberate caution. Only after she had walked out of the bedroom and into the family room did she breathe a small sigh of relief. No pain. Well…not in her head. The rest of her? Not so much. Collin swallowed the discomfort, put on a—if not a happy face, at least not a "cat dragged me in after he partied all night"—look. She could hear voices coming from the living room. Did she walk in as if she belonged there? Did she clear her throat to announce her presence? Knock over a lamp so as not to unduly interrupt a conversation she shouldn't hear?

How about go back to the room until they all go to sleep and then leave?

Collin snarled, *I am not leaving. Yet.* She cleared her throat and stepped into the room.

Lacey looked around and smiled widely. "Collin! Welcome back to the land of the living. You're in time for dinner."

Collin's eyes flared in confusion. "Dinner? I've been asleep all day?" She glanced at the mantle clock. Five p.m. She'd been asleep close to nine hours.

Leesa chortled. "You were asleep on the floor. Jeff wanted to pick you up. Mom said no. She said if you wake her, I'll kill you. Jeff left you alone after that."

Collin felt heat in her cheeks. She ducked her head in embarrassment. "Thank you. You're right. I needed the sleep."

Harmon said, "And now you need food. Which Rich and Arianna have graciously provided." Harmon motioned to the stranger in the room. "Dr. Rich McMannon. Uncle Rich to the kids."

Lacey offered, "He's my neurologist and family friend."

Collin shook the man's hand. "Is your wife in the kitchen fixing dinner? I'll go help her."

Lacey wagged a finger in warning. "Lesson one: when Arianna is in the kitchen, no one goes in. Not even me." Lacey put the back of her hand to her mouth and whispered loudly, "She has her secret recipes, and that's how she keeps them secret."

A voice called from the kitchen, "And when I die, you will all get copies of my favorites. It's in my will. Until then, quit whining." A middle-aged woman came into the family room. She wore an apron over her skirt, her hair pulled in a messy bun. She hugged Collin warmly. "So nice to meet the woman who has finally stolen Jeffery's heart. We were getting worried, there, for a while." She chuckled. "I'm Arianna. I belong with the man over there." She pointed to Rich McMannon.

Collin smiled back. "It's nice to meet you."

Arianna motioned toward the kitchen. "Dinner is ready. Last one in cleans up." Only Leesa scrambled out of her chair to get in line at the door first.

Lacey suggested, "Why don't you sit beside the end? Jeff should be coming along any minute." Lacey held Collin's eyes a moment longer than necessary.

Collin caught the signal. "Thank you."

The backdoor opened, and Jeff came bursting in. "Sorry I'm late!" He offered no reason for his tardiness, however. Instead, he slid into the chair beside Collin and asked, "Did you sleep well?"

"Does a log sleep? If so, yes. Very well. And late. Guess I needed it."

Halfway through the sumptuous meal, Rich studied Lacey

intently. "I can't get over the change, Lacey. I always hoped you'd make it back. But only God could make it happen."

Lacey held her hands out wide. "And He did." Her eyes shone at Harmon. His eyes reflected her joy. Collin felt her heart melt. *Can it be this sweet? After four kids and all the years? Still in love, like teenagers? I want that. I do.*

The dragon screamed; lightning flashed, and Collin's head snapped back. She had enough awareness to scoot her chair from the table, turned, and doubled over in pain. She heard voices of confusion and concern around her but did not bother to decipher them. She focused on one task: *Don't scream. Don't scream.* Well, two tasks: *Breathe* and *don't scream.*

Only as the dragon receded from her consciousness did Collin unclench her fists, unlock her jaw, straighten, look around at the worried faces. "I'm sorry. Post-concussion headache. It will pass."

Rich glowered. "Whoever told you that should have their license revoked." He rose from his chair and stepped in front of Collin. "Look up."

Collin refused. "Dr. McMannon, the headache is gone. They come, they hurt, they go away. I'm fine."

Rich's lips clamped in a straight line. "No, you're not." Rich looked to Jeff. "I want her taken to Sisters of Mercy to be thoroughly checked out—now."

Collin glared at the man. "I will not be ordered anywhere, Dr. McMannon. I had an attack like this at the hospital before my discharge. They checked me out then and found nothing of consequence. I will not have my weekend disrupted over something which comes and goes." She willed her body not to shake, not to reveal the anger she felt. "And Sisters of Mercy is not in the insurance network for state workers. If you think I need further examination, I will call for an appointment."

Rich met her glare with one of his own. "Then be in my office Monday morning at eight a.m."

Collin nodded curtly. "If I can get off work."

Rich scowled at her. "I'll write you a medical excuse. This is not something you want to play with, Ms. Walker. Please. Come in and let me help you."

Collin closed her eyes. *Why is this hard? I can't think straight. Maybe you do need to go.*

She looked back at Rich. "Okay. I'll be there."

Rick patted her shoulder. "Good. "

Collin and Rich returned to the table. Collin tried to avoid looking at Jeff, focusing instead on the meal before her. Jeff leaned against her shoulder for a moment. Enough said.

Dinner ended. The kitchen was cleaned and straightened, dishes done, table centerpieces returned to their decorative positions. Harmon and Lacey escorted the McMannons out; Collin, Jeff, and Leesa found places to sit in the living room. Harmon and Lacey returned to the living room and plopped in their accustomed seats. Harmon's face lost its smile. "Collin, we are here for you any way you need. Let us help you get things sorted out."

Lacey added, "Maybe it would help to identify all the opportunities you're facing right now."

Collin's eyes narrowed slightly, and she couldn't keep the incredulity out of her voice. "Opportunities? Maybe some of them are, but some of them are not opportunities I want to share with anyone."

Harmon said, "All of life is an opportunity, Collin. An opportunity to grow closer to the Lord or to turn away from Him."

I bet he's never had a crazed person try to push him off a cliff in a car.

Isn't that what you were telling Mano? You either grow or you don't. How you grow is up to you.

Collin conceded the point. "I understand."

Lacey suggested, "Writing lists helps me. Kind of keeps things in perspective."

Collin nodded. Her brain still refused to step out of the fog. Lacey dug out a pad and pencil. Old school.

Jeff's face darkened. "First opportunity: someone is trying to kill you."

Lacey noted, "Irrational stalker."

"My trailer court burned," Collin shifted on the couch. "There are over a hundred people who lost all they had. Two hundred when you add in the children."

Harmon leaned forward in his chair. "They aren't your problem to solve, Collin. I know you want to help, but—"

"If they lost it all because someone wanted me, they are my problem. The fire becomes my fault, and it's up to me to make it right."

"Did you set the fire?"

"No. But—"

"Did you force those people to live there?"

Collin squirmed. "I know what you're saying, sir. I do. No, I didn't make them live there. I didn't start the fire. But—"

"You want to help. A legitimate desire. A noble purpose. But helping is a far cry from being to blame. Everything happening in the world is not your fault. Nor your responsibility to correct."

Jeff squeezed Collin's hand. "Listen to him, Collin."

What do they know about you? You are *responsible. Once you know about something, it's your responsibility to change it and make it right. All of it. Any of it. It's all yours. It's always been yours. You fix it.*

Collin closed her eyes. *Speak to me, Lord. Only You. Only Your voice. Help me.*

Where were you when I created the earth? Who made you Me?

Collin lifted her chin to keep back the tears and frustration. "It's always been my fault. Always. Anything I did, anything I saw, anything that happened. My fault."

"You never got credit for anything that went right, though, did you?" Lacey touched Collin's arm. Collin shook her head, unwilling to trust her voice.

Leesa got up from her chair, came over, and sat on the couch beside Collin. She hugged Collin. "I love you, Collin."

Collin drew in a deep breath. "Thank you, Leesa." She looked to Harmon. "Right. Opportunity: I want to help the people dislocated because of the fire. Period."

Harmon nodded. "Good. What else?"

"I have to do something with my grandfather's estate. I have to face the family and tell them—"

"Why do you have to face them?" Jeff turned her to look at him. "Eventually, yes, but why right now? A good lawyer can take care of those details."

Collin tried to think clearly. *Ain't happening, baby.* "The paperwork said I had thirty days to respond before…before something happened. I don't know. I didn't have a whole lot of time to study it." She snorted. "And now I don't even have a copy of it."

"But you know the law office, and you can get a copy." Lacey noted it on her sheet.

Collin began to rock. Little rock. Pebble. "I need to find a place to live. I need to get a car. I need to go back to work. I need to get clothes to wear." She smiled at Leesa. "Thank you for loaning me this outfit. You have good taste in clothes."

Leesa fairly beamed. "I like shopping. Mom likes taking me. I'll help you shop."

Harmon asked, "Of the items on your list, which do you see as the priority?"

Collin scowled. "The crazed stalker."

Jeff added, "Hear, hear."

Harmon nodded. "Agreed. Except it's also the one item you can do the least about."

Collin's eyes narrowed slightly. "Meaning?"

"Short of buying a billboard saying, 'Here I am, come find me,' or parading around town with a brass band, you have no way of knowing where he is. The police are the ones doing the investigating. They are very good at the things they do. Let them handle this."

Collin groaned. Jeff's voice became stern as he turned to face Collin. "Listen to him, milady. You are not a cop. You are not bait. You are the victim. Got it?" Jeff's gaze drilled into her soul.

Who does he think he is? He can't tell you— Collin shut down all the voices of the chorus inside. "I got it. I do. I won't do anything except what the police tell me to do. Promise."

Jeff relaxed back into the couch. The tiniest of voices whispered in Collin's mind, *Got my fingers crossed.* Collin slammed the door in her head.

Jeff looked at his father. "So what does she do about it?

"She waits for the police to contact her."

Collin frowned. "It comes off the list?"

Harmon shrugged. "Not off, but it moves down the priority list."

Lacey suggested, "On a purely practical note, I think you need to get some clothes. Borrowing outer garments is fine. Inner? Not so much." She smiled.

Collin gave a lop-sided grin. "Agreed."

Lacey stood. "I say we table the rest of the items on the list and go take care of item one." She looked at Jeff. "You're staying here. Collin and Leesa and I are going out shopping. We'll be back before nine." The women gathered their shoes, purses (Collin's backpack), and Lacey kissed Harmon warmly. Leesa gave him a daughterly peck on the cheek.

Collin kept the guilt she felt out of her eyes as she stepped into Jeff's arms. He wrapped her in a careful bearhug and kissed her on the forehead. "I love you, lady. We will get through this. Together. You're not alone anymore. Remember. You have family."

Collin kissed his cheek. She wanted to stand like that forever, held in his arms, safe and warm and protected.

But life went on, and she released him. She squeezed his hand and mouthed, "I love you." Then she turned to say good-bye to Harmon.

Collin held the older man's gaze. *You know what he's thinking. You're exposing his wife and daughter to the killer. If something happens to them, what? Maybe you should go alone?*

Harmon smiled at Collin, and his eyes were kind. "Have a good time, all of you. I'll be here when you get home. Jeff will be back at the station."

She promised softly, "I'll take care of them, sir."

Harmon hugged her. In her ear, he said, "Take care of yourself, young woman. God has all of you. I am not worried." He hugged her again. "Go. Have fun. Though how shopping is fun is quite beyond my capacity. I'll see you all later." The three women headed out.

* * *

Jeff waited until the females were gone to ask, "How do you have the guts to let them leave? It's tearing me up. I know they have to, but still…"

Harmon put his arm around Jeff's shoulders. "Been doing it for years. Each time one of this family walks out the door, I know it could be the last time I see you." He chuckled. "Especially you. My prayer is you will marry this wonderful young woman, settle into a boring desk job, and give us at least five more grandchildren."

Jeff shook his head. "I don't know about the five children. Collin and I will be starting a little late for five. Four, maybe." Jeff lost the bantering style. "We've already discussed Leesa. She'll live with us when the time comes."

"I appreciate that. Leesa may well outlive both your mother and me. If she does, I know you'll take care of her."

Jeff hesitated. "Collin told me if something were to happen to me, she would still take care of Lees."

"Do not let this one get away, Jeffery. Why you haven't asked her to marry you yet is—"

"Dad! You know why! I've told you why! I've told the whole world why!"

"Testy, much?"

Jeff dropped his head. "I give up."

SUNDAY MORNING

Collin and the Farrells attended church Sunday morning. They had barely walked into the house when Collin's phone rang. She looked at the number. "May I help you?"

"Detective Jim Russo, here. Maybe I can help you."

Collin's gut tightened. She walked out the back door for privacy.

Detective Russo continued. "We checked out your Patrick Winger. Since he lives in Indiana, we contacted the authorities to let them know we wanted to talk to him. He showed here this morning and said he wanted to address this in person."

Collin sat on the porch. She needed stability. She needed not to pace around the yard like a crazy woman.

Russo said, "He brought affidavits from six people who all swear he attended a family get-together last Sunday night into Monday morning. All six say he never left the premises. Mr. Winger said he holds no grudge against you for thinking he might be involved in your accident."

He holds no grudge against me? Against me? Of all the—

"He hopes he can meet with you to resolve any lingering issues."

Collin listened. She tried to listen without judging, without letting the past color her thinking. *Be objective.*

Fat chance.

When Detective Russo finished, Collin asked, "In your experience, would three hundred million dollars be reason enough for six people to collude to lie on affidavits?"

Silence. "Excuse me?"

"I was informed I have inherited my grandfather's entire estate." She filled him in on the details as briefly as she could. "So I repeat, would a share of three hundred million dollars be enough to collude to lie on affidavits?"

The man chuckled. "For a share of three hundred million, I'd lie on an affidavit. Yes, Ms. Walker, it certainly would. We will keep it in mind while we continue our investigation."

"Thank you." Collin debated a moment. "Did you ever locate the truck owner?'

A long silence told Collin all she needed to know. "I'm sorry, Ms. Walker. We can't comment on an on-going—"

Collin finished the sentence for him. "Investigation. Thank you for letting me know Mr. Winger is in town. I appreciate the warning."

"Always glad to help."

Collin terminated the call. She wished she could terminate the voices screaming *Liar! Liar! Run! Get out! Flee!* It would make her stomach feel so much better. She sat another moment. And another. And another…

Jeff came out to join her. He handed her a glass of water. His glass contained an amber fluid. "Mom made fresh tea. It's unsweetened."

Collin shook her head. "Water is fine." Jeff sat beside her. He said nothing.

Collin didn't make him ask. "Detective Russo called to say my prime suspect has an alibi. Six, to be exact. Which is exactly how many aunts, uncles, and possibly cousins I have, at least who could be rounded on short notice."

Jeff nodded and took a long swallow of his drink. "If you're keeping score, I prefer my tea sweetened."

"I'll make a note of that." She paused. "Patrick is in Oakton."

Jeff looked at Collin, eyebrow raised. "Oh? Detective Russo give you the information?"

"He said Patrick came to town to hand deliver the affidavits. Patrick said he holds no grudges against me for thinking it might have been him."

"Big of him." Jeff drank from his glass again.

Collin eyed him closely. "You're waiting for me to say I'm leaving, right?"

"No. I'm waiting to see the logical, rational thing you are going to do about this 'new opportunity' as my mom would say."

"Logical? Rational? Me?"

Jeff finally grinned. "Okay, it's a stretch. But you've been learning a lot lately, and I thought maybe, just maybe…"

Collin shoved him with her shoulder. "Deserved that. Didn't like it, but deserved it." She looked around the yard, looked at the sky, looked down. "My gut is screaming I should leave before he finds you all. My head isn't far behind on the suggestion." She pursed her lips. "My heart is in full agreement. Which, sadly, means all of me is wrong, and I should wait here for resolution of some kind." She looked at Jeff. "Right?"

Jeff sat silent for a moment. "If it were me…if I were in the situation and you and your family were being threatened, I'd be gone in a shot." He held Collin's eyes. "Which still doesn't make it the right answer. Would you tell me to run off?"

"No."

"Would you want me to run off?"

"No. I get it, Jeff. I'm still here. I haven't run away. I know all the things I shouldn't be doing. What should I do?"

The doorbell rang. Jeff looked toward the front. "No one rings the doorbell anymore."

"I know. Too rude. Wonder who it is?"

Harmon called, "I'll get it."

Collin turned her attention to the questions before her: what should she be doing?

Jeff didn't try to give her advice. He sat beside her, held her hand, and simply let his presence be her support. *Wise man.*

They sat holding hands for nearly ten minutes when Lacey came out the back door and stepped onto the porch. Collin looked at the woman, and Lacey's face seemed guarded. Calm, but guarded.

Mrs. Farrell said evenly, "Collin, there are two men at the door asking for you."

Collin's eyes narrowed. "Asking for me?"

"Harmon has them in the living room. He asked me to suggest you both come in and listen to them."

Collin's flight-or-fight Spidey sense went on full alert. "Listen? Mom Lacey, do they have a gun?"

"No, Collin. Nothing like that. Harmon would never endanger someone's life to save his own." Lacey nailed Collin with a firm look. "Not even to save a family member. Harmon heard them out.

He thinks you two should as well."

Collin wanted to refuse. Wanted to. Knew she should. *Bad. This would be bad. Had to be*. She climbed to her feet. "Okay, Mom Lacey. I'll hear these men out. Because I trust you two." *Lord, don't let this be a bad idea.*

Lacey led the way. Jeff walked protectively ahead of Collin. Harmon and two other men stood as Lacey, Jeff, and Collin entered the living room. Harmon said quietly, "Collin…"

Collin never heard another word he spoke. Her eyes narrowed in on the older man standing before her. Fear struck her like a physical blow. Her stomach dropped three feet. The wind rushed out of her as if she'd been punched.

He looked ancient. More drawn than twelve years should have made him. The lines in his face had deepened to valleys. Thinning silver hair. Not auburn like her own, like she remembered him having. The eyes…the eyes remained as keen and clear as ever. Hard. Still hard. Always hard. The tormentor of her childhood. The source of all her scars and nightmares: Robert Winger.

The younger man at Robert Winger's side moved forward quickly and took Collin's hand. "Caitlin! It is you. We have searched so long to find you."

Collin couldn't speak. The air hadn't returned to her lungs. She could only stare in disbelief. Doubt, suspicion, disbelief.

The man turned to Jeff and stuck out his hand. "I'm Patrick Winger. I'm not sure what Caitlin has told you about me. Probably all true if it covered our early years. I'm here to straighten all that out." Jeff shook the man's hand but remained silent.

Leesa sat in a chair opposite the fireplace. Collin noticed Jeff's sister had a puzzled look on her face. As Patrick turned to address Collin again, "Caitlin—" Leesa interrupted. "Why do you call her Caitlin? She's Collin. She's not Caitlin."

Something broke in Collin at last. She smiled at Leesa. "Thank you, Leesa. My name is Collin now. When these two men knew me, they called me Caitlin." She turned back to the men. "It's legally Collin. Has been for a lot of years. It's what I'm comfortable with."

Patrick said quickly, "Of course. Which is why we had such a hard time finding you. We didn't know you'd changed your name. And none of the people we contacted had ever heard of Caitlin."

And you're surprised why? Collin took a cue from Harmon and

Lacey and sat opposite the two Winger men.

Lacey made as if to rise from her chair. "May I get you something to drink?"

Elderberry wine? With arsenic? Collin snapped the door closed on the sarcasm in her head. She would not crack. She would not crack. She would not give either of them the satisfaction of knowing they had rattled her. *Control. Breathe.*

Both men declined. Patrick moved to the edge of his chair. "Caitlin—"

"Collin."

Patrick ducked his head. "Collin. I came…we came…because we've been looking for you for several years now." His mouth smiled. His eyes didn't. "After I met the Lord, I knew I had to find you and make amends."

Collin's mind whirled again. *Met the Lord? Patrick? Never! He would never… The Lord would never…how? When? Why?* Collin told her face muscles to smile. Some of them complied. Enough so she could say, "I understand the feeling. When did you meet Him?"

Patrick looked at his father and asked, "Three years ago, right, Dad?"

Collin's being lurched for the third time in as many minutes. Well, almost as many minutes. *Dad? Since when? Never 'Dad.' 'Dad' got you a backhand to the mouth. Or a belt. Dad? Who were these imposters? If he calls him, 'son,' I'll throw up.*

Robert Winger stroked his chin. "More like four, Pat."

Pat. Yep. Imposters. Not the Patrick and Robert I knew.

But wouldn't you expect it if they had accepted the Lord?

Collin let the thought rattle around while she said, "Where? How?" *Yeah. Prove it.*

No. No. Wrong. He doesn't have to prove it. Can you prove your faith? Collin shushed the voices. All of them.

Patrick sat back in the chair. "An evangelist came through Fort Newton. I went to the conference so I could argue against his beliefs. Turned out I couldn't. He had it right. Everything he said came straight from the Bible. I left knowing I needed to accept the Lord, make my past right, and find you." Again the mouth smiled, and the eyes didn't. "I've been trying ever since."

Collin forced a smile back. She must have made it convincing, based on Patrick's reaction. "How did you come to be here?" She motioned around the room. "Here, here. How did you find the Farrells?"

Robert Winger's eyes narrowed. "I thought I taught you better. If you don't want to be found, don't put your picture in the paper."

Collin turned to Jeff. "Picture in the paper?"

Robert waved his hand. "On the news. We saw a news clip about how a fearless social worker from Oakton single-handedly took down a serial killer. The photo they showed looked exactly like the age-progression drawing Pat and I have been using to show to people."

Collin frowned. "I did not take down anyone single-handedly. The sheriff, his deputies, Jeff, my crew…they all had a hand in it." She glared at her father. "And I did not authorize anyone to use my picture in anything. I didn't want my name used. I know better, and yes, you taught me well."

Harmon explained, "If it is part of a police report, the news crews can use images without permission. I'm sorry, Collin."

Patrick smiled broadly. "I'm not." The man stood, stepped from behind the ottoman, and moved across to be closer to Collin. "We might never have found you. Even knowing what we did didn't help us. But the name Farrell is identifiable."

Patrick fairly beamed at Jeff. "We searched through every record of a paramedic with that name, then searched out which station you were at."

He looked at Collin and raised his hand. "It's public record. We weren't spying on or stalking either of you." He looked at Jeff. "I gave them my identity and why I wanted to find you. They wouldn't give me your address but did tell me you worked for your dad. So I looked you up"—Patrick turned to Harmon—"and found your address."

Patrick sat back down. "It became a matter of trying to find a good time to come when both Dad and I would be able to be in Oakton for more than a few hours. This weekend happened to work. I never dreamed we would find you already here, too, Cai…Collin."

Collin's eyes narrowed. "You wouldn't have, except Friday night, someone set fire to the trailer court where I live. Four people died."

Patrick jerked at the news. "How terrible. Cai…Collin, I'm so sorry. Accident?"

Collin looked to Jeff. Jeff said, "Preliminary reports are someone deliberately set it. But the investigation is still ongoing."

"Do the police have any ideas who might have done it?" Patrick leaned toward Collin.

Collin leaned away. "Not which they're sharing."

"I am truly sorry, Cai…Collin. Were they friends?"

"They haven't released the names yet. I can't locate everyone I know, so I'm still in the dark as much as anyone."

Patrick's eyes softened. "I'll be praying for them."

Collin nodded, unwilling to give him more than that. She looked at the clock. "It's nearly one. I have some errands I need to take care of this afternoon. Can we meet again later today?" She gave Patrick a half-smile. "I promise. I won't run off somewhere to hide." Jeff squeezed her hand. Whether in approval or dis remained to be told. She asked, "Do you have time? Or are you on a schedule? "

Patrick looked to his father, who nodded. Patrick said, "We have time. When are you thinking?"

Collin rested her head on her hand. "We could meet at 'The Spilt Milk.' Around six? They have a diverse menu. I can get you the direct—"

Robert said, "I know the place." His voice drawled. "Upscale for you, isn't it?"

Collin refused to be baited. "I'll splurge."

"With your grandfather's money?"

"I have my own, thank you. And we can discuss it at dinner if you choose." She stood to dismiss the men. "Thank you for looking for me." She reached to shake Patrick's hand. The man brushed her hand aside, hugged her instead. Collin resisted—barely—the urge to cold-cock him and returned the hug.

Patrick shook hands with Jeff. "Thank you for taking care of my sister. I'm looking forward to getting to know you better."

Jeff replied, "I look forward to it as well."

Patrick looked over to Leesa and made a point to include her in his well-wishes. "Thank you, Ms. Farrell, for allowing me to interrupt your afternoon."

Leesa smiled. "You're Collin's brother. You're not interrupting."

Collin made sure to keep the ottoman between Robert Winger and herself. There would be no hugs there. Not yet. If ever.

Robert nodded to her. "Pleasure to see you again, Katie. I look forward to continuing this discussion."

Patrick steered his father out the door. "Thank you very much, Mr. and Mrs. Farrell, for allowing us to see Cai…Collin. It means everything to Father and me. It does." He shook hands with both husband and wife and closed the door behind himself.

Collin waited until she heard the car door slam, the engine turn over, the tires grind on the pavement… Only when she could no longer hear the motor did she exhale. Unvoiced tension charged the room.

After uncounted heartbeats, Collin quipped, "Interesting. Very interesting." She looked at Harmon and Lacey. "Thank you, and I mean it sincerely. I've played out meeting Robert Winger over and over in my head. It never looked anything like what happened here." She managed a relieved smile. "Which is a good thing. Most of my scenarios ended badly."

Collin stretched her neck and shoulders to relieve the strain on her muscles and nerves. Harmon's shoulders dropped slightly. Lacey began to breathe a little easier. Only Leesa seemed unphased by the drama created with the sudden appearance of the two Winger men. She looked at Collin. "Why did he call you Katie? You're not Katie. You're Collin. You told him Collin. He said Katie. Why?"

Collin kept all emotion from her voice. "He chooses to think of me like a little girl, not a grown woman. He called me Katie when I lived with him." *Only to taunt you. Or as a prelude to a beating. Physical or emotional didn't matter. A beating is a beating.*

Collin smiled. "Thank you for standing up for me, Leesa. I appreciate it." She looked at Jeff and his parents. "And thank you for letting me handle my battle. I needed to confront him, finally."

Lacey remarked, "Didn't sound a lot like a confrontation. Your half-brother seems like he wants to make amends." The woman's eyes narrowed. "Do you believe him?"

"Believe he wants to make amends? Probably. Because he's accepted Jesus? I want to." *I do want to. I want everyone to come to Jesus. Even Robert Winger.*

Harmon cocked his head. "But, you have your doubts?"

The group drifted to the kitchen area and settled around the table. Lacey poured out tea for Harmon and Jeff; Collin got another water for herself. Leesa got out a soda; Lacey frowned at her. Leesa protested, "It's the first one this day. I promise. Only one."

Lacey relented. "Fine. Only one."

Collin answered Harmon's question. "I will admit the timing of their finding me is suspect. Waiting for a convenient time to come here—and the convenient time being the week after Grandfather passes? It's a stretch."

She silenced the voices of derision in her head. "Doesn't mean it's not true. It means it's a stretch. I will get a better feel for it when we talk again this evening." She looked at the clock. "I need to get moving. I need to look for a place to stay on a more permanent basis. Not that I don't love your hospitality. But Jeff needs his home back."

Harmon chuckled. "If it comes to a swap, I can tell you who would win."

Jeff frowned. "You wound me, Dad. You wound me deeply. My own father."

Lacey added, "And Mother. I'd vote for Collin as well."

Leesa threw in her voice. "I vote for Collin. Love you, brother, but I want a sister. Too many boys lived here."

Jeff pretended he'd taken a dagger to the heart. "My family!" He straightened and smiled. "I'd choose her myself. If she'd let me."

Collin studied him for a long moment. A very long moment. She held his eyes, feeling her own eyes cloud over. She whispered, "Yes. I let you."

Jeff stared at her sideways. "Really?"

Collin couldn't speak. She nodded. Her voice cracked. "If you want."

Jeff immediately dropped on one knee. He held Collin's hand in his and asked solemnly, "Collin Walker, will you marry me?"

Collin studied the man of her dreams on his knees in his parent's kitchen, surrounded by the family she'd never had… "Yes."

Jeff leaped to his feet, let out a war hoop audible for a two-mile radius. "Yes!!" He nearly crushed her in his arms. Collin buried her head in his shoulder. She could hear Lacey and Harmon and Leesa all cheering. It didn't matter. Nothing mattered except Jeff. She and Jeff were together. For the start of all their forevers. Nothing but the Lord would come between them.

The Lord and the paralyzing pain coursing through her brain. Collin's body spasmed. She clutched Jeff in desperation, pleading all the while, *Not now! Not now! Please!*

Jeff continued to hold her, whispering in her ear, "I got you, milady. I've got you. Hang on. Hang on."

She hissed through clenched teeth, "No doctors. Not now. Tomorrow. I see a doctor tomorrow. Not now. Please."

Jeff pulled her head closer to his chest. He rocked with her slowly. Collin heard him say, "She's having another attack."

Lacey's tone filled with concern. "Should I call a squad?"

Jeff said, "No. Not yet."

The pain released. Collin straightened in Jeff's arms, pulled her head up. Her voice shook only a little. "No. It's gone. I'm fine."

Harmon said sternly, "You are not fine." He relented. "But you will be. I know." He looked at Jeff. "Run errands with her. Do not let her drive alone." He looked to Collin. "If you have an attack on the freeway, you'll take out more than yourself."

Collin ducked her head in agreement. "Yes, sir. I'll let Jeff be my chauffeur." She looked at Leesa. "Would you like to go with us while I go apartment shopping?"

Leesa smiled. "I'm a good chaperone. You two will not kiss."

Jeff groaned.

SUNDAY AFTERNOON

Jeff and Collin dropped Leesa back off at the Farrell house in plenty of time to make it to "The Spilt Milk" restaurant before six. Collin had debated changing clothes before going but decided against it. Robert and Patrick could see her in the same outfit twice in one day. Vanity had never been one of her shortcomings. There were plenty of other sins, but not vanity. Jeff pulled the jeep into the parking lot, circled to find a good spot for easy access and egress, parked and shut the engine off. He took Collin's hand and prayed, "God, be in our words, our thoughts, our actions. Amen."

Collin asked, "Actions…meaning don't let me throw something at either of them?"

Jeff shrugged. "If the knife fits…"

Collin waited as Jeff came around to let her out. This waiting on the gentleman to open the door certainly crimped her style. She ordinarily would be half-way to the restaurant by the time Jeff got to her side of the car. Maybe they could compromise… *How about if it's raining and he has the umbrella, he can come around for me. Otherwise, I'll manage myself. Sounds fair, right?*

Neither Winger had come in yet, so Jeff asked the host for a table somewhat away from the other diners. Collin wondered if Jeff still feared her acting on her more base nature. She wondered if she should fear the same thing. No. She had made peace with her background. Having it brought to the foreground might be uncomfortable, but the Lord had taken all the shame and guilt and anger away. *"Peace I give you; my peace I leave with you."* His promises never failed.

By six-thirty, Jeff polished off a second basket of warm brown batter bread with melted honey butter, and still, the Wingers were no-shows. Jeff raised his eyebrows at Collin. "You think they stood you up?"

Collin shook her head. "No. By coming late, he thinks he controls the situation. We're the ones who have been sitting twiddling our thumbs waiting on him. We're his captive audience. It's a power trip."

"Poor way to do business."

"When you're in a specialized business like he is, you get used to people catering to your wish and whim. Buyers seek him out, not the other way around."

Jeff shrugged. "Still bad business."

"I agree." Collin nodded toward the door. "And to prove my point, here they are. Patrick may apologize, but Robert won't."

"Good cop, bad cop?"

Collin snorted. "Bad cop, worse cop. But that was then, this is now, right?"

Jeff rose as the two Winger men reached the table. Patrick shook Jeff's hand warmly and moved to kiss Collin. She held out a hand. "Not on a first date." She smiled to take any sting out of the action.

Patrick laughed. "I see how it is." He looked at Jeff and asked, "She do that with you?"

Jeff grinned. "Our first date, she tried to beat my brains out on the basketball court."

Collin held her breath. Surely he wouldn't tell how the rest of the date had gone.

Jeff sat next to Collin. "I'm not sure when we went from combatants to friends." His eyes shone as he looked at Collin.

Collin breathed again. *Why do I doubt him?*

Because he's a man and all men are alike. He'll turn on you before the night is over. Watch.

Robert's face darkened. "Why is he here?"

Collin quipped, "He's my designated driver. I never leave home without him."

"Have him wait in the bar."

Collin watched Jeff's eyes. Not a flicker of anger showed. Collin looked at Robert. "Anything concerning me concerns Jeff. Anything you have to say, he can hear."

Robert's eyes narrowed. "Anything?"

"Jeff knows my past."

"Everything?"

Jeff said, "I know Collin came to Oakton at fourteen. I know she did anything she needed to do to survive. She'll never be condemned by my family or me for the decisions she made to stay alive." He squeezed Collin's hand under the table and looked steadily at Robert. "Any of them."

Patrick started to speak, but Robert interrupted him. "Fine." He turned to Collin. "We know you're the executrix of Fenton's will. Did he abide by Mother's wishes?"

Patrick asked, "Can we order before we start the family feud? I'll have the server bring only spoons. No knives."

Collin studied Patrick closely. *Maybe he had changed. He never joked with me before. And trying to redirect Robert's focus? Hmm.* To Patrick, she said, "I think we're safe. I haven't stabbed anyone in years."

Collin waited to see if Jeff would comment. He smiled and nodded but didn't offer anything incriminating.

The server came. Robert motioned to Jeff. "I'm not paying for him."

Collin knew tonight would be a test of wills and wants. And she wanted to remain calm, cool, and unscattered. She said, "I am covering the meal tonight for all of us. I chose the venue; I'll pick up the tab."

Patrick started to say, "You don't have—"

Robert interrupted. "Fine. I'll have the lobster."

Collin didn't flinch. "Good choice. I hear it's very good. Jeff?"

Jeff nodded. "I've heard the same."

Collin grinned. "No, I meant, what are you having?"

"The ribs. Side salad. Vinegar and oil, please."

Collin and Patrick placed their orders. The server asked, "Anything to drink for this table?"

Patrick joked, "We're all teetotalers here. Water will be fine." Robert glowered at his son. Patrick jerked his head at his father. "Bring him sparkling water."

The server moved off. Robert snarled, "Embarrass me again; you will regret it."

Patrick shrugged. "Nothing to hide here. Right? We're all family. She'd know about it sooner or later. Why not get it all out in the open?"

The urge to placate her father swept through Collin like a cold wind. She recognized the feeling for what it symbolized: fear of making the man mad. His capacity for retaliation went far beyond what the offense warranted. Collin let the memory—and its emotions—pass. She also chose to ignore the subject of Robert's drinking. "What business do you have bringing you to Oakton?"

Robert snapped, "You. Why else would we be in this hole? You heard your brother. We came to find you. Period. Now I want one thing from you: the will."

"I don't have the will."

"You know what's in it."

Collin held her temper. "Grandfather's law firm—"

"That man was no grandfather to you. He was a money-grubbing thief who—"

Patrick said sharply, "Dad! Enough. Fenton Mudd loved your mother very deeply. He made her happy. That's what counts." Patrick looked at Collin. "Forgive him. Since his heart attack, his emotions have been suspect."

Collin looked to Robert. "Heart attack?"

"Why would you care? You wouldn't have come back anyhow."

Collin said as evenly as she could manage, "People change. I've changed."

Robert shrugged. "Old business. Over with. We are talking about now. What is in the will?"

Collin didn't hesitate. Hesitation meant you were lying. Never hesitate. Have your stories straight in your head before you start. "Instructions on how he wanted the estate divided. And who he wanted to divide it. Namely, me."

"According to what formula?"

"It has yet to be determined."

Robert's eyes narrowed. "Determined by who?"

Shouldn't that be whom?

Do not start. Do not even start. Not the place, and there will never be a right time with Robert Winger. Sit, shut up, and behave.

Collin made certain her hands were still. No fidgeting. No tells. "I haven't spoken to Fenton's law firm yet. I didn't hear about his death until Thursday. Friday, my trailer court burned."

Collin's face hardened. "Once I help my neighbors find housing, make sure the kids are back in school and over the trauma of losing everything they own, after the victims have a proper funeral and the families are in some sense taken care of…" Collin took a breath. "Then I will contact Fenton's partners. We will work out an equitable distribution plan, and I will let all the interested parties know what's what."

Robert snorted, "And you'll pay for it all with my money, I suppose."

The food runners arrived and gave everyone their appropriate dishes. The server asked, "Does everything look right?"

Collin looked around. No one seemed inclined to complain, at least not without trying the food first. She nodded. "Thank you." She poked around at her chicken, cut it into small bites, looked at Robert. "You have your money. The money you've accumulated through the years is your money. The money Grandmother had belonged to her. She earned it while she and your father were married. Grandmother willed it to Fenton. Fenton willed it to…to who remains to be determined. You never owned it."

Robert glared. "That money should have passed to me. It always goes to the oldest son. Mother meant it to be mine. She said so. She told me she never intended it to pass to you."

Collin shrugged. "Unfortunately, what she put in writing supersedes anything she might have said or intended. When she passed it to Fenton, she gave it all to him. Legally he could do anything he wanted to with it. He could have spent it or given it away or buried it. He didn't. He kept it safe to pass to the next of kin in the Winger line. Me." *Why, Grandfather? Why?*

Patrick looked over at Jeff and asked, "How're the ribs?"

Jeff nodded. "Excellent. The fish?"

"Excellent." He smiled. "The only thing that would make it better is if it were fresh off the boat, breaded and deep-fried with hush puppies and onion rings."

Jeff grinned. "You'll have to come to the lake and go fishing with Dad and me. Next spring, of course, when the perch are running. I'm not into ice fishing."

"Me neither. Too cold. I can wait until the sun warms the lake enough to melt the ice pack."

Robert glared. "Are you enjoying your little chat about nothing?"

Patrick smiled. "You and Collin are carrying your conversation well enough without Jeff or me. I figured we would have our own family feud. Except we don't seem to be feuding about anything."

Jeff suggested, "I could start one if you like. Who do you follow in the Big Ten?"

Patrick shook his head. "I'm an Atlantic Coast Conference fan myself."

Jeff's eyes sparked with interest. "Oh, ho. Now it gets serious. Pray tell, what shade of blue do you prefer?"

"Who says the color has to be blue?"

"Because there are only two teams in the ACC worth any true allegiance." Jeff paused. "Well, okay, you can include red. But only because of Jimmy V. He's the one memorable thing the Wolfpack has ever produced."

Collin saw Robert's face turning a particular shade of nasty. He seethed, "You can take your basketball and—"

Collin interrupted. "Mr. Winger, you want to know what the will said. More to the point, you want to know who controls the estate. I can tell you the will has been filed with the probate court in Fort Newton."

Collin's eyes narrowed. "As executrix, I will begin the process of examining the document at my earliest opportunity. I cannot tell you when that will be. When I am able to begin, I will. If that does not meet with your approval"—Collin had to bite back the response she wanted to say. She swallowed and finished—"I will take your feelings under advisement."

Patrick clapped. "Bravo! Bravo! Forgive me for thinking you were still the little kid I remember. Well done, little sister."

Jeff chortled but said nothing. Collin held Robert's eyes, not acknowledging Patrick's approval, nor backing down from the elder Winger's glare.

Robert finally dropped his gaze to his plate, then looked to Collin. "When you find opportunity, let me know." For the first time in the evening, his eyes reflected something close to respect. He smirked. "I'm sure your uncles will be delighted to know the family estate is in your competent hands."

Collin finished her dinner, as did the men in her life. The bill came. Collin kept her emotions totally in check when she saw the total. *It's only money. You can't take it with you.*

Yeah, but at this rate, I won't be able to take it far in this life either.

Three hundred million will circle the globe a few times. I think you're safe.

Collin smiled pleasantly at the two Winger men. "Thank you for coming out tonight. It is good to see you looking well. Both of you." She stood to signal the evening over.

Robert held her eyes as if studying her. After a moment, he shrugged. "Yeah. You too."

Patrick gave her a genuine smile. "I enjoyed it. Maybe next time you and I can talk together. We can talk about the important stuff. Like what you're doing, how you're doing. Inconsequential stuff. But fun to know."

Collin nodded. "Next time."

Patrick and Robert left the table. Collin picked up her backpack. She noticed the zipper on the outside pocket had been opened. She never kept anything in that pocket, so why would it be unfastened? Concerned, she looked inside.

A slip of paper with scribbled handwriting had been tucked in at the bottom. Collin lifted it and showed it to Jeff.

"What's it say?"

Collin read, "'Call me. I need to talk to you. Dad has appointments tomorrow afternoon from one to four. Leave a message on my phone.'" A phone number followed.

She looked at Jeff. "What do you think?"

Jeff shrugged. "Patrick wants to talk to you without Robert knowing. Not too surprising, is it?"

Collin tried to reconstruct all the things Patrick had said in both their brief encounters. She stared at the note as if in staring at it, she could see his intention. When that failed, she looked at Jeff. "I don't know. People around Robert Winger don't do well trying to outthink him. He's a wicked chess player. Ruthless."

Jeff chuckled. "He should play against Trey. I'd bet they would be evenly matched."

"If Trey is as brutal as Robert, I pity you taking lessons from him."

"He's not brutal. He has empathy. He feels for me every time he beats me. At least that's what he says."

Collin shook her head. Unable to draw any inspiration from the note, she stuffed it in her purse. She looked at Jeff. "Let's go. I've got the appointment with Dr. McMannon in the morning, and you're back on your regular rotation, aren't you?"

"Yep." Jeff helped Collin into her jacket. "Are you going to call Patrick tomorrow?"

"I don't know."

Truer words have never been spoken.

Oh, shut up.

MONDAY

Collin rearranged the folders on her desk for the tenth time. She glanced at Marne's office to see if the door had opened, in the unlikely event Marne was ready to interact with her staff. Nope. Still closed.

Collin ground her teeth in frustration. Dr. McMannon's admonitions came back. *Lower your stress levels. Keep your blood pressure down. Avoid extreme emotions. Or exertions. Or caffeine. Or life itself...*

He did not say avoid life. He told you to do those things to save your life.

Life without coffee? What's the purpose?

Collin let the voices battle it out. She focused her attention on what she could control: the paperwork in front of her. Lots and lots of paperwork. A week's worth. No one had touched her cases while she'd been gone. Which did not bode well for them being covered if she left the department for good. Short-staffing affected more than the fire department. But the chance of her working and not being paid, as Jeff did, would be non-existent.

The phone on her desk rang. Collin looked at the caller ID: Detective Russo. Maybe he had news? Good news?

"Social Services Office, Walker speaking."

"Walker, this is Detective Russo."

"Yes, Detective. You have news for me?"

The detective paused. Collin cringed. Russo said, "Can you come to the office here to discuss your case? There are some developments we'd like to follow up on."

Not good news. "No, Detective, I can't. I don't have a readily available mode of transportation at present." She looked at the clock. "The next express bus to your office doesn't come for another hour. If I take the regular bus, it will take me twice as long to get there."

"You still don't have a car?"

"No. Not yet." Which technically could be said to be true. The fact she might soon have her license suspended and had been ordered not to drive didn't need to be mentioned right this moment. *Thank you, Dr. McMannon.*

Sarcastic, much? He's trying to protect you.

And every other driver on the road. I got it, I got it. I don't like it, but I got it.

The detective paused. "We could send a car to get you."

"Can you come here? I'm on a tight schedule and need to get caught up on some work." She hesitated. "And I'd like you to explain to my supervisor what's going on. I won't have to explain it twice." *And she'll believe you.*

Again the pause. "I can swing it. We'll be there in twenty minutes. You're on the fifth floor?"

"Sixth. Hidden in the back. I'll have Marne with me in the conference room."

"Good plan. See you in a few." The phone went dead.

Collin slipped the receiver back on its holder. This would be interesting. Not fun, but interesting. She stood, walked to Marne's door, and knocked.

"Go away."

Collin knocked again.

"As you value your life, go away."

Marne's standard admonition. Collin ignored it and opened the door. She walked in, sat across the desk from her supervisor, and took a deep breath. "I need you to meet with two detectives from Homicide and me in the conference room. They'll be here in twenty minutes. I also need you not to ask me a lot of questions before you hear them out."

Marne eyed Collin closely. "They got a warrant for your arrest?"

"No."

"You kill someone?"

"No."

"You try to kill someone?"

"No." *Wanted to a few times, but no.*

"They gonna tell me what this is all about and why I'm wasting my precious time listening to them instead of making out the monthly projections my boss wants yesterday?"

Collin swallowed her smile. "Yes."

"I'll be there."

"I need expedited relief supplies for the people in my…the people affected by the fire." She felt her hands tremble. "Marne, they lost everything. All of them."

Collin hesitated. "I also need a six-month leave of absence. Starting today."

Marne's eyes narrowed. "Six months? That's a long time. You gonna tell me why?"

Collin swallowed hard. "No. Not yet."

Marne shook her head. "Don't know if I can swing it without a good reason."

"Try, Marne. Because if you can't, I'll have to resign. Effective today."

"This has to do with these policemen coming?"

How to answer? "Yes." *Partly, anyhow.*

Marne nodded. "I'll see what I can swing."

Collin stood. "Thank you, Marne. I appreciate everything you've ever done for me. I appreciate you, period."

As she turned to go, Marne called, "Walker…whatever it is, we'll get it straightened out. You're too good an employee to let go."

Collin didn't turn around. She walked to her desk and sat. She would miss this place. She really would.

She pulled out the piece of paper with Patrick's number on it and dialed. As soon as he answered she said, "Patrick. I don't know if I can meet you for lunch yet. Something has come up. I'll know in about an hour."

Patrick laughed. "I'd ask you how you knew what I wanted to ask you about, but I guess it's kind of obvious."

"After your note last night, yeah."

"If you can make it, where should we meet?"

"Someplace I can walk to. Sal's Deli is down the street from my office. If I'm available, I'll meet you there. I'll call you and let you know." She hesitated. "How are you able to take this call and Robert not know?"

"He's in the shower."

"Okay." Collin let it pass. "You're sure he will be in meetings?"

"It's why we're here. Why we came looking for you this weekend. Dad knew we'd be here several days and decided this would be the opportune moment to reconnect with you."

"Where are you staying?"

"The Bradford Inn."

Collin whistled under her breath. "Sort of extravagant for him, isn't it?"

Patrick sounded surprised. "Why would you say that? Dad always travels first class. He always has."

Collin started to correct Patrick's image of her father but stopped. "Right. Okay. I need to get off here. I'll call you back and let you know. Talk to you later."

Marne walked toward her desk, an unhappy look on her face. Collin studied the woman. "They turned down my request for expedited help, didn't they?"

Marne nodded. "I'm sorry, Collin. I know how you feel about your kids. But the department has channels, and regulations, and baggage and bureaucrats and politicians. They won't budge."

Collin nodded. "I thought as much, but it needed to be asked. I'll tap my other sources."

"Sources such as…"

"The faith-based network I know." She smiled. "They only have one Boss to answer to. Works much simpler."

Marne huffed. "Gets more done, too. Well, get on it, girl. Get those people the help they need."

Collin smiled "Thanks." Marne went back to her office; Collin started dialing. "Rob? I need your help." "Brother Golding? I need your help." "Pastor Andy? I need help."

In thirty minutes, she arranged for backpacks, school supplies, clothing, and transportation for the young people in her former neighborhood. The transportation would be good through the Thanksgiving break, coming sooner than Collin liked. Would her neighbors feel like they had anything to be thankful for?

They're alive. That's always a good start.

Truth. Collin heard the buzz of someone being let into the department. She looked to see Detectives Russo and O'Conner being escorted to the conference room by Marne. Collin straightened her shirt, climbed to her feet, and followed them.

I have a bad feeling about this...

Don't we all?

Collin sat opposite the two detectives and waited. Marne did the same. Collin nodded to Detective Russo and said, "The floor is yours."

Depending on his tax bracket, so may the desk, the chairs, and the rest of the room.

If you can't be helpful, be quiet.

Russo pulled out a photograph of a white male, maybe in his fifties. "You know him? Ever seen him around your place?"

Collin studied the photo and shook her head. "No. Do I want to?"

"Probably not. Arnie Lansing. He's the suspected arsonist at your trailer court. Materials used match his style. Except he's never hit anything this large before."

O'Conner added, "Or with so little to gain. From what we can find, there's no insurance policy to collect, no property of value to build on. He's usually a for-hire kind of arsonist. Insurance fraud, property disputes, those kinds of things. This is totally out of his norm."

Russo added, "Not to mention he was one of the victims. Nothing about this fire makes any sense. We hoped maybe you could shed some light on things."

Collin asked, "Where did the fire start?"

The answer confirmed Collin's suspicions. "Under your trailer. You weren't home. Why?"

Collin closed her eyes. "Ice cream. We stopped for ice cream." She looked at the two detectives. "You weren't calling me downtown for that. What else is it?"

Russo's eyes narrowed. "Someone wants you dead. I want to know why."

"As I already mentioned, there's a 300 million dollar will with my name on it. I'm the executrix and the beneficiary. Someone—or someones—would like me not to inherit it. They assume if I die, it will be distributed by stirpes. Which means everyone gets a share."

Collin shifted uncomfortably in her chair. "Except no one in this family ever plays by the rules. Fort Newton could see a murder spree like they're never known before."

O'Conner scoffed. "Right. This isn't some crime drama."

Collin snapped, "And my family's not the Waltons, either. There is no love in this bunch, except the love of money." She backed down the vitriol. "Beyond that, I have no clue why anyone cares about my existence. Much less wants me dead."

Russo asked, "No one in your past you might have crossed, turned in to the police, testified against, sent to prison?"

"No." Collin thought through her past. Her dark past... "No. Besides my family, I can't think of anyone who would want to kill me."

She frowned. "And who would take out innocent lives in the process." She looked at Russo. "I'm supposed to meet with my half-brother"—she managed to say the words without spitting them out—"for lunch at one. Maybe I can get information from him. He's telling me everything is all happy and rosy between us. Maybe he'll tell me who it isn't with...or whatever. You know what I mean."

The absurdity of the situation threatened to crush Collin. She looked at Marne, then to Russo. "It's crazy. They don't need to kill me. All they need to do is wait. I've got a mass in my brain wanting to do the job for them." She shook her head, dropped her gaze to the floor, and whispered, "Oh, Lord, what are You showing me? What do You want me to do?"

Marne exclaimed, "What? What are you talking about?"

Russo, too, looked more than interested. "What's that about?"

Collin said, "Headaches. I've been getting these intense headaches. They knock me to the floor. My doctor saw the CT scan they did after the accident. He saw what he thinks is a shadow and believes I may have a tumor. He thinks it's what is causing the pain. He wants me to have surgery now. Wanted me to have an MRI this morning, then do surgery this afternoon. I told him no."

Marne threw her hands in the air. "Why not?"

Collin threw hers as well. "Because I've got things I've got to do before that happens. Like, take care of my kids. Find out who's killing innocent people while trying to get to me. Figure out what to do with my grandfather's money." She glared at Marne and Russo. "Little things."

The defiance faded as quickly as it came. She dropped her head. "Tell the man I love he should find someone else because there's no guarantee I'll be the same person after the surgery is over." Tears threatened to fill her eyes. She brushed them back angrily. "Little things. You know?"

Marne put her hand on Collin's shoulder. "I'm sorry, Collin. I am. I didn't know."

Collin's chin quivered. "I didn't either until this morning." She drew in a deep breath and said, "I have things to do, Detective."

Russo nodded. "I hear you. We'll take care of the investigation, Ms. Walker. That's not one of your concerns. That's my job."

Collin half-smiled. "I've heard that before." She nodded. "Right. Your job. But I still need to meet my half-brother for lunch. Maybe if I tell him about the tumor, he'll call off whoever it is trying to kill me. Save them the trouble."

Russo asked, "Where are you meeting him?"

"I told him Sal's. But I have to confirm it with him."

"Make sure he comes there. We'll have a man inside, just in case." He smiled at her. "Order the Reuben. They pickle their own sauerkraut. It's delicious."

Collin shuddered. "No, thank you. I'm a ham and cheese person." She stood. "Thank you for coming here, Detective. I'm sorry I can't be more help."

"You've told us all you can. That's help enough. We'll see you later, I'm sure."

The detective looked at Collin. "Person to person, Ms. Walker. This thing with your boyfriend? Don't say no for him. Let him make up his mind. If he loves you, he'll make the right choice. But you gotta give him the chance." Russo paused. "Not my place, I know. Only a thought for you to consider."

Collin smiled at him. "Thank you, Detective. I appreciate it. I do."

Especially since it's the exact opposite of what McMannon said. He said don't tell Jeff, period. If you tell him before, he'll have some misguided sense of loyalty and will promise to marry you no matter what. You don't want to trap him, right? Or do you?

Collin walked back to her desk and punched in Patrick's number. After the third ring, he picked up. "Hey, sis. Are we on for lunch?"

Collin let the "sis" go. This time. She looked at the clock. "Meet me at Sal's at one. It's not hard to find."

"Great. Fantastic! I'll see you at one."

Collin hung up. Another look at the clock told her she had a little over an hour to make the next part of her plan come together. She buzzed the clerk of courts' desk. "Janey? Is Judge Solomon in? Is he…" Collin trailed off. 'Busy' went without saying. She changed her wording. "…able to be disturbed for a few minutes?"

"How few?"

"Five. Maybe less."

"I'll work you in. Now would be your best chance of catching him."

"I'll be right down. Thanks, Janey."

* * *

At a quarter to one, Collin made her way over to Sal's deli. An exceedingly popular take-out joint, it nonetheless had a few open tables in the back room. Sal met Collin at the door. "Hi, beautiful." The man hesitated. "I can still say beautiful, can't I? And not offend you?"

Collin smiled. "I am not offended. Your eyesight could use some correction, but no, I'm not offended."

Sal wiped his brow. "Good. I didn't see you in here last week. What happened? You haven't found someplace you like better, have you?"

Collin shook her head. "I had a little fender bender on Monday. Took the week off to recover."

"Slacker. No wonder this city can't get anything done these days." He led Collin to a table away from the front noise and confusion.

Collin said, "I'll be meeting someone for lunch today."

Sal grinned. "*That* someone?"

"No, not *that* someone. A…relative. On my paternal side."

"Long lost?"

"You could say that." *Wish he'd stayed lost.*

Unkind. True, but unkind.

Sal said, "I'll watch for him."

"If he stays true to family tradition, he'll be late."

A voice called out urgently, "Hey, Collin! There you are!"

Collin's heart leaped, but she hid any outward reaction. "There he is."

Sal directed Patrick to the table and handed him a menu. He didn't bother giving Collin one. She nodded. "Usual. But half the size. And half the soup. I don't have any place to store it today."

Sal ducked his head and left.

Patrick gazed quickly at the menu. "What's good?"

"Everything. And you get a lot of it. Lots and lots of it. I'm always asking for half portions and still end up taking enough home for the next day."

"Impressive, considering how you used to eat. I remember you always were able to put away a meal in a hurry." He smiled as if to take any sting out of the comment.

Patrick looked at the menu. Collin eyed him. *When did you see me eat?* "I guess I've changed some."

"I'll say. You look good, though. You do. More like Dad than your mom."

Collin let it pass. "You look well. Tell me what you're doing these days."

Sal returned with silverware, napkins, and a glass of tap water for Collin. She smiled at him. Patrick asked, "How's the Reuben?"

"Exquisite. We pickle our own sauerkraut."

Collin rolled her eyes. Patrick nodded. "I'll do the Reuben. Diet soda to drink. Onion rings, if you've got 'em."

"Coming right up."

Patrick looked at Collin. "What am I doing these days? Working for Dad, of course." He laughed. "Far cry from what we wanted to be when we were growing up, right? I wanted to be an engineer, Erin wanted to be an astronaut, and you were going to be a jockey. You loved horses."

Collin stared at Patrick for a long moment. "When did we talk about dreams for our futures?" *Horses? I'm afraid of horses. Well, highly respectful of horses. And Erin never said anything about being an astronaut. He hated heights.*

Patrick shrugged. "Must have been at Grandma's. You remember all those family gatherings we had? We'd hide from Dad under Grandpa Jeremiah's desk. We sat there for hours and talked about what we wanted to do when we grew up."

He eyed Collin closely. "You're telling me you don't remember?"

Collin hesitated. "Not so much." *Not at all. Never even once.*

Patrick shrugged. "Whatever. I remember. And I remember when we went on vacation to the Outer Banks in North Carolina. You wanted to go to Chincoteague Island and see the wild ponies. You were so upset when we couldn't reach the island because it's a refuge. You had a nuclear meltdown." He laughed. "Dad tried everything to get your mind off of them. I think he even promised to buy you the island."

Patrick smiled. "Matter of fact, that's what finally got you to stop crying. You had a good time from then on. You told everyone we met, 'My daddy is going to buy me an island with ponies!'"

Collin listened. *"My daddy?" I never called him daddy. Ever. And buy me an island? With ponies? What's Patrick been smoking?* She shook her head slowly. "How old were Erin and I?"

Patrick thought. "It had to be before Grandma passed, so I'd guess seven. Maybe eight at most." Again, he studied her. "You don't remember that, either?"

Collin admitted, "No, Patrick. I don't." *Because it never happened.*

He looked at her with concern. "What do you remember?"

"I remember Erin and I being alone a lot while Robert Winger went away on business trips."

"Dad never left you two by yourselves. If he left for more than half a day, he left me with you two"—Patrick grinned—"so I could keep you out of trouble."

A memory or two of Robert Winger's definition of 'trouble' flashed through Collin's mind. Accompanied by punishment in advance. Collin mused, "Didn't matter what I did. He considered me trouble from the day I drew my first breath."

Patrick's eyes grew wide. He turned his head to one side to stare at her. Sal came to deliver the meals before Patrick could say anything. Collin's sandwich had a double-high stack of ham and cheese on a single roll. Patrick's plate, however, held a triple portion of corned beef topped with a mountain of sauerkraut. A second plate contained another mountain, this time of onion rings. Patrick's mouth fell open as he stared at the offering. He looked at Sal and said, "Now that's what I call a Reuben. My compliments to the chef."

Sal smiled. "Enjoy."

Patrick stared at the plate. "Oh, I'm going to. Believe me, I will enjoy every bite of this." He waited until Sal left. "For days to come, I'm sure. You could have warned me, Caitlin."

"I did. It keeps well."

Patrick took his first bite, rolled it around his mouth, nodded approvingly. He swallowed half of it and said, "That's a gooood sandwich."

Collin took half the meat and cheese off hers, set it to the side, ate slowly. Savor every moment, right?

Patrick swallowed the other half of his mouthful. "I don't understand what you're talking about, Collin. Dad adored you. You were his special princess. You had him so wrapped around his finger Erin and I didn't dare dream of doing anything to you. Not that you didn't deserve it. The way you hassled us!"

Collin chewed her sandwich carefully. "Patrick, you and I have very different memories from childhood." *Very different. Like two worlds different.* "But that's behind us. What matters is who we are now. Let's agree to disagree about what went on before and start a new relationship. Right?"

Patrick hesitated. Collin eyed him sideways. "What?"

Patrick dropped his eyes to the table. "We can. But…I need to know one thing from our past. It's haunted me ever since it happened. Dad won't talk to me about it. But I have to know." He stared Collin in the eyes. "What happened the night Erin died? Why did you run away?"

Run? Run? Collin worked to keep the shock from her voice. She managed, but barely. "I didn't run away, Patrick. I never ran from anything. It's why I—" She stopped. "What do you remember from when it happened?"

Patrick looked at the table again, unable to meet Collin's eyes. He chewed more of his sandwich and downed several of the onion rings. "I remember everything. All of it. Erin and I were playing catch with the football. He wanted to make the JV team and wanted me to teach him to catch. You were jealous he and I were together playing."

He looked to meet Collin's eyes. "You were so possessive of Erin's time and attention. It was pathological, I know now. Back then, I only thought you were a bratty, spoiled girl who always got her way because Daddy gave you everything you wanted."

Patrick shrugged. "Sorry, but that's what I felt. Erin felt the same way. He'd beg me to play with him so he wouldn't have to play dolls with you."

Dolls? I never had a doll in my life!

Patrick continued, "He and I spent an entire summer building a model car, engine and all, only him and me. He kept it on a shelf in his room."

No car. Never. Ever.

A larger portion of Patrick's sandwich disappeared, along with half the onion rings. "Anyhow, we told you you couldn't play, we had to practice. You screamed at both of us. Erin told you to go away; he didn't want to see you. He threatened to tell Dad you were stealing money off his dresser if you didn't leave us alone."

Patrick looked at her. "Were you?"

Collin shook her head. "No." *Not after the first time I touched something on his dresser. Three broken fingers on my right hand; two on Erin's left to make things clear.*

Patrick shrugged. "Whatever. It seemed to scare you off. You disappeared, anyhow. We threw the ball around. I tossed it to Erin one last time, and you came tearing out of the bushes behind him. You leveled him. Erin hit the ground, and…"

Patrick took another mouthful of sandwich. He chewed it, swallowed. "It's still hard to tell, Caitlin."

He's deliberately not saying your name right.

Ya think?

Collin took a bite to settle her emotions. "I understand. Go on, if you can." *Did you rehearse this? Or are you making it up as you go along?*

"You sure you want me to?"

"I'm sure. Go on."

"Erin yelled. You lashed out, kicked him in the head, then ran off. I never saw you again. I stayed with Erin. Someone called the ambulance. I rode in with him to the hospital. Dad met us there, and we stayed with him until…until he passed."

Patrick looked down, then looked at Collin. "Dad took me home. I went looking for you, but you were gone. Everything in Erin's room had been torn and smashed. The car we built was in a billion pieces all over the room. Pictures had Erin's face crossed off, scribbled out, ripped in two."

Patrick shook his head. "I'd never heard of a psychotic break before, but I saw one that night."

Collin took it all in silently. *Say something. Anything.* "What did you do next?"

"Dad said you would come out of it and come home when you realized you'd killed Erin. You'd be devastated, and we would need to be there to help you get the treatment you needed. But you never came back."

Patrick looked at her. "Where did you go? How did you get to Oakton?"

Collin finished her sandwich. All the voices were silent. Collin looked Patrick in the eyes. "I don't remember it that way at all."

Patrick nodded. "Dad said you wouldn't. When we first looked for you, he warned me. He said guilt for killing Erin would cripple your mind. The only way you could reconcile what happened would be to deny all of it."

Patrick's eyes filled with sympathy. "He said you'd create a false narrative about being mistreated and abused. But also one about how much you loved Erin and how he meant everything to you. You'd never hurt someone you loved so much. You wouldn't. You couldn't. So you didn't. In your mind, anyhow."

Collin kept the tremor out of her voice. "My mind did a really good job of it because that's not what I remember at all. None of it. Even before Erin's accident."

Patrick finished his sandwich and the rings. "That's what Dad said would happen. Your mind worked backward to change everything to fit your new version of how things were."

Convenient. He has an answer for everything, doesn't he?

Pull it together. You've still got one avenue of escape.

"Since we don't have an objective observer who saw it all, we'll have to leave it as it is." Collin lifted her head and squared her shoulders.

Patrick hesitated. "What if I showed you pictures?"

"Pictures of what?"

"Of the four of us on vacations. We went lots of places together. Or how about pictures of Erin and me doing stuff? Building the car together. Stuff like that. Would pictures help you remember?"

Patrick pulled out his phone. "I've got them here. On my phone. I scanned the photos into my phone. I figured it would be the easiest way to show them to you."

Of course, he has pictures. You didn't expect him to come unprepared, did you? This is Patrick. Robert 2.0. Collin held her hand out for Patrick's phone.

Her half-brother pulled up his gallery of pictures, went to a specific file, and handed it to Collin. "There. You can see them for yourself."

Collin began to scroll through the photos slowly. Very slowly. The first picture tore her heart. *Erin.*

Her twin brother stood waving to the camera, his eyes full of life and excitement. The picture had probably been taken not long before his accident. To have the first picture she saw,,, Collin closed her eyes to stem the burning tears.

Patrick apologized. "I'm sorry, Collin. I didn't mean for these pictures to upset you. Maybe we should do this another time. Somewhere more private?"

Her gut burned with the realization all this had been a set up to elicit her exact response. And she'd fallen for it. The cruelty snapped her emotion from sorrow to fury. Cold fury. The kind that serves vengeance cold.

Collin gave Patrick a half-smile. "No, I'm fine. Seeing him shocked me, that's all. I haven't had anything but my memory of him all these years. Thanks for showing me this one first." *I won't forget this. Ever.*

She scrolled through the rest of the photos. They did, indeed, show Patrick with the twins on many, many occasions. More than Collin would have thought possible. There were multiple pictures of Erin and Patrick together, working on a model car. The one Patrick claimed she'd destroyed? Probably. Many of the photos showed Caitlin in the background pouting or wearing a look which could only be called disgust and anger. *What's the theme? What's he trying to prove?*

All the pictures had Patrick and Erin front and center, with Caitlin off in the distance. To be sure, there were a few—very few— of her by herself or with Patrick or Erin, but none of the three of them all happy at the same time. Nor were there any of Robert Winger with the children. Collin squinted at the picture in front of her. "Who took all these?"

"Dad did."

"All of them?"

"Maybe not all of them. But most of them."

Collin handed the phone back to Patrick. *Your defense, counselor?* The pictures all looked authentic. Of course, with electronic media, it would be hard to tell. The locations resonated with some of her memories of where she and Erin had played, or more correctly, had been, but nothing sparked in her about Patrick being there or her father taking pictures. All of it remained a blank. Which meant... *Which means what? They're real? You aren't?*

Patrick asked, "So what do you think? Any of those pictures look familiar?"

Time. I need time. Collin sidestepped the question. "Did Robert Winger say I would remember because of them, or did he insist my psyche would continue to protect me, and I'd deny all memory of any of it?"

Patrick took a long swig of his drink. "Does it matter? I'm interested in what you think."

"No, you brought him into the equation when you said he told you what I would do and why. I'd like to know what he told you I'd do now, today." *What does he expect me to do?*

Patrick finished off the sandwich. He chewed for a moment. "He said you would continue to deny it. I said you wouldn't. I said since I had proof with the pictures, you would accept my version, no matter how much it hurt, and would deal with it accordingly." His eyes probed hers. "Am I right? You're not afraid to admit your life has been built on a lie, are you?"

Collin breathed deep. *The Lord is your life. Remember?* "My life—now—is built on the Lord and what He's done for me. That's the only life I'm concerned about. What went before is gone, Patrick. Erin is dead. Knowing the past won't bring him back."

Patrick lowered his voice. "I know. But there's no statute of limitations on murder."

Collin's eyes flew wide, then narrowed. "Are you threatening me?" *Murder? Murder?*

Patrick backtracked quickly. "No, no. Never. Of course not. I'm not saying I would ever accuse you...but the uncles never believed Dad's story about it being an accident. With you back in the picture, who knows what they might do?"

Collin looked at her watch. 2:30. "I've got to get back to work, Patrick. Can you get away tomorrow, same time, same place, and we'll discuss this more?"

"I'll be here."

Collin motioned to Sal. He brought her box without her having to say a word. With deliberate and measured motions, Collin placed the extra ham and cheese in the box, closed it, and stood. *Keep moving. Keep breathing.* "I'll see you tomorrow." Patrick stood as well; Collin went to the front counter to settle the bill.

Sal smiled. "And how was it?"

Don't show anything. Collin put her best smile on her face. "Like it always is, Sal. Perfect. So perfect, he and I will be back tomorrow."

Sal put his hand to his chest. "Two days in a row, you'll come? Can I stand the excitement?"

Collin nodded. "I'm sure you will." She faced Patrick. "I've got today. You pay for tomorrow."

Patrick gave her a small salute. "Thanks, Sis. See you."

Collin walked out of the storefront. Patrick headed for the parking lot. Collin turned down the street and walked back toward work. The sidewalks had emptied. Thoughts raced and tumbled and snapped and crackled... Collin refused to allow any single inclination to take center stage for more than a second or two. Her feet operated on muscle memory alone. Step.

Step.

Step.

You can do this. His words change nothing. Keep moving.

Step.

Step.

Tires screeched. A bright red car jumped the curb and race toward her. Collin stared at the vehicle, unable to comprehend the danger.

Move!

Instinct kicked in. Collin jumped forward and put a street light between herself and the car. It swerved, slammed into a trash bin, raced down the street.

Collin stared after the car, still unable to process anything. A plainclothes policeman rushed to her. "Are you okay, Miss Walker? Did you get a plate number?"

Collin looked at the man in confusion. "Plate?" She gazed down the street. "Plate? No. No. I...I don't think it had any."

The policeman spoke into his headset. "Yeah, she's okay. Missed her completely. No ID."

Collin drew a breath. "I have no idea who it might have been." She looked at the officer. "May I go back to my…" *Where? What do I have? Office. I still have an office…* "Office? Detective Russo knows where I am."

Another consult on the headset. "Yes, ma'am. I'll walk with you."

Protecting the guilty? How ironic…

Shut up. Shut up. Shut up. Shut up. Shut up…

Collin maintained her silent chant all the way to her building, to the elevator, into her office, finally to her cubicle. Only after she sat did she stop. She closed her eyes and went deeply internal.

Peace. Peace I gave you. My peace is yours.

Did I do it? Did I murder my brother?

What do you know? At this moment, what is real?

The desk is real. I feel it. Don't I?

Do you?

Yes. Collin ran her hands across the cold grey metal. *I feel it. It's real. My chair is real. The floor is real. This place is real.*

Is there work for you here, now?

Yes.

Do it. Do the work you have been given to do. Do the next thing. One moment at a time.

Collin drew in a long breath, let it out slowly, and began sorting the files in front of her.

* * *

Five o'clock. No word from Marne. Collin gathered what few personal belongings she had brought into her cubby over the years, stuffed them in her backpack, and walked to the supervisor's office. She knocked.

"Go away."

Collin called out, "I'm leaving, Marne."

Marne opened the door. Her eyes were red from crying. She hugged Collin. "Come back when you get it all straightened out, Walker. You'll always have a place here. I'll find a place for you."

Collin's throat tightened. "Thanks for everything, Marne. I…"

She stopped. All the words she wanted to say wouldn't be enough. She hugged Marne again, turned, and walked out.

MONDAY EVENING

She took the elevator to the Security Office. Shafer, the building's oldest watchman, smiled as he retrieved the suitcase she'd left with him in the morning. "Have a good trip, Miss Walker. See you when you get back."

Collin smiled at him, not trusting her voice not to quaver. She managed a "Bye" and walked out the door.

She strode down the street and across the Memorial Square to the economy express motel. Collin rented a room. *Ground floor, please, and I'll be here three nights.* Wi-Fi password is leavethelighton. No pets, please. And no smoking. Right.

Collin closed the door behind her. She did a quick check under the beds, in the closet, in the shower, dropped the security lock and chain in place, and threw the bolt for good measure. The sliding windows had additional barriers to unauthorized admittance, so she left them alone. Convinced the space was safe, she backed against the wall and slid, curling into a ball. "Lord, what are You showing me? What am I supposed to do with this?"

She stared at the ceiling. "We went over this. Over and over and over… I did not kill Erin." Collin's voice cracked. "How many times did You tell me I did not kill him? Every time I started accusing myself, You came through and said it was a lie."

Collin dropped her head to rest on her knees. "It's not true, is it, Father? What Patrick said about me, about all of it. It's not true, right?"

Crushed. Patrick's words. They crushed her. His words. The pictures… "Oh, God. Oh, God. Oh, God." Collin covered her face with her hands. Tears flooded her cheeks.

"Is it all true, God? Is my whole life a lie to hide the fact I murdered Erin?"

No answers came. The voice of guilt whispered, *Now you see it. You murdered him. Deliberately killed him. I've been telling you all along. You knew the truth.*

Head down, Collin crawled from the wall to the bed. She kicked her shoes off, pulled some of the pillows beside her, curled up with them, and sat in silence. Her phone pinged. Jeff. Collin ignored the call. No one could come between her and this indictment.

Accused. Evidence presented. Defense?

I can't remember.

We, the jury, find you—

Collin gripped the pillow harder. Her hands shook. She rocked back and forth, faster and faster, sobs wracking her body. "I did not murder my brother. I did not murder my brother. I did not murder…"

Prove it! Patrick has pictures! Lots and lots of pictures! Lots and lots of pictures over many years. What have you got? Nothing! You've got nothing!

Collin's wrist popped. She glared at it. *Annoying thing. Hasn't been right since I broke it back—*

Collin stopped rocking. She became still, staring at her wrist. Her wrist she'd broken when she was ten. Collin circled it around in the air. Once. Twice. She pulled up her right shirt sleeve and traced two surgical scars: one ran up her wrist, one ran from her elbow to her shoulder. Her eyes narrowed. She pulled up the left sleeve. Two more surgical scars; two more broken bones. Collin's face drew hard. Her jaw clenched. *Where were the casts?*

Casts? You never had a cast

Collin smiled, but a cold, satisfied smile. *Right. There were none in the pictures. But if I were Daddy's princess, wouldn't there be?*

Collin sat back against the bed. Her head nodded in time to her words. "The surgeon from the clinic said all the bones were broken pre-puberty. Most of them hadn't healed right. Like they weren't put in casts. Which they weren't. Because Daddy"—she spit the name—"never took me to the doctor for a broken bone. Brother Golding insisted on the reconstructive surgery so my bones would grow properly. After I 'ran away.'" Collin sneered out the words.

She rolled to her knees and reached for her phone. Fury filled her heart. She would nail Patrick to the wall. She would flay him up one side and down the other, front to back…she would—

She would stop cold. Her mind pulled her up sharp. Surely he would have an answer to the accusations. He'd never leave out something so obvious without having an answer. And with Robert to back him, she'd still be wrong. No. Better to ask him in person. When he couldn't rely on Robert to bail him out. She would wait until tomorrow. Then she would plaster the walls with his carcass—

Love your enemies. Do good to—

"Not this time. Not now. That's not what this is about. This is war. You know it, I know it."

Her phone pinged. Jeff again. Collin picked it up. "What?"

Jeff's voice came back, unsure. "Uh, Collin? Are you okay?"

Collin backed the attitude down a notch. "I'm okay. It's been a…long day. I'm sorry I jumped at you."

Jeff continued to be cautious. "Is it okay to ask what happened today?"

Collin settled back against the bed for support. "I had my appointment with Dr. McMannon. I went to work. I got things arranged for the kids. I met with Detective Russo. I went to lunch with Patrick. Someone tried to run me over on the way back. I finished my shift and quit my job. I'm staying at a motel. How did your day go?"

Jeff's voice snapped. "Someone what?"

"They missed. Let it go. I'm trying to."

Prolonged silence. "Sounds like a bad day. You want to tell me about it? Piece by piece?"

Collin dropped her eyes to the floor. "No. Yes. Some of it. What do you want to know?"

"All of it. What did Rich tell you?"

"Let's do Rich last." Collin felt some of her anger melting into despair. "The county won't expedite help for the kids in the trailer court, so I called on the faith network. The rescue mission is going to provide the school children with backpacks and supplies. The Tabernacle Church will provide them with transportation to school from wherever they are so the kids at least have some continuity."

"Are you funding all of this?"

Collin drew in a long breath. "Some of it. The rescue mission will distribute the school stuff, but I'm buying it. I have some money put away of my own."

Jeff's voice became, if anything, more cautious. "Will you allow my family to help you? Anonymously, of course. We'll split the cost."

Pride shouted, *No! I'll do this myself!*

Practicality whispered *It's for the kids. Be smart.*

Collin closed her eyes. "Yes. I can use the help. As long as we split it 50-50."

"Of course. So that turned out okay. Right?"

"Right. It was the only thing that did."

Jeff's voice became gentle. "Quitting had to be hard."

Tears threatened to undo Collin. She brushed them back angrily. "Beyond hard. I love my job. Or, loved it. But Marne couldn't give me a leave of absence. So I resigned."

"Can you go back when all this gets settled?"

Collin looked at the ceiling. "Yes. No. Maybe. I don't know. I could get rehired. But could I honestly do my job? Could I still say to the kids, 'I know what you're going through'? And they believe me?"

Silence. "I don't know, milady. Maybe we try to face those fears when the time comes. But not now. Okay?"

Collin could sense Jeff walking on eggshells. She bit her lip. "Detective Russo says the fire started under my trailer. The arsonist died in the fire. Russo believes someone wants to kill me."

Jeff's voice grew dark. "Did he figure that out before or after someone tried to run you over?"

"Before. The miss and run came after lunch. The driver didn't even get close. Jumped the curb, hit the wall, and kept going."

"Okay. But what are the cops doing about all this? What is Russo doing to keep you safe?"

Collin shook her head. "He's not. I'm sure he would like me to go into protective custody or something. But I won't. Period." Collin made the emphasis emphatic.

And Jeff got the hint. "I see. Okay. I get it. No hiding. What happened at lunch?"

All the emotions of the afternoon returned. Full force. "Patrick told me all my memories of the past are a lie. Robert never abused me. Patrick lived with us. We were all a happy foursome. Except I had a pathological obsession with Erin and hated him paying attention to anyone else." Collin forced the anger to continue, ignoring the growing sadness and self-doubt. "He says I deliberately…I caused…I murdered Erin." The words were out. The horror of the thought smashed through her defenses, leaving her raw and exposed. "I killed my brother. And I didn't even remember it."

Jeff's voice hardened. "Never. You would never do that, Collin. I know you. You loved your brother. You would never do anything to hurt him."

Tears rushed down Collin's cheeks, fell off her chin, and puddled on her knees. "You say it because it's what I told you. But what if it's not true? What if I did kill Erin and made up my past to cover it? How could you know?"

"Because I know you. I know your heart, your soul. Lady, if you had killed Erin, the Lord would have brought it to you long ago. He would. He loves you too much not to. Patrick can say anything he wants to because there's no proof one way or another."

"He had proof. He showed me pictures of us all together. Well, mostly together." Collin's throat tightened. "He said—"

"I don't care what he said, Collin. You did not kill your brother. It couldn't have happened. Ever. I don't believe it. And I don't care what kind of pictures Patrick shows you. And why would he even bring it up?"

Collin could hear Jeff getting heated. She shifted on the floor to get more comfortable. "Because, as he said, there is no statute of limitations on murder. My uncles might accuse me of murdering Erin. To keep me from getting all the money, you see."

"Let me guess. Patrick is doing this out of the goodness of his heart, right?"

While it felt good to have someone else as angry as Collin herself, Collin knew she didn't need to agitate Jeff as well. "I don't know why he's doing it. He says he wants to help me."

"You believe him?"

Collin hesitated. Looked into her heart, her soul. "No." It came out a whisper, not a declaration.

"Collin, you know better. You did not kill your brother. You didn't. You know it. Get it in your being. You did not kill Erin."

Collin swallowed hard. "Right. I'm going to ask Patrick why there are no pictures of me in a cast. I broke a lot of bones—or had a lot of bones broken, anyhow—growing up. None of his pictures show me having a cast anywhere. He'll have to explain that."

Confidence began trickling into her backbone. Collin sat straighter. "I'm going to ask him who is trying to kill me. We'll see what he has to say about it."

Jeff's voice echoed her confidence. "You do that. I'd love to be there." Pause… "I could be there if you wanted me to."

"Not without messing up your schedule. Detective Russo says he'll have plainclothes officers in the restaurant. I'll be safe enough."

"Will Patrick?"

Collin laughed. "Oh, I have no idea. If I followed my first inclination, no, he wouldn't be. But I'll let him live. Unharmed, I promise."

She heard Jeff's chuckle. Good. They were both off the ledge. Better for both of them.

"So tell me about what Uncle Rich had to say."

Collin's laughter died. Reality reared its ugly head. Choices. *Tell him.*

Don't tell him. You don't know anything for certain anyhow. It's McMannon's guess.

If you tell him, you'll trap him. You don't want that.

If you don't tell him, he'll never believe you about anything else.

Collin hugged a pillow tightly and began to rock. A little. "He, uh…he thinks there might be…there could be something…maybe…" She bit her lip. "He thinks there's a tumor."

As if to prove a point, the pain slashed through her head. Collin gasped. She could hear Jeff demanding, "Collin? Talk to me, lady. Tell me what's happening. Talk to me."

As quickly as it came, it left. Only this time, her nose gushed with blood. Collin lifted her head up, pinched her nose in the stop-a-nosebleed position she'd been taught, and scrambled to her feet. She called out, "Hang on. My nose is bleeding." She moved to the bathroom, ran a towel under the cold water, and placed it across her face. She went back to the room and flopped on the floor again. "I'm back. Haven't had one of those in a long time."

"You had a nosebleed? How long has that been going on?"

Collin spaced her words. "I said I haven't had one of those in a long time. It's new. Ignore it."

"I think you ought to call Uncle Rich."

"I'll see him in the morning. I can tell him."

"Another appointment?"

"He wants me to have an MRI. Just what I need. Ping pong balls bouncing around me. That should be a thrill a minute."

Jeff's voice became placating. "Collin, if Uncle Rich thinks you need it—"

"It's a good thing. I know, Jeff. I know. I don't have to like it. I won't like it. But I'll go and have it done. That's why I'm staying at this motel. I can walk to the hospital from here." *Since I can't drive.*

Jeff said, "Right. You need a car. Mom wants to give you hers. She's not driving it."

"And I won't be, either. Depending on the results tomorrow, Dr. McMannon is writing to have my license temporarily suspended."

Silence. "He thinks it's that serious?"

"He's afraid I might have an episode while I'm driving and take out half a dozen people with me." Collin dropped the sarcasm. "He's right, of course. I shouldn't be driving. So I'm walking."

Jeff paused a long moment. "If the MRI results show the tumor, when does he want to do surgery?"

"Tomorrow. MRI or not. He wants me to go into surgery right away. Tonight. He honestly suggested today. I told him no. In the kindest way I knew. Without biting off his head."

Jeff paused again. "I want to be with you for the MRI."

"Sorry. One customer to a tube. We won't both fit."

"Collin—"

"It's fine, Jeff. It is. I'll call you as soon as the results are in. And I'll let you know what Dr. McMannon wants to do." She hesitated. "And what I decide to do."

Prolonged silence.

"I understand why you want to wait, milady. I get it. I agree. I'll stand with you against Rich for this one week. Then, wrapped up or no, you have surgery. Understand? I don't want to lose you."

Collin swallowed hard. Her voice barely made a sound. "What if you do? What if I don't come out…the same. Would you still want me? If there's no me left?"

Jeff didn't hesitate. "I love you, Collin. I will always love you. I'll learn to love whoever you are. Because I know your heart and soul will never change. You will always be you deep inside. Nothing can take that away."

A single tear rolled down Collin's cheek. "I love you, Jeffery

Farrell."

"I love you, Collin Walker."

The silence felt whole and good.

Collin broke it. "I should get off here. I need to get to bed early. Doc scheduled the MRI at six a.m."

"Promise me you'll eat, milady. None of this 'not eating to be in control of something' stuff. You need food. You need sleep. Got it?"

"Got it, pushy. I love you, Jeff."

"Love you, lady."

Collin tossed the phone on the bed. "Now, which fast-food establishment shall we grace with our presence tonight?"

Considering it could be your last meal, make it a good one.

Aren't you a bundle of sunshine?

"Chicken. Let's do chicken. They have the best shakes, anyhow."

Collin pulled her shoes back on and headed for the door. She stopped, looked around at the room, then grabbed a sheet of paper off the nightstand. She carefully tore off a small piece and folded it over. She slung her backpack over her shoulder. After a second thought, she picked up her laptop from her suitcase, stuffed it in her backpack. More weight. Collin walked out the door. Before closing it, she slipped the small, folded piece of paper into the hinge side of the door. Low. Too high, and the intruder sees it. Low. Very low.

Collin closed the door.

* * *

Jeff lay his phone on the dresser. *Tumor? Why Lord? Wasn't Mom's stroke enough to deal with? Why again?*

Jeff kneeled beside his bed. "God, please. Please. I am 100% convinced Collin is the one I'm supposed to marry. I asked You before to stop the relationship if she wasn't the one. You haven't. I love her, Lord. Please. Please."

He wanted peace to flood over him, with the sure knowledge all would be well. But it didn't. *Walk by faith.*

"I'm trying, Lord. I'm trying." Jeff got up and walked into the family room to tell his parents the latest news. It was the only thing he could do. It was all anyone could do.

* * *

Collin returned from dinner. She reached to unlock the door, stopped cold. Her burglar alarm lay on the floor. All of Collin's survival instincts went on high alert. Her eyes narrowed, her breath quieted, her hands stiffened. She looked up and down the hall to see if someone from housekeeping might be about. Considering the time, after seven p.m., there shouldn't be anyone in her room.

Call the police.

Don't be ridiculous. There's no one in there. The wind dropped it.

Call the police.

Yeah, and look like a complete idiot when there's no one there. Paranoid, that's what you are.

The argument in her head took only a matter of seconds. Collin pulled her backpack off and held it in her right hand. She pushed the door open slowly.

Collin could see into the bathroom. The shower curtain hung open, as Collin had left it. The mirror's reflection told her the space behind the door presented no danger. *Where are you hiding?*

Behind the wall. Beside the bed, waiting for you to pass by.

Call the police.

Don't call the police.

Collin moved quietly up the hall, stopping short of the end. She readied herself, took a deep breath, swung her backpack around the corner with all of her might.

A loud "oof" rewarded her. Collin spun into the room, faced her intruder. For one instant, time froze. Collin saw a large man, dressed in black, with a nylon mask over his face. The man doubled over from the blow but straightened quickly. Collin shoved the backpack into the man's face, stepped back, and shouted, "Police! Police! Call 911! Help! Police!!"

The man shoved the backpack away. He had a knife in his right hand and slashed at Collin. All of Collin's self-defense training came alive. She kicked the arm aside, kicked savagely at the man's knee.

The man went down but came up stabbing at Collin's middle. Collin jumped back, turning aside to dodge the knife. For one brief instant, she considered a high-kick to the head but immediately dropped the idea. Chances were good she would be the one who got hurt. Instead, she waited for the man to swipe the knife at her, spun inside his arm to grab the knife-hand, wrapping her arm around it and pounding it on her knee. She continued to yell, "Police! Police! Call 911!"

Her defensive move caused the man to drop the knife. He lunged for it; Collin tried to kick it away. The man grabbed Collin and violently threw her to the floor. Collin rolled away from the vicious kick which followed. But quarters were tight, and she could only roll far enough to escape one strike. She rolled back into the man, grabbing his legs and yanking him to the floor.

He fell, striking his head on the wall. It bought Collin enough time to get to her feet, and with fists locked together, smashed them across the attacker's ear. The man went limp. Collin stepped back from him but didn't let her guard down. *Not for a moment.* She yelled again, "Someone call 911!"

Before she could finish her yell, two uniformed officers came sprinting into the room. Both had their guns drawn. One pointed it at Collin and ordered, "Hands! Let me see your hands!"

Collin raised them to show she had nothing. She motioned to the lump on the floor and said, "He tried to stab me. He broke into the room when I left and waited for me to come back. His knife is under the bed."

The officer who covered Collin motioned for his partner to look under the bed. In the meantime, he backed over to check the man on the floor. He told his partner, "This one is alive." He returned his gun to its holster.

Collin lowered her hands very carefully. "I didn't try to kill him. But I think he wanted to kill me."

Collin's attacker began to stir. The officer made sure the man had nothing in his hands, pulled him to his feet. Collin's attacker stood, steadied himself, and lunged for the open door. The policeman yelled, "Halt!" but Collin's assailant made it around the corner and down the hall. Both policemen ran down the hall after him.

Collin sat on the bed and waited. They would be back. Much paperwork and many questions remained to be filled in before this would be over. She thought about calling Detective Russo to give him a heads up but decided against it. *No sense starting an interdepartmental squabble over who has jurisdiction. Let it ride.*

A sharp "crack" of a gun startled Collin. She jumped to her feet but sat back down. No. *I will not go out. I will stay out of the fray. I will be a good girl and let the police handle it. I will—*

Wanna bet?

Collin ignored the temptation to move. She waited in place until the senior officer came back into the room. His partner didn't. Collin asked, "What happened? I heard a gunshot."

The officer's eyes narrowed and his jaw set hard. "Who are you? What are you doing here?"

"My name is Collin Walker. I rented the room here because the trailer court I lived in burned over the weekend." She made sure both her hands stayed in plain sight. And didn't make any sudden moves.

"And you have no idea why this man would choose to assault you?

"I have an idea, but I don't know for certain. I think someone sent him to kill me."

"Why?" The officer's face darkened even further than before.

"I inherited a great deal of money. Some people object to that. They would like to see me gone."

"What people?"

Collin decided the questioning needed to be tempered. "Detective Jim Russo is following the case. He will want to know about what happened here tonight."

"Why would he be following this?"

Collin sighed. "Because this is the second attempt on my life today and the fourth in two weeks. Like I said, some people object to my inheriting the estate."

The officer's eyes continued to narrow, and he scowled. "What people?"

Collin stared at the man, measuring him. "People Detective Russo is following. If you talk to him—"

The officer said sharply, "A sniper shot your assailant as he came out the front door. One shot. Killed him just like that." His eyes could have burned through metal. "What is going on in my district? Who are you, and why is someone powerful enough to hire a sniper after you?"

Collin closed her eyes. She breathed out. Breathed in. Breathed out. Breathed in. "Officer, I would love to answer all your questions if I could. But I can't. I'm a social worker...I was a social worker until this afternoon."

Collin could feel the effects of the tension and exertion creeping over her. Her body began to tremble. Then shake. She swallowed hard. "Please. It's been a very long day. I'm cold, and I'm tired, and I need…I don't know what I need." The shaking rattled her teeth. *I will not break. I will not break. I will not cry. I will not break…*

The officer took pity on Collin. He walked her to the hallway, pulled the duvet with him, and wrapped her in it. Collin nodded in appreciation but did not trust her voice to thank him. Yet. She curled up under the warmth. Still, the shaking continued. Collin leaned against the wall for support, slipped to the floor, and curled into a ball. *I will not break. I will not break. I will not…* She rocked back and forth in time to her chanting.

* * *

Collin had no idea of the time when a familiar voice called to her, "Ms. Walker. You in there? I need you to talk to me."

Collin looked up from her defensive position. Her voice had stopped shaking, at least. "Detective Russo. They did call you. I told them they should."

Russo kneeled beside her. "You okay to get up?"

Collin nodded. "Yeah. I think I'm together again. I needed…I needed time."

"Understandable." Russo extended his arm. She took it. He pulled her to her feet. Collin kept the bedspread wrapped around her for warmth. Russo led her to an empty room, where Collin sat on the bed. She could see a crowd of people in the hall. There were more plainclothes policemen in evidence, as well as two uniformed officers. She looked around for the officer who had questioned her at first but didn't see him.

Collin looked to Russo. He said, "Tell me what happened if you can. Start after you left your office."

"I walked from the office to here, rented this room for three nights. Came in here. Had a mental breakdown. Jeff called, and I got better. Left to go for dinner at the Chicken Roost. I always leave a tell in the door."

"Always?"

Collin nodded. "Yeah. When I got back, the tell had been moved. Which meant someone had been in my room. Or might still be there.

I checked the bathroom. Nothing. So I knew if someone were there, they would be around the corner. I had loaded my laptop in my backpack, so it would be fairly heavy. I swung it around the corner and caught him by surprise. Then , we danced around until I got lucky and knocked him down. And yes, I hit him while he was down." She saw Russo smile. A little smile. Very little. But smile, he did.

Collin cocked her head to the side. "Where do we go from here?"

"Still not ready for protective custody?"

"Not yet. Close. But not yet."

Russo chuckled. "I figured as much. How about a safe house where you can stay, and no one knows you're there?"

Collin thought about it. "Will I be able to walk to the hospital for an MRI in the morning?"

"Not from where the house is. But we can arrange for a car to pick you up, take you, and bring you back. What time is the MRI?"

"Six."

Russo whistled low. "You're not asking much, are you?"

Collin shrugged. "Asking a lot would be asking for your driver to take me wedding dress shopping. I won't subject whoever it is to that. I do need a couple of things, though."

"Such as?"

"I need to get in touch with my grandfather's law office. I want a complete copy of the will to look at. I also need to have lunch with my"—Collin couldn't bring herself to say it— "with Patrick. One o'clock tomorrow. Sal's Deli again. I have two questions to ask him."

"Only two?"

"Two will be enough."

"We'll get you there."

"I'm sorry this is getting so convoluted, Detective Russo. I swear I was a simple state social worker two weeks ago."

Russo shook his head. "That's what they all say. Come on, Walker. Let's find you someplace safe to stay."

TUESDAY MORNING

Eight a.m. Tuesday. Jeff's phone pinged. Not Collin. She'd already called after the MRI and her discussion with Rich McMannon. Jeff shut out the memory of the conversation. Well, not the conversation, but the despair. *Trust the Lord. Don't try to figure it out on your own. Accept His way is best. Let Him be God.*

Jeff looked at the caller ID. Trey. *This early?* He offered a *Lord, guide me*. "Trey. Pretty early, oh tutor mine."

"What's going on? What's happened? When I saw you Saturday you were going to be living at the station. This morning they tell me you're gone, and no one knows for how long. Make it good, Jeffery."

"Are you where you can talk?"

"Would I be calling you if I wasn't?"

Jeff frowned. "Rather talk to you in person. Can you meet me at the community center?"

"When?"

"Whenever you can get there safely and not run into any more dressers."

Silence followed. "Give me about an hour. I'll be there by nine. Nine-thirty. If I'm not, you'll know why."

Jeff pocketed his phone. Working off his tension at the community center beat sitting here, jumping every time the phone pinged. He walked to the kitchen where his parents were sipping coffee and reading. Harmon had a Nat Geo magazine in front of him; Lacey had Popular Mechanics. Jeff looked sideways at his mom's reading selection. "What's with the magazine?"

"I'm expanding my education. Men aren't the only ones who need to know what makes appliances tick. Or whine and scream and shake."

Harmon looked up from his reading. "The washer, again? We should get a new one."

Lacey's eyes narrowed. "We should. But since we haven't, I need to make this one work a while longer. And I think I can."

Jeff kissed the top of his mom's head. "I'm sure you'll figure it out. I'm going to the community center to shoot hoops, then meet Trey. Do you need anything while I'm out?"

Lacey smiled. "A new washer. But it can wait."

Jeff turned to his dad. "You?"

Harmon shook his head. "No. How long will you be gone?"

"A couple of hours. If you need me, call me." He hesitated, his hand on the doorknob. Jeff turned back to face them. "I love you both."

"Love you too, son."

* * *

As always, a pick-up game had already been started when Jeff got to the center. He tagged in after about five minutes. The no-holds-barred nature of the competition suited Jeff. He pounded the pine hard, pounded his opponents harder. Collin being in hiding when she and Jeff ought to be planning their future ground on his nerves. *It's not right, Lord. It's not supposed to happen like this. We're supposed to be—*

A sharp shoulder to his chest banished all the "supposed tos." He "oofed" as the wind got partially knocked out of him. It took a moment to get his breath back. *But I hear You. No supposed tos. Only what is. And what You want. I remember. Thanks.*

The combatants played another half hour when Jeff tagged out. He needed to cool down before Trey arrived. And get his head back in whatever game he and Trey were playing. Jeff scooped his warm-up suit off the bleachers and headed for the locker room.

Only to see Trey in the doorway. The younger man's eyes danced in joy as he watched the warfare continuing on the floor. He pointed with his chin. "Purple shirt's got game. Or would have, if he knew how to pass the ball."

"I've tried to tell him."

"Won't listen?"

Jeff pointed to the wall. "It hears better than he does."

"Yeah, well. Some people are like that." Trey spun his chair around. "Meet you in the game room in ten."

"You got it."

Jeff showered—well, splashed and dashed—and hustled into the game room. Trey occupied a table nearest the corner, away from windows and doors. He had the chess pieces out and ready. Jeff slid into the seat opposite him. "How's the eye?"

"Better. I can see out of most of it."

Jeff frowned. "Not a good answer, Trey."

"It's as good as it's going to get for now." Trey moved a pawn, moved a bishop, moved a knight. He arranged the board to look as if the two men were playing a match. He looked at the board. "So what's going on? Cap'n at the station said you were going to be off for a while. Something happened, didn't it? To Collin?"

Jeff felt an internal peace and permission to talk. "Someone tried to kill Collin yesterday and again last night. Detective Russo believes her accident on the freeway and the fire were both attempts on her life as well. He's had her moved to a safe house until they can catch the…" Jeff struggled with what he wanted to say but couldn't.

Trey's face darkened. His fists clenched in his lap. "No leads, right?"

"Not yet. Detective Russo is doing all he can. He's a good man. I trust him."

Trey chewed his jaw. "How is she doing?"

"She's mad. She hates being cooped away from the action."

"Have you talked to her? Since she got moved?"

"Talked to her this morning. After her…her doctor's appointment."

Trey's eyes narrowed. "Doctor? For what? Those headaches?"

Jeff looked to the ceiling before answering. "She's…she's got a…mass… in her brain. Her doctor wants her to have surgery now. Yesterday. She won't agree until she can clear up the will issue and catch the killers. Or killer."

Trey's face went pale. His voice became hollow. "A mass? Like a tumor? And she's waiting on a will?" Trey pounded his fist on the table. "Is she insane?"

"She's Collin."

"Can't you talk to her? Make her have the surgery?"

Jeff's jaw tightened. "Don't you think I would if I could? This is her decision. I can't make it for her."

Trey's knuckles grew white as he clenched the arms of his chair. "She can't do this. She has to have surgery. She has to. The estate doesn't mean anything. Doesn't she know?" He looked at Jeff, pleading in his eyes.

Jeff spat out the words. "That's not what her biological family is telling her. All that matters to them is what's in the will." He laughed bitterly. "I wish I could see Patrick's face when she tells him if she dies, the whole thing goes to the Rescue Mission."

Trey's face lit. "She's going to tell him what? When?"

"Today at lunch. He's been filling her head with garbage about her childhood. How good she had it, how much her father loved her, how jealous she acted whenever Patrick and her brother spent time together."

Jeff had to unclench his fists. "He even called Erin's death murder. Said Collin tackled Erin, kicked him in the head, breaking his neck."

Trey's eyes emptied of light. He whispered, "He said what? He told her she…murdered her brother? Murdered him?"

Jeff nodded. His hands shook in time to his voice. "She loved her brother. Still loves him."

Trey's whispered, "She didn't believe Patrick, did she?"

Jeff wished he could put more conviction in his words. "No. But it hurt her. Deep."

Trey closed his eyes. The younger man drew in two breaths, opened his eyes again. They glinted hard in determination. "It's not right. It's not. This has to stop."

Jeff eyed Trey sidelong. "What do you know, Trey? Are you somehow involved?"

Trey placed his fist on top of Jeff's hand and tapped it. "I can't tell you. Yet. I need you to trust me, Jeffery. Another day. Or two. But I need you to trust me. And not tell anyone what we've talked about."

"It's hard, dude. This is Collin's life we're talking about…or not talking about."

Trey hesitated. "I don't know how this works, but can you ask your God to tell you to trust me? Would He do that?" Trey shrugged. "I mean, would you trust me if your God told you to?"

That may be the only way I'll trust you, Trey... This is all out there.

Jeff exhaled. "If God tells me to trust you, yes, I'll trust you."

Trey urged, "Ask Him. Ask Him if I can be trusted." Trey stopped; confusion tinged his eyes. "How do you ask Him? And how will you know the answer?" The younger man's face shaded red. "I guess I didn't think that part out very well, did I?"

Jeff grasped Trey's shoulder. "I'll ask Him. And I'll know His answer." Jeff bowed his head. *Even the dumbest sheep knows the voice of his shepherd. I admit I'm not one of Your brighter ones, Lord. Collin's life is on the line here. Show me what to do. I trust You. Do I trust Trey?*

Jeff listened. And listened. And listened. He opened his eyes and looked at Trey. "Don't let me down, Trey."

"I won't." Trey turned his chair away, turned back. "Oh, checkmate in two moves. White wins."

Jeff shook his head. "Which one am I?"

Trey grinned. "White. I'll be in touch."

* * *

Collin sat on the floor of the safe house, staring at the documents in front of her. She dug through the legalese to see what she actually had to distribute, besides control of the corporation. Nothing she read compare to the worth seven lives…and hers to be the eighth if the killer had his way. Fenton had left the running of the munitions corporation to the three Winger sons, as promised. In her lifetime, Grandmother provided loans to each son for them to purchase land and to build their homes. Her repayment terms were ridiculously low. So low even Collin could afford them on her budget.

Collin shuffled the papers around. Ledger sheets showed none of the Wingers had repaid Grandmother according to the agreement; Fenton subtracted the "balance due" for each property from what the sons would otherwise have received from the estate. *Cause for murder?*

Maybe of each other, but why come after me?

Collin shuffled the papers again. They instructed her to leave all the law books with the firm; made sense. The art collection went to the local museum after each relative had selected one piece to keep for themselves if they so choose. Collin could select who got first pick. *Wonderful…*

Unless the Mona Lisa is hanging on the wall, there's no artwork there worthy of murder.

Or donation, either, if you ask me.

I didn't.

Collin cleared her throat. "If you can't be helpful, be silent." She continued down the list of personal effects to be distributed to various entities, most of them charities. *Good.*

The last page described items Fenton had wished Collin to have for herself. A very sizeable life insurance policy. Bank accounts, bonds, the family home…all more wealth than she could have ever imagined owning, but still less than the Winger sons were worth. *So why are you coming after me? What did I do?*

Collin dropped her head into her hands. "Oh, Grandfather. What do you want from me?"

Wrong person to ask. Try again.

Collin sat straight. "Lord, I'm missing something. I know I am. Show me, please. Show me what's worth the taking of seven lives to stop me from getting it. I don't understand."

No answer jumped out. Nothing fell from the sky; no voice whispered in her ear. Collin exhaled deeply, slumped her shoulders, and went back to reading. She read until her alarm went off, telling her it was time to meet with Patrick. Collin dressed appropriately for battle and called for the driver. She wouldn't be alone. Felt like it, but there would be unseen forces at her back. Heaven and Earth had her. How much safer could she be? Collin squared her shoulders and headed for the deli.

Once she arrived at the deli, Collin sat at the same table as she had the day before. *Twenty-four hours before. Before I lost all control of my own life.*

Control is an illusion. You control nothing. You never have.

She glanced at the clock: quarter after one. Maybe Patrick wouldn't show. *You can only hope.*

Sal came by and asked, "You want I should bring you your order while you wait?"

Collin started to say yes when Patrick rushed in. "I'm here. I'm here. Don't start eating without me!"

Sal laughed. "Same as yesterday?"

Patrick nodded as he took the chair opposite Collin.

"What kept you?"

"Traffic. This town is impossible to navigate at lunchtime. Everybody and their brother must be out today."

Collin shrugged. "It's Oakton. We have our rhythm." She smiled as politely as she could. "Did you have a busy day yesterday after Robert came back from his meetings?"

"Not too bad. Appointments went well, so we celebrated by going to an AA meeting. Keeps us both level."

Collin waited as Sal brought Patrick's order and set it on the table. Sal set a cup of soup in front of Collin. "You sure you don't want some bread with this? Or a cracker, even?"

Collin smiled. "No, Sal. Thanks. I appreciate everything you do for me." She swallowed anything else she wanted to say. Not here. Not now. Later.

Collin waited until Patrick dove into his sandwich before starting her soup. It took all her training in self-control to smile pleasantly at him.

Patrick swallowed a major portion of his sandwich. "You look awful, Caitlin. Hate to say it but you look ragged. You not getting enough sleep?"

Collin gritted her teeth. "You might say that. Having someone try to kill you will keep you up at night."

"Kill you?" Patrick's mouth fell open. "Someone tried to kill you?"

"Fourth time in two weeks."

Patrick's eyes widened. "Really? You're not kidding me, right?"

"No. Not kidding. I want you to give a message to whoever it is who wants me dead. Tell them I have a will, made out by the leading Probate Judge in Oakton. If I die, everything in Fenton's estate goes to the Downtown Rescue Mission. Everything." She nailed him with as fierce a look as she could muster.

Patrick shook his head. "I don't know what you're talking about, Caitlin. No one is trying to kill you. Honest." He looked sidelong at her. "Are you sure about this? It's not some mistaken—"

Collin cut him off. "The police tell me my 'accident' wasn't.

Someone murdered the owner of the truck which ran me off the road. When they found the truck, they found the guy who stole it inside, shot to death. The fire at my trailer court started under my trailer. The arsonist who set the blaze died in it. Along with three others. That makes six people dead."

Collin couldn't keep the edge out of her voice. "Yesterday, after lunch, a car deliberately jumped the sidewalk and tried to run me over. Last night, a man broke into my room when I went out, waited for me to return, and tried to stab me to death. He failed."

Collin chewed her cheek. "He made a break for it. When he ran outside, a sniper killed him. One shot. One kill." Collin leaned forward to Patrick. "Now, you tell me, Patrick, are the police crazy, too? Am I imagining all of this the same way you told me I imagined my past?"

Collin lay her hands flat on the table. "You tell whoever it is to lay off, or the estate passes to the mission. Tell your father and his brothers I will announce the distribution of the contents of the will tomorrow. Arrange a convenient time for a conference call. Get them all together. I want this thing over."

Patrick sat back, his eyes still wide. "Caitlin, I don't know what to say. If there is someone after you, it isn't anyone in the family. I swear it." He shook his head. "Do the police have any leads?"

"One or two. Who in the family has sniper training?"

Patrick laughed. "Come on, Caitlin. You honestly suspect—"

"Who has training? Winger is a munitions company. You make guns. I remember going to the firing range more than once. Your father and his brothers were dead shots. But killing someone with one shot across a plaza takes special skill. Who has it? You?"

Patrick's eyes grew round. "No! No! Never! I'm a disappointment to Dad because I can't hit the broad side of the barn I'm standing in." He looked at the table. "If anyone could make a shot like that, it would be Gareth, Richard's oldest. He trained in the military. But why would Gareth want to kill you? It doesn't make sense, Caitlin."

"None of it does, Patrick. Seven people are dead. Someone wants me to be the eighth. I won't let that happen."

Collin could feel a headache coming on. Not a lightning slash but rolling thunder. Building. Always building. She was running out of time.

"There is still the matter of whose memories are correct." Collin leaned back in her chair. "You showed me your pictures. I have pictures, too. Pictures of broken bones. Broken before puberty." She nailed Patrick dead in the eyes. "How many bones did I break, Patrick? There were no pictures of me in a cast. If your father thought of me as his princess, and I had him wrapped around my finger, why are there no pictures of casts? If I were the brat you say I was, wouldn't I have blamed you and Erin for any injuries? And wouldn't your father have punished you and Erin in a manner you'd not soon forget?"

Collin pushed back from the table. She needed to leave now. "I'm going. Tell the family what I said. Call me and let me know the time." She threw a business card. "There's my number. It's my cell. Call it."

Collin walked to the front of the deli. She pulled Sal aside. She kept her voice low. "I need a favor. A quiet one, okay?"

Sal's eyes widened, but he nodded. "Sure, Collin. What is it?"

"You see the man at the end of the row of stools at the counter?"

"In the suit? Plainclothes cop?"

Collin shook her head slightly. "They are so obvious. Yeah, him. Will you tell him I'm ready to leave, and I'd like him to bring the car around to the service entrance? I'll meet him there."

Sal's eyes narrowed. "Are you in trouble? Do you need help?"

Collin assured him, "It's all good, Sal. It is. Or will be if you give him the message."

"Sure thing, sweetheart." Sal started off, then stepped back. "It's okay if I call you sweetheart, isn't it? I didn't offend you?"

"Not offended, Sal. Thanks."

Collin watched as Sal went to the man at the counter and passed her message. Her driver didn't look at her, but nodded to Sal, dropped money on the counter, and walked out. Collin closed her eyes and bit her lip against the pain continuing to build. *Not here. Not now. Please. Hold it together. Another day, please. One more day. I'll have the surgery. I promise.*

The pain continued to build. Collin moved behind the counter, into the kitchen itself. She ducked her head to the cook, walked through the storage room, and stood by the service door. She could see her chariot and driver pull into the alley and stop near the exit. He threw open the back door. Collin hustled out and slid into the waiting back seat. Only when the door closed and the locks clicked did she feel safe.

Collin leaned back, dropped her head on the back seat, and closed her eyes. The driver asked, "Safehouse?"

"Yeah. Unless you want to take me shopping for wedding gowns."

"Sorry, not my department."

"Right." Collin exhaled softly.

* * *

Two o'clock in the morning, Collin lay staring at a ceiling she couldn't see. She'd done all she could for the day: she'd called Jeff after lunch with Patrick. Discussed his reactions. Discussed his denials. Came to no certain conclusions. Called Detective Russo. Same story, different verse. Called Fenton's law office for advice on how to set her distribution plan in order.

It had been an afternoon of legal divisions of holdings and shares and property and who knew what. None of it explained the attempts on her life, let alone the killing of seven others. She tried to swing the facts a dozen ways and whys but always came back to nothing. Nothing explained it.

Collin's phone pinged. She checked it out of habit. No one texted her at this hour. Must be a wrong number. Fat thumbs?

A series of random letters and numbers shone on the screen. *What the—?* Collin slid her glasses on her face and looked again.

$[a(c+o)]^{NE} = 1$

Algebra? Who in the…

Collin's eyes went wide. She grabbed the phone and pulled it closer. *No.*

$[a(c+o)]^{NE} = 1$

Collin's hands shook. Her whole body began to tremble. "No. No. It can't…"

$[a(c+o)]^{NE} = 1$

Collin grabbed a piece of paper and copied the equation. Did she remember? She wrote it out, scratching out letters and symbols until she had it the way she remembered it. Her fingers refused to obey her as she tried to text back the answer on the keypad.

$[ac+ao)]^{NE} = 1.$

Collin pulled her knees to her chest and rocked back and forth. "It can't be. It can't. It can't be."

Five minutes.

Ten minutes.

Fifteen… the phone pinged. Collin snatched it and stared at the numbers.

[acne+aone)] = 1.

She whispered, her voice echoing back twelve years. *"That's not how you distribute exponents in a polynomial."*

"That's what makes it brilliant, Cane. No one will be able to figure it out."

Collin didn't need the paper. Her hands still shook as she typed in the final equation.

[cane+Aone] = 1

Cane plus A-One equals one. Erin was alive.

Collin grabbed a pillow, buried her face in it, and wailed, "Why? Why? All these years? All this time? Lord, You knew! You knew, and You didn't tell me! Why?" Great wracking sobs broke through her body. "Oh, God. Oh, God…why?"

Collin snapped out of her anguish. In desperation, she pounded in, "WHERE ARE YOU????????"

She stared at the phone. "Come on, come on. Answer me. Tell me where you are."

Five minutes later, the answer came. "Safe. Trust Jeff."

Collin stared at the phone. "Trust Jeff? What's that supposed to mean? Erin…"

Another message came across. "Love you."

And then, nothing. Collin held her breath waiting. Ten, fifteen, twenty minutes. Nothing else came through. Collin whispered, "Love you, A-One."

She collapsed on the floor. She laughed. She cried. She slammed her fist into her pillow over and over and over. Tears—some happy, some angry—spilled from her eyes. Collin buried her head in the pillow and screamed. And screamed. And screamed.

Until there was nothing left inside. A sense of quietness filled her. Not peace. Quietness. She'd emptied all the emotions. *Now what?*

Call Jeff. Erin said to trust him, so call him.

Collin looked at the clock. Three a.m. and a little. She picked up the phone and tapped in Jeff's number. She waited for his groggy, "M…hello?"

Her voice shook with anger. "You knew Erin is alive and didn't tell me? How could you do that? Where is he? Tell me!"

It took a minute. Or two. "Collin?"

"Where is Erin? You knew, didn't you? Didn't you?"

"Ummm. Are you alright, Collin? Has something happened?"

Collin twisted the corner of the blanket, rocking all the while. "I'm perfectly fine, Jeff. I'm not crazy, I'm not off my rocker."

No, you're rocking fine.

Yeah, and I'm getting seasick.

Collin stopped rocking but not twisting the blanket. "Erin is alive."

Long silence. Jeff's voice took on a much more alert note. "Erin is what?"

"Alive. I know it. You knew it, and you didn't tell me."

"Uh…how? How do you know it?"

Collin stopped. It had been part of the pact, part of the equation. *"You can't tell anyone we have a way to know we're really ourselves. All twins make some test…and everyone expects them to have one. So we have to say we don't even have one. That way, they can't torture it out of us. Got it? We never tell anyone. Ever. Not even when we die. Promise."*

Collin breathed out slowly. "He said trust you. Trust you. How do I trust you when you keep something—"

"Collin, I do not know Erin is alive. If…if I knew, I would never keep it from you. Never."

Collin sat still. Perfectly still. She stared at nothing, focused her mind. "He said to trust you. But if you don't know he's alive…"

She heard Jeff moving around in his room. "Collin, milady, please. Tell me you're okay, please? Nothing has happened since this afternoon has it?"

Collin dropped her eyes to the floor. The fire ebbed. "You don't know. You don't." She drew in a deep breath and said, "Erin is alive. He passed me a message. He told me he's safe, and I should trust you. He knows you. You have to know him. You have to."

She heard a chair creak. "If he knows me, he hasn't told me who he is."

Collin bounced her phone from the call to the text. "$[a(c+o)]^{NE}$

= 1" Collin chose her words carefully. "I know he's alive, Jeff. Maybe he hasn't revealed his true self. I'm sorry I yelled at you. I'm sorry I doubted you. But I do know he's alive."

Silence followed. "If you say he's alive, I believe you. But...I wouldn't tell anyone else yet. If he's hiding, there might be a good reason. Maybe we should let him make the next move."

Collin dropped her head. "You're right. Okay. I won't say anything." A thought occurred. "Grandfather must have known." Tears stung her eyes. "Why wouldn't he tell me? Why would he let me keep believing Erin had died? Why would Grandfather keep me away from the family?"

"I don't know, milady. I don't. Listen, please try to get some sleep, Collin. Rich wanted you not to get worked up over anything. Sleep tonight, call me in the morning when you get up. Maybe in the daylight, we can figure it all out. I'll be waiting for your call."

Collin stared at the phone. "You don't believe me, do you?"

"I do. Yes. If you say you know Erin's alive, I believe you. I have to."

The fire threatening to explode faded. Collin nodded, even though she knew Jeff couldn't see it. "I love you, Jeff Farrell."

"I love you, milady."

Collin ended the call. She piled the blankets and pillows on the floor. She curled in them, wrapping herself in a tight cocoon. She kissed the phone. "I love you, A-One. Stay safe, little brother."

* * *

Jeff lay the phone on the dresser and stared at it. And stared. And stared. *Now what?? Has all the stress pushed her over the edge? Is she nuts?*

Jeff did the only thing he knew how to do. He hit his knees, bowed his head, and prayed.

God, You showed me Collin is the woman to be my wife. I know You did. I have no doubts, no questions about that. But I can't marry a crazy person, can I? If she's mentally unstable or psychotic or I don't know what...if she's suffering some sort of mental break, I'll get her all the help she needs. Help me understand, Lord. Show me Your will for this, please.

Jeff sat back on his haunches and prepared to listen. For the rest of the night, if that's what it took. He would not leave this spot until he had his answer. Period.

WEDNESDAY MORNING

At seven a.m., Jeff's phone buzzed. He stood with a muffled groan and retrieved it from the dresser. "Good morning, milady."

"Morning yourself."

Her voice sounded cheerful. Too cheerful? Jeff strained to detect any hint of something extra in Collin's voice which might indicate her mental state. "Did you get some sleep last night?" Jeff sat on the edge of the bed.

"Yes, I did. Ended up sleeping on the floor, but I did sleep."

"Why on the floor?" The fact he'd spent the night on the floor would go without mention.

"That's where the covers were. And the pillows."

"Makes sense, I guess." He paused. "How did you sleep?"

"Fine. I'm a little stiff, but otherwise, I'm okay."

Do I ask her about Erin? Or let it go and...

"I know what you're thinking, Jeff. I'm not crazy. I didn't have some kind of breakdown last night. I do know Erin is alive." Collin's voice sounded firm and sure and as rational as ever. "I'm taking your advice and not telling anyone. Yet. We'll let this thing play out and see what happens next."

Jeff thought hard. "What is your schedule today? What are you doing?"

"Patrick said he would have his father and uncles ready for a conference call at around eleven. I'm going to go over the will again and see what I'm missing. Unless it is the money. Once this call is over, if there are more attempts on my life, I'll know it wasn't about the estate itself."

Jeff's phone began to buzz, signaling he had a second call. He looked quickly. Trey. "Collin, I have to go. Trey is on the other line.

He's been in some sort of…trouble…and he may need help. Okay? I love you, Collin."

"I gotcha. Love you, Jeffery Farrell."

Jeff switched over to Trey's call. "I'm here, Trey. What's up?"

Trey's voice sounded unnaturally exuberant. "Jeffery, my man! How are you doing this fine morning? Did I wake you? I hope so." Trey laughed, but it sounded forced to Jeff's ear.

Jeff said, "No, dude. I'm awake anyhow. What's going on?"

"Nothing. Nothing at all. Wanted to talk, that's all. You're not at the station anymore, so I figure I better call you instead. Oh, and the dresser you volunteered to fix? It's still acting out, I don't think a carpenter will do it. It may need an exorcism, you know? Thing is possessed."

Jeff's eyes narrowed. He chose his words carefully. "Sorry to hear that, Trey. I know furniture can be a real hassle. I'll look for a good exorcist for you."

"Or a magician. They seem to be good at making stuff disappear."

Jeff wasn't sure what thread Trey was spinning. "I'll look into it."

Trey laughed again. Definitely forced. "You're funny, Jeffman. You'll look into a magician who makes stuff disappear. How are you going to see him? Look into it. Good one."

Jeff chuckled cautiously. "Yeah. You know me. Always joking around."

"You weren't joking around about knowing where your lady friend is, were you? You do know where she's moved to since the fire, right?"

Jeff nodded to himself. "No, I'm not joking. I'm going to marry her. I better know where my wife-to-be is."

"Very good, Jeffman. Very good. I know you're paranoid about telling me these things over the phone, so I won't ask you for an address or anything. But hey, maybe we can meet at the community center later. We can play chess like we did last night, and you can tell me about where she is."

"Sounds like a plan, Trey. What time would you like to meet me?"

"Well…oh, wait. First, I want to know, you said your best man's last name's…Russ…no, um…Ossur. I get names turned around. But not your dad? I'd like to meet this Ossur before you tie things up with your lady friend. I'll see if he's got the right stuff, you know? Wouldn't want you to get married without the right posse behind you."

Jeff's jaw tightened. *What? Ossur?* Jeff's eyes widened. *Russo. Ossur. Got it.* "Nope. No worries. Ossur's the man I can call on when I need him."

"Good, good. Glad to hear it. Um…we need to decide where to meet today. I get lost when I come by myself sometimes. You might have to look for me."

Jeff thought fast. "How about the side door, on Fitzroy? It has a ramp."

"Fitzroy? We have a street named Fitzroy? Weird. What kind of name is Fitzroy?"

"Irish, maybe?"

"I don't know, Jeffman. Tell you what, if I come by myself, I'll come in the side door. But if I get turned around again, I'll have someone bring me in the front door. I meet the strangest people when I'm lost." Trey paused. "Some of them I'd like to lose. But you know how it is. When someone is helping you, you kinda have to go along with them."

"I hear you, Trey." *Do I ever.* "What time can you make it?"

"Now?" Trey forced a laugh. "Nah, I know you got things to do, first. Places to go, people to call. How about ten? And bring your posse if you dare. We'll see if they're up to snuff."

"I'll do that, Trey. You hang in there, my friend. I'll see you soon."

"Make sure you tell your lady friend you love her. Oh, tell her I love her, too. She'll get a kick out of it."

"She might. See you, Trey."

"Toodles."

Jeff disconnected the call. He stared at the phone, replaying the last conversation in his mind. How to make sense of it? Jeff pulled on his clothes while he chewed on Trey's words. *When did I mention Detective Russo to Trey?* Three minutes of deliberation later, Jeff remembered. *Yeah. Last night. When I told him about Collin being in hiding. All Trey's remarks about wanting to meet Detective Russo…*

Jeff's eyes narrowed. He pulled his shirt over his head, picked up his phone, and hit speed dial. The phone on the other end rang once.

"Talk to me, Mr. Farrell. What's going on?"

Jeff drew in a deep breath. "Detective Russo, I need your help."

"I'm listening."

* * *

Collin turned her head from side to side, trying to loosen the tension in her neck and shoulders. She had her computer up and ready and signed in. She needed the "go ahead" the other players in this drama were ready. *I hope they're feeling half as nervous as I am.*

Doubtful. They know what they're doing. You're the one guessing.

Do NOT show them you're nervous. If they sense weakness, they'll eat you faster than a lion jumping on fresh meat.

What a disgusting analogy.

You prefer white on rice?

The computer pinged. A notice came: "Patrick Winger has joined the conversation." *One.* Rapid-fire, she read, "Robert Winger has joined the conversation." "Richard Winger has joined…Rupert Winger has joined the… Garth Winger…Gareth Winger…" *That's everyone. Except Erin. Where are you?*

Robert stared at her. "Is there a reason we can't do this face to face? What are you hiding?"

Collin kept her voice calm. "Myself. I'm certain you've talked to Patrick, so you know why I'm staying isolated."

Rupert smiled at the screen. "Caitlin. It's so good to see you! You look beautiful, girl. Like your mother."

Richard asked, "What reason? I don't know why. I don't want Robert having knowledge I'm not a party to. He doesn't deserve any preferential treatment."

Collin bit her tongue. She counted to five. "None of you deserve anything. Fenton left everything to me. Period. I get to decide how to distribute it."

She folded her hands under the table. "The reason I'm in hiding is there have been several attempts on my life in the past week. The police are working on the case, have some leads, and think it best I stay out of the line of fire for a while. I agreed."

Rupert asked, "What does that have to do with us getting together? Surely none of us are suspects, are we? We're your family. We love you. We'd never do anything—"

Collin interrupted. "You're right, sir. You didn't do anything. When a 14-year-old girl went missing, none of you came looking for me. No one tried to find me, no one put in a missing person's report. I dropped off the face of the earth, and you were all content to leave me there."

She looked at Garth and Gareth and added, "You two are excused because you were young at the time. I'm sure you were told something credible, and you had no reason to disbelieve your parents."

Gareth nodded. Garth wouldn't look at the screen to meet Collin's eyes. *What's that about?*

Not the time or place. Move on.

Collin continued, "I have reviewed the will. I have reviewed the financials for the family corporation. I've looked at them, anyhow. The first thing I realize is I have no clue how to manage this corporation. So I'm not going to."

She could see the smirk on Robert's face. Richard's face reflected the same smugness. Rupert proved harder to read. Collin went on. "As owner, it's my responsibility to put people in positions of authority who can keep the company running profitably. I owe it to the employees who depend on Winger Enterprises for their livelihood."

Robert sneered, "Cut to the bottom line, princess."

Collin refused to be baited. She held the pages of the will for the men to see. "This gives me the authority to hire, fire, transfer, suspend, or otherwise do what I deem in the best interests of the company. Right now, what I deem best is the three of you"—she looked at Robert, Richard, and Rupert—"continue in the roles you have. But only until I can have an independent audit done. Then, any adjustments needing to be made will be carried out."

She felt the tension increasing in her neck. She prayed, *Please. Not now. Not yet. Please.*

Collin didn't wait for feedback. "The first item I'm changing is the structure of the shareholdings. Each of you holds a one-third interest in the company. I'm reducing the ratios from 33% to 25%.

The final 25% will be divided between the second generation Wingers. Meaning Gareth, you will receive five percent, Garth, you will receive five percent, and Patrick, you will receive five percent. I will hold the remaining ten percent."

Her proposal received the reactions she had anticipated. Gareth and Patrick's eyes lit, and smiles crossed their faces. Brief smiles, of course, but there nonetheless. Garth continued to look away from the camera.

Rupert asked, "What about the rest of the holdings? I know Fenton had investments outside of the company."

Richard interjected, "Made with Grandmother's money. Which makes it our money. What about all of that?"

Collin smiled without mirth. "Actually, no, it doesn't make it your money. It makes it my money. I repeat, the will gives everything to me. Every last dime is mine. Every single one of them. I can do what I like with all of it, or none of it. It's mine to give away or keep. I know how good a lawyer Fenton was, and I'm convinced everything in this will is above challenge." She stopped. "You can challenge it, but you will lose."

She felt no joy in the victory, no sense of retribution. Her road to freedom from the Winger past tracked a different path. "Grandfather left instructions to me about how he wanted things carried out. Some of them I am following. Some I am not." Collin saw looks of extreme interest on Rupert and Richard's faces. "The deeds for the land you built your homes on will pass to you free and clear. The loans for the construction of the houses will be torn up.

"Contrary to Grandfather's wishes, you owe nothing. I forgive your debt. Someone took my debt and paid it. I follow Him, and I'm doing the same."

Garth looked up. His eyes met Collin's for the first time. His face remained devoid of emotion. The eyes were empty. Dead. The man looked dead. *Why? What am I missing?*

Rupert asked, "Are you going to continue to pay the taxes?"

Collin looked at her uncle. "No. Once the titles pass to you, you will each be responsible for property taxes, utility bills, maintenance, and every other expense which goes with being a homeowner." She smiled. "Welcome to the real world."

Richard scoffed. "Like you would know what the real world is like."

Collin's eyes narrowed. "Yes, Mister Winger, I do. More than anyone else in this conference. Which is why the money being used to pay your expenses will now go to underwrite homeless shelters, women's homes, recreation centers, and food kitchens. In short, will be used to help people who need help."

She didn't wait for the men to react to the new arrangement but continued, "Next item. Grandfather Fenton's home has been secured and is being guarded to prevent theft. I will designate a representative to escort each of you through the house. You may take any painting you desire, and a single piece or set of furniture." She begged the tension mounting in her head, *Please. A little longer. Please.*

Looking at the men, she added, "You can fight it out amongst yourselves who gets first pick. Once you've all had your chance to get out what you want, the remainder of the furnishings will be donated or auctioned off."

Robert snapped, "I want the desk. And all the papers inside of it."

Collin breathed in and out. "I am going to go through the house before you all are allowed in and remove those things I want for myself. When I'm done, you can have anything you want."

Robert growled. "Those papers concern the business. You can't have those."

The pain in Collin's head continued to build. She needed to get off the call. Now. "You can address any questions to Brenden Aster. Good afternoon." Collin clicked out of the conference, put her head in her hands, and pressed on both sides. She retrieved and swallowed the medicine for pain, lay on the bed, curled in a ball, and closed her eyes. She whispered, "Erin. Where are you? Please, God, let me see him before…before anything. Please."

* * *

Jeff scrunched his shoulders to his ears, rolled his shoulders backward and forward, shook them out. It didn't relieve the tension, but it made him feel like he had done something other than stare at the front entrance to the rec center. 10:20, and Trey hadn't shown yet. What happened? Had the 'dresser' figured out what Trey planned? Would Trey even be allowed to leave? What if…

"Jeffman! Hey, Jeffman! I'm here!" Trey motored up the front entrance, noticeably accompanied by a muscular gentleman wearing a deep frown. When he saw Jeff looking at him, he immediately changed to a smile. He leaned forward and said something in Trey's ear. Trey shook him off and continued to call, "Jeffman! I'm here! Don't start the game without me. Of course, you could, and I'd still beat you. How you doing, Jeffman?"

Jeff stepped forward to greet Trey and his escort. Jeff grinned at Trey. "Yeah, yeah, I know. I know. You'll beat me again, and I'll keep coming back for more." There were several more bruises on Trey's face than the last time Jeff had seen his tutor. Jeff looked at the other man, stuck out his hand. "Jeff Farrell."

The man extended his hand. "Mert Johnson. Trey knows he shouldn't be out like this. But he insisted, so I agreed to accompany him. To keep him out of trouble, you know?"

Jeff nodded. "I know." *More than you think I do.* Jeff looked to Trey. "I've got the board set up in the back. And no, I didn't start without you."

As Trey rolled his chair toward the back, he asked, "Did your posse show?"

"Yeah, they're here when you want to meet them. Thought we'd play a match first."

"Good idea." Trey positioned himself across the table behind the black set.

Jeff tried to not look surprised. Trey always took white. Always. But sitting in front of the black set meant Mert would have to find somewhere else to stand instead of glowering over Trey's shoulder. *I see. Lord, help me see everything I need to. Help me hear everything I need to hear. And keep me sane.*

Mert scowled at the arrangement. "How'm I supposed to watch over you?"

Trey shrugged. "Watch from the other room. We're not going anywhere. You can see me fine from the breakroom. I swear I won't try to make a break for it, Mert." Trey smiled at the man, who simply scowled deeper.

Mert stepped closer to Trey. "Right. Be smart." He looked at Jeff and smiled again. "He's a good man. But he needs to be watched over."

Jeff nodded. "I understand." Mert walked off to the break area, and sat, making sure Trey stayed in his line of sight.

Jeff looked at the board. He kept his voice as low as his eyes. "What do you need me to do, Trey?"

Trey shook his head and moved several pieces. Jeff moved his as well, so anyone watching would think the men were playing. Trey asked, "Where are your people?"

Jeff continued to stare at the board, careful not to obey the impulse to look around for Russo. "Detective Russo is playing backgammon in the next aisle. He has three men with him around the room. I think there's one in the breakroom as well."

"Can he hear us?"

Jeff shook his head. "I have no idea what technology he has. I'm not assuming anything, though."

"Wise man." Trey knocked a pawn off the board. "Man, I'm sorry. I'm getting so clumsy these days."

Jeff bent to retrieve the piece. Trey bent as well. "Mert isn't alone. He thinks I don't know, but he brought backup. I don't like the setup, Jeff. Too many people could get hurt."

Jeff and Trey both straightened. Jeff asked, "What do you want me to do?"

"Play it out. I'll see how good your man is about listening."

The men played several minutes without talking. At least it would look like they were playing. And taking time. And not talking about Trey's bruises. Or the way he winced when he moved. Jeff noted and raised an eyebrow. Trey shrugged. "Zumba. I'm not as fit as I used to be. Ignore it."

Jeff scowled. "You sound like Collin."

Trey ducked his head. "It's fine, Jeff. They need me. They won't kill me. Not as long as they think I'm giving them the information they want."

"Which is?"

"At this point, anything. I can't tell them the one thing they really want, which is where Collin is."

Jeff snorted. "Join the club. I don't where she is, either."

"That's not a bad thing, you know."

"It is if we're going to get married."

Trey moved a piece, shook his head. He raised his voice. "Jeffman, you aren't paying attention! You're so focused on protecting your queen, you never move from defense! Your queen is surrounded by bishops and knights and pawns. No one is going to break through your arsenal to get to her. Get your head in the game, Jeffman."

Jeff swallowed a smile. "What would you have me do, oh wise one?"

"Get off defense and go on offense. Follow my moves, even. Have you ever thought about that? Huh? Shadow my moves."

"I should follow your moves?"

Trey groaned. "Not you! Never you! That's what pawns are for! Oh, Jeffery, the pains I take to teach you." He picked up his king and whispered in its ear. "Will he ever learn? Is he even listening?" Trey held the little king to his ear as if to hear the king's answer. Trey nodded. "You're right. I should give him a break. This is not the place for heroics. We'll have to make it another time. But soon. Soon." Trey looked at Jeff and grinned. "Soon, my precious. Soon."

Jeff nodded. "I hear you, Trey."

Trey ducked his head. "Keep her safe, Jeffery. That's your job. Keep her safe. After this is all over…well, never mind."

Trey pushed back from the table. "Since this game is going nowhere, introduce me to this Mr. Ossur who's gonna be your best man. I'd like to meet him."

Jeff kept his head down. "Ossur?"

"Go with it, Jeffery. In case Mert has a background I don't know about."

"Right." Jeff stood and motioned to Detective Russo. "Over there. Come on."

As soon as Trey moved, Mert appeared from the break area. He moved over to Trey's side, making sure to be included in the introductions. Jeff caught Russo's attention and said, "Trey, meet Jim Ossur. Jim, Trey Weller. Mert Johnson."

The men shook hands all around. Trey smiled at Detective Russo and asked, "So, you're the one keeping my man Jeffery straight, huh? You got his back, right?"

Russo nodded. "Yep. Keeping him safe."

"Good thing. He needs it. Hey, Jeff tells me you're interested in firearms. You like to go to the range and shoot. True?"

Russo shrugged. "I like to plink at targets, yeah."

Trey nodded. "Good man. Mert, here, he's a pretty good shot. At least he tells me he is, right, Mert?"

Mert frowned. "He's not interested in my shooting."

Trey laughed. "Oh, come on, Mert. Don't be so humble. I heard you tell Stan you could hit a moving target from…I can't keep those distances straight. You tell me a thousand yards, and it means nothing to me. Tell me in something I can visualize. Like, one city block? Two? Three?"

Mert lay a hand on Trey's shoulder. Jeff watched as the man's knuckles whitened as he squeezed harder and harder. *Trey isn't flinching at all. Like he doesn't even feel it. Or…won't show it. And who does that remind you of?*

Trey shrugged. "I remember now. You told Stan you hit a moving target from three blocks away. A single shot, dead center. That's something to be proud of."

Detective Russo nodded to Mert. "Good shooting. We should go to the range and drop some targets one of these days."

Mert shook his head. "Can't. I'm on assignment with the guy here. Can't leave him by himself. He gets into trouble on his own. Can't do anything without assistance. He's helpless without me around." He looked at Trey and practically threatened, "Right, Mr. Weller?"

Trey looked at Russo but answered Mert. "Right, Mert. I need you to keep me alive."

Jeff wondered who the interplay was for. A thought hit him. He prayed, *Lord, make this from you or shut my mouth.* He looked from man to man. "I've got an idea. Why don't we get together somewhere less crowded so we can talk? My folks are out of town. How about we meet there around five? I'll have pizza."

Trey jumped in. "No anchovies. Or black olives. Or shrubbery of any kind."

"Meat lover, huh? Okay." Jeff looked at Russo. "Your preference?"

Russo smiled. "No pineapple. But how about we meet at my place? It's closer. Yours is out on the southside. Mine is at least still in the city limits."

Jeff shrugged. "Sure. Is this too short notice?"

"Nah. It'll work better for me this way."

Jeff looked to Mert. "Any pizza preferences?

Mert shook his head. "I don't think this is a good idea. Trey, you know you have therapy in the evening. It's not smart for you to be out twice in one day."

Jeff threw a prayer Heavenward. "Collin's going to call me around six. She said she'd like to talk to you sometime, Trey. Maybe you can get her to move our date up." Jeff smiled at Trey. "I know you're good at talking people into things."

Mert's eyes lit. He looked at Trey and said, "It won't hurt you to miss a day of therapy."

Trey's mouth drew into a firm line. "No, no it won't. "

Jeff rubbed his hands together. "Great. I'll bring the drinks as well. Sodas?"

Mert asked, "Beer?"

Jeff nodded. "Sure. Any preference?"

"Cold."

Jeff chuckled. "I hear ya. Okay, I'm gonna head out. Jim, thanks for coming this morning. Trey, I'll see you later."

Russo nodded to Trey. "Good to meet you, Trey. I look forward to talking with you more tonight." He looked at Mert and said, "And I want to hear more about your skills at the range. Maybe you can give me some pointers. I'm always looking for improvement."

Mert shrugged. "Yeah, maybe. We'll see how it goes."

Russo looked at Trey. "My house is on Gentry. Number 113. It's on the west side, the third lot in. It's all new construction, so not a lot of mailboxes with addresses on them."

Do not look confused. Do not ask him what he's talking about. Nod and say, "That's the one." And act like it is. Jeff nodded. "That's the one. I'll see you there. About five, right? With pizza." He headed out the door, turned left, walked to his jeep, and climbed in. He dropped his head to the steering wheel and groaned. *Lord, what have I gotten myself into? Where is Russo sending us?* To the implied question, Jeff answered, *Yes, I trust him. I trust You more. Be in this, please.* Jeff started the motor, put it in drive. *Surrounded by bishops and knights and pawns...* He headed for home.

* * *

Jeff arrived home, walked through the side door into the kitchen, grabbed a soda, and sat at the table. *You don't need a soda. You need a beer.*

Jeff stared at the can of soda. Beer? He chuckled. "Beer. Me drinking beer. Right.”

Harmon walked into the kitchen. “I thought I heard someone in here.”

Jeff motioned to the seat across the table. “Sit. My brain told me I needed a beer to deal with these ‘opportunities’ as Mom calls them.”

Harmon’s eyebrows rose. “It did, now did it?” He took the seat opposite of Jeff.

“Yeah.” Jeff looked at his dad, looked at the soda again. “That’s how it happened the last time, too. One beer to take the edge off. Another to sleep at night.”

Harmon nodded. “No one would blame you. All the stress you’re under…”

Jeff saw the set of his father’s jaw and knew exactly what the older man thought. He shook his head. “Of course not. But it didn’t help, did it? Once I started, I couldn’t quit. I didn’t want to quit. I wanted to stop feeling anything.”

“And you did. For how long? A year?”

Jeff looked at the floor. “I guess. Most of it is still under the fog.” He looked at Harmon. “If you and Mom hadn’t thrown me out, I don’t think I would ever have stopped on my own. Beyond the Lord’s intervention.”

“Hardest thing I’ve ever had to do, son. Hardest thing ever.”

Jeff looked at his dad. “Did I ever thank you?”

Harmon smiled. “A time or two. Or more.”

“Yeah, well, it’s never going to be enough. I owe the Lord, and I owe you.”

“Some debts are a pleasure to forgive.”

Jeff looked at the floor. “I don’t know what’s going on, Dad. Collin’s hiding from a murderer…a professional hitman. Who hires a hitman in real life? Who takes out innocent people and doesn’t care how many? This has to be about more than money, doesn’t it? I mean, the whole Winger family is rolling in luxury and excess. Why would they care? It’s got to be more than money.”

Harmon sat silent. “Maybe there’s something else in the will. Something someone doesn’t want to be seen or found. And they’re afraid a secret will be exposed. Or they will be.”

“But what? They’ve all seen the will.”

“True. But there might be something in there directed to Collin only she will recognize." Harmon stretched. "Wasn't she going to tell the Wingers the distribution plan today?"

"Yeah. And?"

"If there are no more attempts on her life, it would mean money was the issue, and now it's resolved. But if they keep coming after her, it's something else in the will."

"How is she going to know? Step out in public and see if they shoot at her?"

Harmon smiled. "I think she's smarter than that. I trust the police to be smarter than to let her. You have to trust others, Jeff. No matter how hard it is."

Jeff shook his head. "Nope. Not gonna do it. This is my to-be-wife. I don't trust anyone with her except the Lord. And even He's on notice."

Harmon laughed. Jeff smiled. "Okay, that's an overstatement. It's hard, Dad." Jeff debated. "I got myself involved."

"How so?"

Jeff detailed the morning and the plan for the evening. Harmon took the information in silently. Jeff finished and looked at his dad. "Stupid, right?"

"I think you've shown great restraint, Jeffery. You haven't grabbed anyone by the shirt collar and demanded they talk. You haven't punched anyone out...or threatened to. I think, all things considered, you've done well. This, however, stretches the limits." Harmon lay his hand on Jeff's arm. "I understand the why. All I ask is you be very, very careful. And keep your head down."

Jeff nodded. "I will. No heroics."

"Good. One last request."

"What?"

"Bring home the leftovers. I'm dying for a pizza. This healthy diet your mom has me on is killing me!"

Jeff shook his head. "You got it, Dad. You can eat it in my room. She won't go in there."

"Deal. I love you, Jeffery."

"Love you, Dad."

* * *

Collin sat at the desk, looking at the pile of papers in front of her. She had been over and over the will and nothing jumped out. She pushed back her chair and groaned. "Jeff! Where are you?" *Where he's supposed to be. Staying safely away from you.*

Collin dropped her eyes at the rebuke. *You're right. You're always right. Why can't we run away from all of this? Elope?*

Eloping sounds wonderful. Now is good, too. Call Jeff and see what he's doing. You know he'll be in favor of it.

Sure. Sure. In the middle of this turmoil and mayhem, the two of you are going to blissfully drive off somewhere and get married. Riiiiight.

It still sounds wonderful.

Collin pulled back to the desk. She sat and waited for peace to fill her. For the calm assurance all was well, and all would be well…but it didn't come.

Trust Me. Even when I'm silent. Trust Me.

"I do, Lord. I do. It's hard."

Gethsemane was hard. I know hard. Trust me.

Collin's head dropped to her chest. "I do. I will." She picked up her phone and speed-dialed Jeff. She got his voicemail. Collin rolled her eyes and groaned. She closed her eyes, "Watch over them. Keep them safe. Please."

Trust Me.

Collin pulled out the sheaves of paper of her grandfather's will. She sat on the bed and began reading the first page. The next page. The next.

Collin shifted from sitting on the edge of the bed to lying on her stomach on the bed. To sitting on the bed propped against the headboard.

To sitting on the floor propped against the mattresses.

Collin set the papers aside and stared at the ceiling. "Lord, I don't know what any of this is about. I can't even talk to Jeff the way I want to with me in hiding and him only You know where."

Collin sat in silence for several moments. She let the past few days run through her head, trying to put the pieces into a puzzle which made sense. But nothing fit. Nothing…

Collin pulled her phone out and looked again at the texts she had received.

"WHERE ARE YOU???"

"Safe. Trust Jeff."

Safe from what? Or who? Trust Jeff about what?
About knowing Erin is alive? About knowing where Erin is?
None of it made any sense.

Collin shuffled the papers of the will around. Maybe if she read them back to front, they would make more sense. The last few pages were filled with lists of where special items were to be donated. Collin waded through list after list until a particular request caught her eye. Collin recognized the names of her grandfather's many canine companions.

"It is my wish the cremains of my faithful companions Jesse, Sarah, Brandy, and Alli be scattered in the following locations· Jesse loved to lay under the arbor in the back of the property on Willow. She used to follow me out and stay there for hours. Please scatter her ashes around the area. Sarah preferred the garden. She would help dig the carrots and potatoes. Scatter her ashes around the perimeter. Alli..."

Collin smiled, but her lip trembled. "You did love your dogs, didn't you, Grandfather? Making sure they're taken care of to the end."

The list continued with four more names and locations for the disposal of their ashes. Then a third list. In the middle of the instructions, she came upon a name she didn't recognize. *"Bury Full Disclosure, my beloved cat, under the steps to my workshop. He left all his prize kills for me there. It will make me happy to know he is properly laid to rest."*

"Cat? Grandfather hated cats. He swore no cat would ever live in his house or on his property. Cat?"

Collin read the instructions again. *"Bury Full Disclosure, my beloved cat..."*

Collin's eyes narrowed. "You scattered all the others...but you want to bury the cat. Why? What made the cat special?"

Does it matter? Who cares about a cat? You have more important things to think about instead of worrying about a crazy man's obsession with a cat.

Collin stared at the words in front of her. *Who names a cat Full Disclosure?*

A lawyer?
Someone wanting to make full disclosure about something.
Collin grew still and silent.

WEDNESDAY EVENING

Jeff pulled to "Mr. Ossur's" house at 4:30 as directed, three boxes of pizza in hand. He resisted the strong urge to look around for the surveillance he knew had to be around somewhere. The prickling at the back of his neck nagged him. *Bad idea. Bad.*

Jeff walked to the door and knocked like he knew he belonged there. "Hey, Jim! I got the pizzas."

The door opened, and Detective Russo, now in blue jeans, waved Jeff inside. "Come on in. You're early."

Russo closed the door. Jeff handed him the boxes and said, "Like you told me."

"Exactly. We've got a few minutes to go over the plan. Tell me."

Jeff drew in a deep breath. "Trey and Mert come. We sit, we talk. We eat pizza. Mert drinks beer, but not too much. At six, Collin calls. She talks to Trey, who gets it out of her she and Luna, a new friend I've never met, are going to shoot hoops at the rec center on Eleventh and Shaw. It's usually quiet there, so she can get in a good practice. I repeat the address and time, so Mert hears me. We watch to see Mert pass the information somehow to someone. Your team is all over the rec center, and you have a double for Collin. Someone tries to take her out; you catch them. We get the signal from your team, and you arrest Mert for his part in it. The bad guys go to jail, and I get to see my fiancée again." He looked at Russo. "Right?"

Russo nodded. "Exactly how the script is written, yeah. Now…"

Jeff added, "If it goes wrong, I let you do all the talking."

"Good. And if it goes really wrong…"

"I keep my head down and don't get shot."

"Perfect."

Jeff let out the breath he didn't know he had been holding. "How do you do this day in and day out?"

"Practice. Lots of practice." Russo pointed to the kitchen. "After your call, I got the drinks for you and the beer for Mert." The man smiled. "Always happy to help a brother stay clean and sober." He returned to his more focused self. "Get a soda, so you have something to do with your hands besides twisting them. Walk around the house; you need to be able to navigate through here as if you've been here before. Did you bring the other jacket I asked you to bring?"

"Yeah. It's in the jeep."

"Bring it in here and throw it on the bed in the spare bedroom. I'll bring it out to you later. Like you left it here the last time you were here."

Jeff stepped out and got his spare jacket. He went on a walkabout in the house, familiarizing himself with the layout, the furniture, the pictures, the trophies…you'd have thought someone lived there. Jeff picked one of the bowling trophies and examined the nameplate. Sure enough, it read, "Jim Ossur, high score 282." Jeff shook his head. *Lord, my head knows You have this. Make my gut know it, too. Don't let me screw up, please.*

Jeff walked back to the central "open concept" living/dining/kitchen area. Everything visible at all times. *Like they know what they're doing.*

Jeff grabbed a soda from the fridge, sat in a comfortable chair, and put his feet on the table. Russo nodded. "Now you're getting the idea. Nothing going on here except four guys eating pizza and talking smack. Keep that front and center in your head. No surprises."

Jeff took a long swig of his soda. "Right."

The sound of a car engine came up the street. Jeff started to move; Russo ordered, "Sit. My house, my job to look." Jeff settled back into the chair. Russo looked outside. "White van. Handicap plates. They don't transport him in style, do they?"

"They haven't transported him at all since I've known him. He came to the rec center by MobiMobile most of the time. I had to sit with him to make sure the transport came back and got him."

Jim nodded. "Sounds about right."

"Mert's been beating on Trey."

"I saw the bruises. Here they come."

Russo threw the front door open. "Welcome! Come on in. Did you have any trouble finding it?"

Trey motored up the ramp to the house. "Nice touch."

Russo smiled. "Thank you. I designed it myself."

"Really?"

"No. Picked it out of four models being offered. My dad's getting up in years. I need to look down the road when he might have to come stay awhile."

Mert shook his head. "GPS works even out here. Didn't know there was this much undeveloped real estate in the city."

Russo laughed. "It'll fill faster than I want it to. The brokers tell me this will be all the rage in another year or so."

Jeff didn't get up. "Hey, Trey, Mert. Make yourself at home."

Trey glared at Jeff. "Looks like you already have. You think you own the place?"

"It's my second home. Well, third. After the station." A twinge of longing niggled at Jeff. *I miss the station.*

Russo pointed to the kitchen bar. "Pizza's there. Fridge is there. That's as much service as you're going to get. Help yourself."

Trey turned his chair in circles. He nodded in approval. "Very nice layout. I could almost live in a place like this."

Mert ignored the small talk and went straight to the fridge for a beer. He didn't offer to get Trey a drink, nor did he bother to serve Trey any of the pizza. Russo stepped to the plate before Jeff could get out of his chair. "Trey…meat pizza, right?"

"Good memory." Trey looked at Jeff. "He's a good man. I'm trusting him more to take care of you."

Jeff nodded. "Me, too."

Mert asked, "You got cable yet?"

"Dish. It's not hooked up yet. Friday, they tell me. Been here a month, and it's always, 'Friday.' I do have a streaming service."

Mert growled something uncomplimentary. He took a seat close enough to Trey to be intimidating without actually sitting on the man. Trey's eyes glared. "A little room, huh, Mert? 'Joined at the hip' is just an expression." He looked back at Jim. "What were you saying about Friday, Jim?"

Mert moved a seat further away. Jeff swallowed his smile and took a drink of soda to keep from laughing. Trey looked at Jeff. "Did you say Collin would call tonight?"

"Yeah. I thought with your silver tongue you could talk her into moving the wedding up. I'm not having any luck with her."

Trey shook his head. "Not a good plan, Jeffery. Never let another man negotiate between you and your woman. Keep the lines of communication open, and the interlopers out."

Jeff eyed Trey sideways. *That wasn't the plan.* "You know all this because?"

"I'm wise, Jeffery, my man. Wise. I know stuff. Like I don't want your lady to hear my voice in her ear. She has to believe it's all you, mon."

What are you doing, Trey? Wait, what did you say? 'I don't want your lady to hear my voice.' Because she might recognize it? Or you? Jeff studied Trey a moment. "I'll have to consider that, Trey." *Very carefully.*

Russo sat between Trey and Mert. "Who do you like in the college championships?"

Trey quipped, "The cheerleaders."

Jeff threatened to throw a pillow at Trey. "Degenerate."

Trey shrugged. "He asked."

Russo looked to Mert. "What about you?"

Mert shook his head. "I don't follow college. Only the NFL."

Jeff looked at the man sideways. "How do you live in Oakton and not follow college? There's not a professional team in Ohio anyhow."

Russo warned, "Browns fans might object."

Jeff grimaced. "I rest my case. Come on, Jim. OSU can beat the Browns on a bad day for the college, and the best day for the Browns."

Trey's mouth fell open. "Blasphemy!"

"It's truth."

Trey asked, "What about the Bengals? Don't they count as a pro team?"

"You seen them in the playoffs in the last ten years?"

"No."

"Again, the case rests. No pro teams in the state. Gotta follow college."

Mert didn't seem interested in the discussion. Jeff looked quickly at Russo. Jim turned to Mert. "I'm more interested in sharpshooting. Where did you train, Mert?"

Mert chugged his beer and got a second one. "Around. I did a stint in the Army a few years ago. Didn't like taking orders, so I got out. But I learned the basics there. Taught myself from then on..."

Jim whistled. "Takes some real discipline to train enough to hit the kind of distances Trey says you hit. Did you hit a moving target three city blocks away?"

Mert thought about it. "Yeah, maybe. Might have been further. I don't know for sure. No one measured it at the time."

"Too bad." Jim shook his head. "Could have been a record or something."

"Myeh. I don't keep records. All that matters is I hit what I aim at. That's what counts. Bringing down the target."

Jeff felt his guts twist. *Like Collin?*

Jeff's phone pinged. His face lit as he looked at the number. "It's Collin."

Trey offered, "Duh. We can look at your face and know."

Jeff ignored him and answered the phone. "Hello, milady." He walked into the kitchen but left the speaker on.

Collin's voice came back to him. "Hi, yourself. Miss you, Jeff."

Jeff tried to keep the yearning from his voice. "I miss you, too, lady. How'd your day go?"

"I got the relatives all squared away on the will. There shouldn't be any more dissension or discussion about who gets what. That part is over. And I couldn't be happier."

"Good, Collin. I'm happy for you. Does this mean we can move the wedding up? Actually set a date and keep it?"

"I'm sorry, Jeff." Collin's voice sounded contrite. "I am. I didn't mean to make this harder on us. But with everything going on, and thinking the Wingers wanted me dead because of the will, I had to be careful."

"I understand. But we can plan it now, right? Set the date, invite the guests, all those things?"

"Sure, my love. Look, Luna and I are going to go to the rec center over on Eleventh and Shaw. They stay open late, and I can get in the exercise I need so badly. They even have a sauna for afterward. You want to come join us?"

Jeff chuckled. "No, I don't think so. I'm not sure co-ed saunas are a thing in Oakton."

Collin laughed. "You're probably right. Anyhow, Luna is picking me up in a few minutes, and we're headed over there. We should be there by six-thirty and done by eight. I'll call you when she brings me home."

"Sounds like a plan. You be safe out there, okay? Don't take any chances."

Collin's voice softened. "Never. I love you, Jeff. Miss you."

Jeff hung up. He turned away from the others. He knew the emptiness in his heart would be reflected in his eyes. It took him a moment to pull it together and turn back around. "There. Finally. I can say with certainty where my bride-to-be is, at least for tonight. The first time in a week, it seems."

Trey shook his head. "You better figure out how to keep better track of her, Jefferyman. You can't go around losing your wife all the time. You need to know where she is at all times."

Russo looked at Trey, his eyes questioning. "What makes you the expert on wives and husbands?"

"I told you, I'm wise. I know things."

Mert stood. "I gotta use the water can."

Russo said, "Last door on the right at the end of the hall."

Mert nodded and left the room. Russo continued his interrogation of Trey. "So you know things. What things? From where? Who taught you anything?"

Trey rose to the challenge. "I read. I read all the latest magazines, listen to podcasts, follow the twitter-verse. I'm on things, I tell you."

Russo snorted. "Sure you do. When's the last time you had a date, wise man?"

"With a real woman? Uh…,never."

"That's what I thought. Don't talk theory without knowing real-life application."

"What's real-life got to do with anything?"

Jeff shook his head. He kept his eyes off the back of the house, off the back room where Mert would be calling in a location for a hitman to kill his wife-to-be. From where Mert would emerge, smiling, having completed his assignment for the night. *Lord, I can't do this much longer. I'm going to crack, I know it. Keep Your hand over my mouth, Father.*

Russo and Trey continued to spar. Jeff went to the fridge for another soda. He turned around to see Mert coming back into the room, a broad smile on his face. It took every ounce of discipline Jeff had to not come across the room at the man. *How can people be so cold? So calculating. So evil?*

Russo motioned to the pizza. "Come on, guys. Eat. There's plenty there."

Mert looked around the room. "You got a clock here?"

Russo nodded. "In the kitchen. It's six-ten."

"Thanks." Mert grabbed another beer and returned to his chair. Jeff noted the man pull his cellphone out and lay it on the arm of the chair. *Waiting for the signal it's done. You've killed my lady.*

Jeff got up and walked to the back door. "I need some air." He pulled open the door and stepped outside. The bitter cold air slapped him. *Thanks.* He stood and drew in deep, painful draughts of air, trying to still the rampaging nerves inside his gut. He heard the door open and Trey's wheelchair bump over the door jamb. He rolled up beside Jeff on the landing.

The chess tutor kept his voice low. "Hang in there, Jeffman. This is all going to be over soon. You and Collin can go back to planning your future." Trey dipped his head. "I'd promise, but mine isn't the assurance you need, is it?"

Jeff shook his head. "No, it's not. But I'll take it." Jeff looked to his tutor. "What about you, Trey? What happens to you when it's all over?"

His tutor lowered his eyes. "I don't know. I don't. Not sure what I'll do. Can't go back where I came from. No one there will want me anymore. None I would trust." His voice became bitter. "Pack of vultures and snakes…"

Trey's bitterness disappeared as quickly as it began. "I wasn't much better. But it's too late now. I'll find something. Looking out for myself is what I do best, I guess."

Do I call him out on it now? If I'm right… Lord, give me wisdom or shut my mouth. Again.

Jeff stuck his hands in his pants pockets to get them warm. "You have family and people here, Trey." He stared at the younger man. "Or is it Erin?"

Erin would not look up to meet Jeff's eyes. "It doesn't matter now. I screwed everything up. There's no way Cane will accept me back."

"Are you kidding me? Accept you back? Erin, she's never let

you go. She loves you. Losing you is the one hurt in her life the Lord hasn't been able to heal completely. Two a.m. this morning, she calls me. She about came through the phone to kill me for not telling her I knew you were alive. Which I didn't."

Erin looked up, hope in his eyes. "Really?"

"Why would she think I knew you were alive?"

The younger man's cheeks reddened. "Uh, poor choice of words on my part. I may have told her to trust you… I didn't think that part through very well."

Jeff grunted. "Ya think?"

Erin put his hands out in defense. "Hey, things at my end were a little dicey. I did the best I could."

Jeff grunted. "We'll discuss it again later. Let's get inside before we both freeze."

Trey turned around and headed inside. Jeff paused long enough to look into the sparkling heavens. "Thank You."

Inside, Russo and Mert were sparring about firearms, which ones were best for distance, for power, for avoiding windage or drop… Jeff ignored the conversation, got a second slice of pizza, and sat at the breakfast bar to eat it. Happy thoughts. Think happy thoughts. *Where should we hold the wedding? If I invite everyone I know, we'll need the downtown arena. If she adds everyone she knows, we may as well rent the Horseshoe. Which we can't do until football season ends. And it stops being twenty degrees out.*

Six-thirty came and went. Seven came and went. Seven-thirty… Jeff forced himself to stop looking at the clock. Watching it didn't make it go faster. Didn't bring the night to a close, didn't get them any closer to ending the nightmare. *Patience. Patience. Right. Patience.*

Russo's phone buzzed. Jeff nearly jumped out of his shoes. Russo ignored the call. "They can send it to voicemail. I don't answer my phone when I'm with friends."

Jeff turned away toward the wall. He knew his expression would reveal far more than he wanted to. Like, wanting to throttle Russo. To grab the phone and answer it for the detective. Wanting to crow at Mert for failing to kill Collin… No, he would do none of those. He would breathe, he would control himself, he would remain calm.

If only his hands would stop shaking.

Mert's phone pinged. The man looked at it and nodded to

himself. "Well, this has been fun, but we gotta go. Gotta get Mr. Weller home and in bed."

Russo stopped him. "Uh, you've had three beers. I don't want to be responsible if something happens while you're driving home. You need to wait at least another half-hour before you go."

Mert snorted. "Three beers is nothing. I'm not drunk."

Trey jumped in. "I'm not riding with you until you've waited half an hour. It's dark out, the streets don't have lights, and I'm not taking chances. I'll take myself home before I get in a van with you."

Mert scowled at Trey. "You'll do what you're told. The agency which hired me gave me responsibility for you. Which means you'll do what you're told."

Russo raised a hand. "Let's not get ugly here. It's only half an hour. You can wait that long. Cops are pretty strict about impaired drivers. With the streets being icy, they can't always tell if it's your driving or the bad roads. But they tend to pull you over first and ask questions later."

Mert glared at Trey. "Fine. Half an hour."

Jeff consolidated the pizza into smaller portions, setting aside a couple pieces for his dad as promised. He looked at Trey. "You want to take some of this home?"

"Can't get out of bed to get it at midnight, so won't do me any good."

Jeff looked to Mert. "You?"

"Nah. We got plenty of food at the house."

Jeff raised an eyebrow at Russo. Jim said, "Sure. It'll probably be a long night."

Mert ignored the comment. He busied himself, looking at his phone, checking the time. When the half-hour expired, he stood. "Okay, Mom, can I leave now?"

Jim grinned. "You sure you want to leave all this excitement?"

"I'm sure. Let's go, Mr. Weller."

Trey gave Jim a quick salute. "Been fun."

Jeff caught Trey's hand. "See you tomorrow?"

Trey looked from Mert to Jeff. "I'll let you know. Don't know what tomorrow will look like at this point."

Jim went to the back room to bring out the jackets. He stepped between Mert and Trey. "Trey, is this your jacket?" The detective held three jackets.

Trey looked it over. "Not mine."

"Mert?"

"No."

Jim shrugged. "Fine." He threw the extra coat back into the bedroom. "One more thing before you go."

Mert swung back to look at the detective. "What?"

Jim caught the man's free arm and twisted it behind him. "You're under arrest for conspiracy to commit murder. You have the right…"

Mert shoved hard against Jim, knocking him into Trey. The caretaker pulled a gun from behind his back.

Jeff's eye's widened. He grabbed for the gun arm, trying to deflect what would otherwise be a point-blank shot at Russo.

The shot went wide. Detective Russo untangled himself from Trey and grabbed Mert's arm as well.

The men struggled.

Shots were fired.

More struggle.

More shots fired.

Finally, Jeff and Detective Russo were able to wrestle Mert to the ground. Jeff jumped on top of Mert's gun arm. Jeff slammed Mert's hand over and over against the floor until Mert dropped the weapon.

Russo wrenched Mert's free hand behind the caretaker's back and slapped a handcuff on him. Jeff twisted Mert's other arm to Russo, who cuffed the other hand as well.

The detective stood, breathing hard. He glared at Jeff. "You call that keeping your head down?"

Jeff trembled all over. "I… I… aye, yai yai!"

He turned to look at Trey. "You okay, Trey? Erin?"

Jim looked from Jeff to Trey. Jeff noted the detective's eyes narrowing.

Jeff looked to Erin. The chess tutor couldn't have been more white. His eyes were wide, frozen in fear. He didn't move. Jeff dropped to look Erin in the face. "Erin? Are you okay, man? Talk to me."

Erin looked at Jeff, but his eyes stayed wide, and his mouth hung open. Jeff caught Erin's arm. "Erin. Talk to me. Are you okay? Are you hurt?"

Life flooded back into the tutor. "How should I know? I'm numb from the waist down. How'm I supposed to know?"

Jeff went into paramedic mode. He examined what he could see of his friend, checking arms and legs, front and back, to make sure there were no signs of bullet holes or bleeding. Only after he had convinced himself Erin hadn't sustained any damage did he nod. "You're good. Nothing touched you."

Russo called in his backup. Jeff heard him order, "Go around to the back of the house. I know the light is on in the front, but drive around and come in from the east."

The detective pulled Mert to his feet and sat him in a chair. Russo finished reading Mert his rights. "You want to talk now or downtown?"

Mert ignored Russo and glared at Erin. "Chose the wrong side, loser. I'll be on the street in twenty-four hours. Where will you be?"

Russo looked out the front window, peering through a slit in the curtains. "I wouldn't be so sure about being on the street. Not alive, anyhow. Your bosses don't leave loose ends."

Mert's eyes narrowed. "What are you talking about?"

Russo enumerated. "We found the driver who ran Collin off the road shot to death. The arsonist who set the trailer court on fire died in the blaze. They're still waiting on the autopsy report, but I'll bet there's no smoke in his lungs. And last night's botched knife attack? Someone silenced him before he got out the door. You think your bosses are going to take a chance you'll stick around to name names?"

Mert smirked. "I'm not worried."

The backup team came in. Russo motioned for them to take Mert. The officers stood Mert up. Russo studied Mert. "The only reason you wouldn't be is if you were the one responsible for the clean-up. But you would be an even greater liability, wouldn't you?" The detective cocked his head. "All the more reason to make sure you never got arrested."

Russo looked to the officers holding Mert. "Take him to the station. But walk him out through the front door. Make sure you give him plenty of room. Don't get between him and the lights. In case someone wants to know if he's still alive and in custody."

Mert glared at Russo. "You got nothing."

"You'll be the first one to know. Take him out, guys."

Jeff's eyes widened. He looked at Erin, and his tutor's eyes reflected the shock Jeff felt.

Russo motioned for the front door. "Get him out of here."

One of the officers threw the door open and partially pushed Mert forward.

Gunfire sounded. The doorjamb splintered. The officers dropped to the ground, pulling Mert with them. Mert screamed in fear and anger. "Get me out of here! Those…"

Jeff ignored Mert's colorful description of his bosses, whoever they were, as the officers hauled him out the back door. The three men in the house waited silently until the cruisers pulled away. Jim walked to the front door, snapped the light off and on three times. Jeff saw a light across the field flash in response.

Jim turned the light off. "Well, this should prove informative."

Erin started at Jim, comprehension dawning in his eyes. "You set it up! Your own guys were out there!" The tutor began to chortle, clapped his hands. "Well played, sir. Well played. We need to play chess together. Well, against each other. You will be someone worth playing."

Russo shrugged. "A little persuasion works wonders."

Jeff shook his head. "But shooting toward your own guys? What if…"

Russo shook his head. "Blanks. Squib charges on the door frame. They'd hang my hide if I pulled a stunt like that for real."

He looked at his watch. "Forensic team should be here shortly. Once they arrive, we'll take a trip downtown, and you can give me your statement…" Russo trailed off. "Mr. Weller? Mr. Winger? Which is it?"

Erin lost his enthusiasm. "Winger. But only until I can change it like my sister did. I'm done with this family."

Jim's eyes narrowed as he looked at Jeff. "How long have you known about this?"

"I didn't until tonight." Jeff motioned toward Erin. "He confirmed it. I suspected something this morning when Collin told me she knew Erin was alive." Jeff looked at the floor. "I thought she'd lost her faculties, but she insisted. I had to believe her. Or else marry a crazy woman."

Erin studied Jeff. "You'd marry her even if she were wrong or hallucinating?"

"Yes. Even then."

Erin shook his head. "You're a good man, Jeffery. Strange, but good."

Forensics arrived. They took over the house while a transport van took Jeff, Erin, and Detective Russo to the police station. Russo led Jeff to a room with a stenographer. "My partner Nick is going to come in and help you give your statement. I want you to tell him everything you know about Trey slash Erin. When you first met him, what questions he asked you, what he ate…don't leave anything out."

Jeff grew somber. "Where will Erin be?"

"With me. I've got questions to ask him about his involvement in this whole affair."

"Is he under arrest?"

"No. Not yet. Not until we hear what he has to say."

"You know they held him prisoner, right? He couldn't have left on his own. He's not capable—"

Russo held out his hands. "All that will be taken into account, Jeff. We need to know what he knows,. And if he had an opportunity to do anything with the information. I'm well aware he's your friend."

"He's going to be my brother-in-law. And if I don't do everything I can to protect him, Collin will never forgive me."

"We'll take good care of him. Trust me, Jeff."

Jeff groaned. "Why does it always come back to trust? Why?"

Jim laughed and clapped Jeff on the shoulder. "Some lessons need to be repeated before we get them right."

"I hear you."

* * *

Jeff told Detective O'Brian everything he could remember about Trey, and about Erin. In reflection, besides the "where does Collin live, what does she do" questions, most of Erin's queries during their weekly chess matches centered on "what is she like?" Questions, Jeff realized, which had nothing to do with finding and killing her, but with rediscovering the sister Erin had lost.

Only after Jim's partner felt sure Jeff had told him everything he could remember did he kick him loose. Jeff found a deserted breakroom and sat to wait for Erin. Or news of him, anyhow.

He looked at his phone. Ten-thirty. Too late to call Collin? Doubtful. She would be waiting on news of what went down at the "house." Jeff lived, the bad guys were in custody, all was well in the world again.

Jeff dialed. Collin answered immediately. "Hi, love of my life." Jeff felt the thrill her voice always gave him sweep over him.

"Hi yourself, milady."

"How are you?"

"I'm good. Safe. Unhurt. Everything went according to plan. The bad guy is in custody and most likely pouring out his guts about who hired him."

"It went that well?"

Jeff smiled. "Yes, it did. I'll fill in all the details when I see you. And soon, I know."

Collin's voice sounded tired. "Good, Jeff. I'm glad you're okay. And I'm glad this is going to be over."

"Are you okay, milady?"

"No. But I will be. I think I found something in the will. I want to see if you read it the same way I do."

"What is it?"

"Nope. Not going to tell you in advance. Don't want to sway your opinion. When you and I can get ourselves in the same room at the same time, I'll have you look at it and see what you see."

"Not fair."

"Is too."

"Is not."

"Is too." Jeff heard the laughter in her voice. Good. He'd made her smile. At least for a little while.

Collin cleared her throat. "Um…did…did Erin make his…move?"

"Did he come out of hiding? Yes. He's been very instrumental in bringing this to a conclusion."

"You saw him? Talked to him?"

"Yes, milady. Don't get jumpy."

"Jumpy? Because you've seen my brother who's been dead to me for twelve years and I haven't? Because you talked to him? You know where he is, and I don't? Why would I get jumpy?"

Jeff backtracked. "That's not the word I wanted to use. I

mean—"

"I'll show you jumpy, Jeff Farrell. Next time we're on a basketball court together, you're going to learn a whole new definition of jumpy. I can't believe you didn't call me the moment you knew it was him."

"Things were a little…um…dicey." *Worked for Erin. Maybe she'll buy it from me?*

"And how are things being dicey an excuse? Jeff, I…"

Collin's voice trailed off into silence.

Jeff waited a moment. "Collin?"

Nothing.

"Collin?"

Nothing.

"Collin!"

"Stop shouting at me! Give me a minute. My nose is bleeding."

Jeff seethed. *Not right, Lord. Not right. I should be there with her. I want to be there with her. Why are we apart?*

Collin came back on the phone. "I'm here. I should get off and clean my mess."

"Call Rich. He needs to know about this." *For once, listen to me. Please. Please?*

"In the morning. I'll call him in the morning."

"I love you, lady. I do. I don't want to lose you. Please call him now."

Her voice was adamant. "In the morning. I want to see you first. Then I'll call him."

"Tomorrow, then… I'll see you, then you'll call him. Right?"

She didn't argue with him. "Yes, love of my life. I'll see you tomorrow. I love you, Jeff."

"I love you, Collin. Sleep well."

"'Nite."

Jeff closed his eyes. "Lord, please. Please. Don't take her from me. Please. It's Your will, I know. I know, okay? But please."

The Lord knew the rest. Jeff would leave it there.

* * *

Jeff made one more phone call; he called home to tell his parents how things stood. He would either be bringing a second body with him when he came, or he'd be spending the night at the police station. He'd let them know as soon as he knew which it would be.

The clock in the breakroom neared midnight when Jim Russo and a subdued Erin Winger came in looking for Jeff. Jeff's eyes narrowed as he waited for the verdict.

Jim gave it. "He's free to go. So long as he stays in town. Or where he can be reached when we need him."

Jeff took a long look at Erin. "You okay, dude?"

Erin nodded but said nothing. Jeff looked at him closer. Erin dropped his head. "Can we get out of here, please?"

Jim Russo said, "We'll have a transport van take you back to get your car, Jeff, and take Erin here wherever he needs to go."

Jeff's eyes dared Erin to challenge him. "He'll come to my house. The folks are expecting us both."

Erin looked up, then down again. "Fine." Something must have pierced through the younger man's funk. He raised his head. "Thanks, Jeff. I mean it. I appreciate having a place to go."

Jeff gripped Erin's shoulder. "We're going to get this all straightened out, Erin. Whatever we have to do, we'll do."

Erin nodded, but it lacked conviction.

Jeff looked at Russo; the detective shrugged. He left the room, presumably to arrange for the transport van.

Jeff eyed Erin. "What's going on, man? What's wrong?"

Erin wouldn't look at him. "All those questions he asked. I realized what a jerk…what a coward…what a Judas I'd been to Cane. You say she never stopped loving me. I quit caring about her when Robert convinced me she'd run out on me. Left me to die." Erin's voice reflected his bitterness. "I gave up on her. She never gave up on me."

"Um, bro…she thought you were dead. You could never be any different than she remembered you. I'm sure Robert Winger painted quite the picture of what Collin had become, or what she might be doing. Give yourself a break, man. Collin will. Trust me, she isn't going to stand for you beating yourself over it."

Erin raised his head, his eyes searching Jeff's. He must have seen whatever he needed, for he looked down and nodded. "Right. I shouldn't beat myself. I'll let her beat me for it."

Jeff sighed. "She's going to beat both of us for not spilling the whole story to her immediately after the affair with Mert ended. She wasn't happy being left out of the loop. Trust me."

The two men headed down the hallway to find Russo. Erin asked, "You think we can see her in the morning?"

"I'm hoping. I'm planning on it, anyhow." Jeff remembered the exhaustion in Collin's voice. "She needs to get to surgery. Maybe seeing you will motivate her."

"I'll do my best."

"That's all anyone can ask, my friend."

THURSDAY MORNING

Collin waited politely for Jim Russo to come around and open the car door for her. *Practice.*

The voices inside refused to play. All the walls, all the defenses were sliding into the black pit of pain her brain had become. But there were things to do, still. She'd rest when the last jobs were done.

Russo pulled the door open, a folio of papers under his arm. Collin slid out. Her hands trembled. A little. Slightly. Not much.

As they had prearranged, Russo walked to the entrance with Collin a shadow in his wake. She made sure to stay behind him, shielded from the front window. Being only seven in the a.m., the sun had done little more than peek over the horizon. A horizon of naked tree limbs and tree trunks added to the not-daylight.

Russo stepped to the Farrell household and knocked with purpose and vigor. Collin winced. *That ought to raise the household. And the neighbors.*

The door opened almost at once. Jeff stood in the entrance. He smiled. "Good morning, Detective."

Before Jeff could utter another word, Collin stepped from behind Russo. Jeff's eyes flew wide open. His mouth dropped. Collin slipped into his arms and buried her head on his chest. Jeff enclosed her in a bear-hug carrying all the emotion Collin knew they both felt. Joy. Sadness. Desperation. Hope. Fear. Love…

Jeff crushed his lips into Collin's forehead. "Oh, milady. I have missed you."

Collin whispered, "Aim. This once. Aim."

Jeff leaned and kissed her full on the mouth. They stood together forever. A lifetime. Or until Russo cleared his throat. "Can we come in?"

Jeff broke from Collin. His eyes sparkled. "Of course."

One joke. You have to muster one joke. He will expect one. Or he'll know how bad you're hurting. And there will be a fight. Collin stopped. "Who made the coffee?"

"Mom did."

"Okay. We'll come in."

Jeff chuckled and hugged her again. "It's good to have you back, Collin."

He has no clue. Keep it that way for as long as possible. As long as necessary.

Russo and Collin stepped into the living room. Harmon and Lacey sat in their respective chairs but rose as the threesome entered. Lacey beamed as she took Collin in her arms. "Child…it is so good to see you. We have been praying for this day." She held Collin at arm's length. "You look exhausted."

All the snappy comebacks went AWOL. She nodded. "I am. I need a cup of coffee, the four of you to read something, and then I'm checking into the hospital." She looked around. "Where is Leesa?"

Harmon folded his paper. "We thought it best for her to visit her brother in the Canton area for a few days. Mike has four young children, and Leesa loves to be with them."

Unspoken were the reasons why the Farrells thought it best to send Leesa away. No one needed to explain them. They just were.

Lacey led Collin to the couch and sat her down. Jeff followed close behind. Jim and Harmon exchanged handshakes and introductions. Harmon looked at Russo. "Coffee, Detective?"

"Black, yes. Please." Jim took the seat Harmon pointed to as the older Farrell headed for the kitchen. He called back over his shoulder, "Collin, black, too?"

"Yes, sir. Thank you." She hesitated. "Pop Harmon."

She heard the chuckle of appreciation from the other room.

Another voice called out, "I take mine with creamer and two sugars, please."

Collin froze. Her head turned in minuscule increments toward the hallway from where the sound had come. She felt her mouth go slack…the rest of her remained paralyzed. A wheelchair rolled into the room. Its occupant…its occupant… Collin could only stare.

Hallucinating. You're hallucinating. He's not real. Not. Real.

The young man in the chair tried to smile. He cleared his throat. "So, how's your algebra these days?"

Collin whispered without thinking, "Better than yours. You can't distribute polynomials that way."

"Ah, but that's what makes it brilliant, Cane. No one will ever figure it out."

The words, the magic words to break the spell and set her free. Collin dropped to the floor beside her brother. She hugged him around his middle, burying her head in his chest. She didn't cry. She sobbed. Great wracking sobs tore through her and wouldn't stop. All of the tears of all of the years…all cascading in a torrent threatening to drown her and her brother.

Erin stroked her head. He muttered, "I'm sorry, Cane. I'm sorry. I'm so sorry…"

Collin looked at him. "Where have you been? I thought you were dead! He told me you were dead. Patrick. He told me I had killed you! What happened? Where did they take you?"

If she could ask enough questions, the apparition would never vanish. Collin buried her head in his chest again. "I missed you. I missed you so much."

Erin's voice cracked. "I'm sorry, Cane. I…"

Collin sat back and stared at her brother, breathless. *Alive. He's alive. I'm alive. We're alive.*

If you don't get moving, you won't be. The mounting pain in her head ticked off the seconds remaining.

She wiped her eyes on her sleeve, pulled herself to her feet, and hugged Erin again. She took several breaths to gather the shards of her self-control back together. What there remained of it. "We can talk all about how we were lied to and what they did to us and how we survived later. What matters is you're here." She squeezed his hand. "I love you, little brother."

Time. Time. Get on with it. Cry later.

Collin turned to the others. Her voice cracked. "Detective Russo can fill you all in on the case as it stands."

Erin came into the room proper. Harmon returned from the kitchen with a tray and three cups of coffee. Jim took the coffee from Harmon. "Thank you, Mr. Farrell. Much appreciated." He took a sip from the mug. "Mert gave us enough information to get warrants issued. Robert, Richard, and Rupert Winger were all arrested and booked on federal charges of murder for hire, murder for hire across state lines, murder, arson, and a few dozen other charges we thought of. The actual charges will be announced when we finish the investigation. They are currently being held without bond. We have seventy-two hours before they have to be formally charged. It gives us time to round up all those sidekicks Mert has been telling us about."

Jeff asked, "Patrick?"

Jim shook his head. "We don't have enough yet to book him on anything. Granted, Collin identified him in the surveillance photo, but it's not enough to hold him. The police in Fort Newton have been alerted and are happy to cooperate with us if we need him back here. If you hear from him, let me know."

Jim looked at Collin and nodded. She took a deep breath. "Right. I read through the will again last night, and I think I found something." She read the passage about burying Full Disclosure. Collin looked up. "There's one thing."

Erin snorted. "Yeah. Grandfather Fenton hated cats. Hated cats. It's a fake."

Collin nodded. "That's what I thought. Grandfather buried something under the stairs, and the information in the cat's box tells us what it is."

Jeff's eyes lit up. "So all someone has to do is go and dig up what's under the stairs? Great. We can…"

Jim Russo raised a hand. "You need to take it slower. Find the box with the cat first. Find out what's been buried. You don't want to disturb evidence, and let guilty parties walk on a technicality. It's waited this long. It can wait long enough to do this right."

Harmon raised a finger. "Won't Collin need a warrant?"

Russo shook his head. "No. She's the legal owner of everything on the property, and the property itself. She can open any box she wants. She may think what's in the box points to a crime, but she has no actual knowledge it does. The box is in the clear. What's buried, not so much."

Jeff insisted, "But Collin doesn't need to be there, right? She can send a designated representative to find and open it."

Jim nodded. "Yes, she can."

Which left her only one issue to resolve. "Jeff, will you go with

Erin and find whatever is in the box?"

Erin exploded. "No, and that's the stupidest request you could ever ask of him! He's going to the hospital with you. He's going to hold your hand, he's going to walk you to surgery, he's going to sit in the waiting room and do the prayer thing. He will go nowhere else until you get out of surgery and are declared fine. Do you hear me?"

Her brother moved to stare Collin dead in the eyes. "Do you?"

Collin dropped her head. "Yes, A-One." She turned to Jeff. "I'm sorry. I'm not thinking clearly."

Erin continued. "And I'm not going anywhere except the hospital, either. I'm going to be Jeff's shadow the whole time. I am not losing you again."

Her twin picked up her hand and squeezed it hard. "You are going to do what the doctors tell you when they tell you. You are going to get that thing taken out of your head, and you are going to live to be an old, cranky woman. Now get up and let's get out of here."

Jim Russo touched her shoulder. "With your permission, I'll go." He smiled. "I've been with this case long enough. I want to see the end of it. And I can probably call in some markers from the guys in blue in Fort Newton."

Collin breathed out again. "Thank you, Detective. Brenden Aster has the keys and the permissions you'll need." More needed to be said, but there wasn't time. *You have to make time. Do it.*

She forced the words. "Tell him I gave you the code. It's Grace." Collin cringed against the pain hammering inside. "I give you full permission to go anywhere and do anything on the property." Collin kept her eyes closed but motioned to the others in the room. "You're witnesses." *That's all there is, folks.* She dipped her head in surrender. "I'm ready to go."

Jeff grabbed the keys to the jeep. "Dad, call the hospital and tell them to expect us."

Lacey kissed her son. "I'll call Rich and let him know he's needed." Lacey also kissed Collin in passing. "I'm praying for you, Collin. God is with you."

A single tear escaped the prison walls that once were Collin's eyes. She let Jeff lead her outside to the jeep.

Jeff maneuvered Collin into the front, lowered the seat so she could recline almost flat. He reached across and buckled her belt.

Collin listened as Jeff assisted Erin into the backseat, threw the man's folding chair into the cargo area, and jumped into the driver's seat. Collin closed her eyes and whispered, "I hurt. I hurt so bad." She heard a slap on the roof of the jeep. She opened her eyes to see Jeff fixing his red rotating light on the top. "No sirens. Please. No sirens."

Jeff squeezed her hand. "Understood."

How long the trip took, Collin had no clue. She measured it less in time and more in how many times her head bounced on the seat, and how many waves of pain threatened to wash over her and drown her in their wake. Drowning would be a mercy.

She could hear Jeff's repeated, "Hang in there, Collin. Hang on." Erin encouraged her from the back seat. "Do what he says, Cane. You can do this. I know you. You're stronger than any pain. You can do this."

Just desserts would be to scream her brother's ears off. But screaming would hurt Collin more than Erin, so she swallowed the urge and tried to visualize herself above the pain, riding the crest, sailing smoothly into shore. It almost worked…could have worked if Jeff hadn't hit the last pothole. She moaned. "Lord, help me. Please."

* * *

Jim Russo spared a glance from the road ahead to look at the clock. *Aster said we'd reach the driveway in half an hour at most. Where is it?*

Nick pointed to an opening between two twisted and gnarled maple trees. "There. Has to be it. Haven't seen anything else even resembling a driveway around here."

Russo pointed the car down the well-rutted drive and wished they had brought a four-wheel-drive vehicle. The constant rain-freeze-rain-freeze-snow-rain pattern of the past few months had done a number on even the most well-maintained roads. No telling how many times they'd been graded before now. He dodged and braked and climbed and sank and dodged…

Nick bounced his head off the roof of the car. "Watch it! Russo, where did you learn to drive? Why are we even here?"

Russo tried to go around a fissure which snuck in from nowhere, ending in an even deeper pit. He gunned the engine and accelerated up the side of the rut, banging his partner's head once again. "Sorry."

Nick responded with several curses to Russo's ancestors and any descendants Russo might one day have. Russo grimly ignored the profanity and kept his eyes fixed on the 'road.' "We're here to find the evidence we need to make our case against the Winger brothers as airtight as we can. If Collin is right"—he jerked the steering wheel left, right, left again—"there should be an explanation for all these murders. And it should be under the steps to the workshop."

"If and should aren't gonna play well before a judge, you know." Nick braced himself for another rut.

Russo nudged the car forward in inches. "And if Collin is right, all will be made clear in the cat box."

Jim could hear the skepticism in his partner's voice. "Right. A cat named 'Full Disclosure.' You sure this isn't some sick joke? Another way to draw her out of hiding so they can kill her?"

Jim saw a breach in the road's walls. He aimed for it, prayed, and willed the car to climb up and out of the cratered pathway. The undercarriage screamed as it scraped over the muddy claws of the furrow but held together. Jim pulled the car into a level, graveled area, free from obvious pits. A log-cabin mansion, three-story house in the middle and two-story wings on the ends, sat nestled in the trees. A mailbox, carved to look like a sleeping Labrador, declared it the "Mudd" residence. A helicopter pad sat to the right of the house. No wonder the road was impassible. No one used it.

"We're about to find out. Let's go."

Nick and Jim walked toward the house. Jim searched the area for some sign of the security team Brenden Aster said would be patrolling the grounds. Collin gave Jim the code to let the guard know they had permission to enter, and Aster gave him the keypad code to get inside. So why hadn't they been challenged?

Jim slowed his pace. His eyes narrowed as he looked for any sign of a guard. Or a security system of some kind. Nothing. No cameras. No guards. Something was wrong. Jim muttered, "And we haven't even gone inside yet."

Nick turned to Jim. His eyes reflected uncertainty. "What's wrong, partner?"

"No security. There should be a security team here."

Nick glanced around the area. "Yeah? So, where are they?"

"That's what I want to know." Jim pulled out his cellphone and called Brenden Aster. He put it on speaker so Nick could hear as well.

"Detective Russo. You found the place?"

"We're here. There's no guard. No cars, nothing."

"Hmm, not good. Let me call the company, and I'll call you back."

"Right."

Jim disconnected the call. Nick cocked his head. "Trap?"

"I don't know. I think we should stay out here until Aster calls back."

"If they intended the trap for Walker, seeing us should make whoever it is stand down, right? We're not their target."

Jim grimaced. "Except they don't seem to mind collateral damage."

"True."

Russo's phone buzzed. "Talk to me."

Brenden Aster's voice sounded terse. "Someone called and canceled the contract effective today."

"Who would have the authority?"

"Collin and myself. The company said Collin Walker gave them notice she no longer required their services."

"And they verified her identity how?"

Aster growled. "They won't tell me. The representative assured me all safety protocols were followed. Someone either knew the code or..."

Jim snorted. "Money talks."

"So I've found. I'm still digging into it. Shall I send the local mounties out to you?"

Nick shook his head. Jim shrugged. "No need at this point. If we run into anything, we'll call."

"Heard and understood. I'll be in touch."

Jim put his phone away. He looked at his partner. "What? Why no backup?"

"We're Oakton's finest. I think we can handle a dead cat."

Jim shook his head. "You're so sure we're not going to find anything. Put some money on it."

"Fine. We find nothing, you buy dinner. For a week."

"And if we do?"

Nick's eyes circled as he thought it over. "I cook for a week."

Jim burst out laughing. "And that's a win for me how? Forget it."

The men reached the front door. Everything looked fine. Jim rattled the handle. Locked. "Go around back and see if there's any sign of…anything."

"If a vampire cat jumps out—"

Jim pointed to the back. "Go." He shook his head as Nick disappeared around the corner. Jim keyed the code he'd been given. The door opened. Jim called out, "Anyone home? Hello?"

No answer. *Is there ever?* Jim put his hand to his shoulder holster but didn't draw his weapon. This wasn't a crime scene, and he didn't anticipate it becoming one. He pushed the door wide and continued to announce his presence. "Hello? Anyone here?"

The entryway emptied on a parlor. It was a woodworkers paradise: chairs, benches, tables all built from natural oak…floor to ceiling oak bookcases with glass which slid up and back to protect the contents…a massive oak rolltop desk. Jim ran his hand over the top of the desk. *Handmade.* All of it. Impressive. Very impressive.

He looked around at the walls. There were framed pictures of Labradors and Shepherds and herding dogs, all with the same older gentleman. Dogs. Lots of dogs. Lots of dogs. *But nary a cat to be seen.*

The parlor opened on one side into a living room; the other opening led to a game room. Billiard table. Poker table. A chess set with ornately carved pieces, some easily ten inches high. Jim walked over and hefted one of the pieces. Hand-hewn, too. Jim could see Erin learning the game from his grandfather. *Who wouldn't want to play with a set like that?*

Focus. Russo scanned the game room for urns or ash receptacles but saw none. A quick check of the living room also turned up nothing. At least nothing looking like a cremains holder. Could there be a library? Did Mudd keep his pets with him in his bedroom? *Not in the kitchen. Never.* Jim shook his head at the thought. No.

He circled his way through the house. The prickling at the back of his neck warned him he was being watched. By who, for what, remained to be determined. But Jim heard the faintest traces of footsteps shadowing him from room to room.

He put his hand to the pretend mic in his ear. "Yeah, Nick. I haven't found it yet. Have the team on standby, so when I do locate it, we can get right to work. Yeah. No, I haven't checked the bedroom. Right."

Jim worked his way across the lower floor to the staircase spiraling to the second floor. He resisted the urge to turn around, to confront his follower. No. Not yet. Guided by some sense Jim recognized as outside himself, he climbed the stairs without looking back. He pressed his hand to his ear again. "Yeah, I'm upstairs. Come on up when you finish the perimeter."

It bothered Jim Nick hadn't come in yet. *What could he be doing?* As there hadn't been any shots or shouts, Jim continued on his course. *Nick can take care of himself.*

The staircase ended on a landing separating into four bedrooms. A quick look in each gave Jim the impression the one farthest down the hall should be the master and the possible location of the boxes. He started to head there but stopped. Jim stepped into the nearest room and examined it.

A guest room, of course. But decorated in a more feminine style. A queen canopy bed, sans canopy, sat in the middle of the room. The ruffles on the faded pink bedspread had lost most of their starch. A dressing table without a mirror sat between two mahogany dressers. The smell reminded him of his great grandmother: the powdery scent of extreme age. A windowed alcove had been turned into a reading nook its embroidered seat nearly bleached white from direct sun.

Jim walked to the bench which served as seating and pulled up the cushion. Underneath, the bench had a hinged lid. Jim pulled it up and looked inside. Only books. Again, the tang of time long past whispered. Jim reached inside and rummaged through the selection. He pulled out a thick, much-read copy of something whose title wasn't English.

"Got it." Jim smiled. He put his hand to his ear. "Nick, I got it. Yeah, it's here. I'll bring it in a minute."

Jim turned around to find his stalker standing in the doorway. The man…young man…couldn't be more than seventeen or eighteen. Still a kid. He held a pistol in his hand but had it pointed at the floor. Fear, shame, uncertainty…all played across the youngster's face. His eyes darted back and forth from Jim to the hallway to Jim to the book in Jim's hand. The young man pointed his gun at the book. "G…g-ive it to me." His hand shook in time to his verbal stutter.

Jim looked at the book. "This? You want this?"

The man-child swallowed hard. "G…g-ive it to me."

Jim debated tossing the book to the kid and disarming him when he went to catch it. He decided against the strategy. *Someone could get hurt by accident.* Jim handed the book to the intruder. "Here. I don't know why you would want it. Not much of a plot."

The youngster looked from the book to Jim, to the book, to Jim…his hands continued to shake. "What's in it?"

Jim shrugged. "I don't know. Words." Jim sat on the bench. "What's your name?"

"You d-d-on't need to know."

"I do, though. If you're going to kill me, I'd like to be able to tell whoever I meet at the Pearly Gates who sent me." His eyes narrowed as he studied the man. "You're a Winger, right? One of Richard's sons. Probably the youngest. So you would be…Garth. Right?"

The boy's eyes flared, then widened in fear. "How d-d-o… you know me?"

"Your cousin, Collin. Well, you knew her as Caitlin. I know her as Collin. She told me about you. Well, not you, per se, but her Uncle Richard had two sons." Jim reached slowly into his pocket and pulled out his ID. "I'm working on the murder case she's involved in." He tossed the ID to Garth. Garth looked at it, and his eyes widened. The young man tossed the ID back to Jim, staring at him, even more guarded.

Jim kept his tone light and conversational. He crossed his arms over his chest. "Let me see. I bet you got picked to wait here and follow Collin when she came. You were supposed to wait until she found something, then you were to take it." Jim cocked his head. "Were you supposed to kill her, too?"

Garth moved further into the room and leaned against the wall. "Yes."

Jim shook his head. "No way. You're not a killer. You'd never pull the trigger. Would you?"

Garth's eyes sparked. He pulled himself to his full height and glared at Russo. "I would. I could d-d-o it.

"No, Garth. You couldn't. Like you're not going to kill me." Jim uncrossed his arms, leaned on his hands to look less intimidating. "You're not the killer type. I've seen them. So why did they choose you?"

Garth hung his head. "I d-d-rew the—"

"Short straw?" Garth nodded. "I bet it they rigged it."

Garth cocked his head. "What do you mean?"

"Your father and his brothers are too smart to leave a job like this to the youngest member of the family. They play the odds. The sure odds. And they cover their tracks. Pulling the security away from the place…leaving you here alone."

Jim mused a moment. He saw Nick standing in the hallway, gun drawn, question in his eyes. Jim shook his head at Garth but signaled Nick at the same time. Nick nodded and stepped back slightly, remaining out of sight.

Jim stood to pace the floor. "But why? What did they want to happen?" Jim looked at the floor as he paced. He looked up. "I got it. Security is gone. You come to check out the house. While you're here, Collin arrives. You think she's an intruder, so you shoot her. Security comes in moments later, thinks you're an intruder, and shoots you. No witnesses, no loose ends. All neat and tied up, and the Winger brothers get away with murder. Again."

Jim stopped his pacing. "Sound about right? I mean, what were you supposed to do after you killed Collin?"

Garth's eyes grew wide. "Nothing. Wait. They said someone would come and take her away. And no one would ever know I did it."

Jim shook his head. "Yeah, that's what they all say. But we always do figure it out. Sooner or later, we do figure it out."

Garth dropped his head. "I don't want to kill anyone." He looked at Jim, pleading in his eyes. "But what can I do?"

Jim reached out for the gun. Garth hesitated, handed it to him. Jim patted the boy on the shoulder. "Good man. Tell me, where did your grandfather keep the pets he had cremated?"

"His dogs? In his bedroom. On the nightstand. And the dresser. And the table. I think some are in the closet. He had a lot of dogs."

Jim smiled. "Yes, I'm sure he did. Tell me, did he ever mention a cat?"

Garth shook his head hard. "No. Grandfather hated cats. They were always digging in his garden and making it their cat box. He never met a cat he liked."

Jim nodded. "So I've heard. Show me where those boxes are, will you, Garth?"

As Jim and Garth walked out into the hallway, Nick joined with them. Garth's eyes widened again when he saw the second man. He looked from Nick to Jim, fear returning to his face. "You had a partner?"

Jim nodded. "Always. We never leave home without them."

Nick reported, "Place is deserted."

"Yeah. But I'll bet it gets busy real fast if a gunshot goes off." The three men…well, two men and a man-child…reached the master bedroom. There were, indeed, cremains boxes placed all around the room. Shelves lined the walls, and boxes lined the shelves. Boxes were stacked on the dresser, on the nightstand…a look in the closet revealed even more.

Nick groaned. "You've got to be kidding me. What did he do, run kennels? No one has this many dogs…and loses them all in one lifetime. No one."

"Exactly what I'm counting on. Look for a small box…no, wait…" Jim stopped. He turned a slow circle and looked around. *You were a chess player. You're still playing, aren't you?* He looked at his partner. "You want to pass a message, but you want it to be so only one person understands it. People know you hated cats. Would you use a cat as a message?"

Nick's eyes half-closed. His jaw worked back and forth. "No. It would be too obvious."

"So, how would you pass it?"

"Didn't Walker figure it out? I thought that's why we're here— to get what she figured out."

Jim studied the boxes again. "Maybe…maybe the cat would lead her here, and she could find the real clue."

Nick rolled his eyes. "Come on, partner. You're trying to make this more than it is. Let's look for the cat and be done with it…"

Jim shook his head. "I want to play a hunch first." Jim turned to Garth. "Will you help him look for a box saying 'Full Disclosure' and is supposed to have a cat inside?"

Garth's eyes grew wide. "You want me to help you?"

"Right. We can use your help. Will you?"

Garth looked at the floor. He looked up. "You think they would kill me?"

"I think they've killed a lot of people, and one or two more would be no stretch if it kept them from being found out."

Garth looked back at the floor, nodded his head. "I'll help you look."

"Great." Jim looked at the overabundance of boxes. He chewed his tongue a moment. "I'll be right back. You two start here."

Nick grunted and started pulling boxes out of the closet. Garth cocked his head at Jim. Jim waved him off. "Help Nick. I want to check something."

Jim took the steps by twos on his way back to the game room. He stopped to stare at the chess set. The board was in play, but only one piece had been captured: the white queen's knight.

Jim stared at the placements. "This isn't a real game. No one has all of their players engaged at the same time…and only one taken." Jim picked up the white knight, turned it over and over in his hands. *What did it mean? What did the old man want Collin to know?*

A thought nudged him. Jim searched the walls for pictures of animals. Dogs and dogs and dogs and a horse and dogs… *A horse?* Jim examined the picture more closely. The mare stood in the typical "here's my prize horse" stance, a handler in white presenting her to the camera. Jim dropped his gaze to the caption. "Chessie…" *That's it. That's the message. That's what we need to find. Not the cat.*

Jim took the steps the same way he'd come. He started to call out to Nick, but caution stopped him. *What if...* Jim walked into one of the spare rooms, looked around, walked back into the bedroom where Garth and Nick were busy pulling boxes out of the closet and placing them on the floor. Both men looked up when Jim came in.

Nick's face told Jim he had no love for the task he'd been given. "You find what you were looking for?"

Jim shook his head. "No. Wild hare. I'm wondering if it would be better to bring the ones you've already checked across the hall. Then you won't go through them twice. It'll save time."

Nick muttered something under his breath. He glared at Jim. "I have to move them twice, so I don't read them twice? Is that your idea of saving time?"

"Yeah. It's how Siskal would have done it. We can stack them in there for now. I'll help you get the first bunch moved." Jim directed Garth, "How about pulling out some more to look through while we move these?"

Garth nodded. Nick picked up four boxes and waited as Jim picked up four more. The two men transported the cremains containers across the hall and into the bedroom, around the corner and out of earshot of Garth. Nick set his load down. "What's going down? Siskal, huh?"

"Okay, sorry to drag Siskal out of the blue. We're not looking for Full Disclosure. We're looking for Chessie. Or for a box with a horse on it. But a horsebox would be obvious, and Mudd didn't want anyone to find it except Walker. I'm playing a hunch." He paused, looked to the room across the hall. "Two hunches. If you find it, don't let on you have. Carry it in here same as any other. But let me know. I'm going to be cataloging these for our report."

Nick smirked. "The report we're not writing?"

"You got it. Let's keep everything calm as possible."

"No problem."

Nick went back to the other bedroom while Jim sat and began writing names in his notebook. *Lord, guide our search. And give me wisdom about Garth.*

Box after box came in with no suspicious markings. Only dogs. Or what looked like dog cremains. Jim doubted whether all these were truly dogs Mudd had lost. Nick had been right. No one lost this many dogs in a lifetime. Not and named them all.

Nick came in the room carrying three boxes, Garth behind him with another two. Nick set his at Jim's feet. "We're coming to the end of the boxes. Maybe half a dozen left. What do you want to do when we get to the last one?"

Nick nudged the bottom one slightly. Barely. "I told you this would be useless. All this looking and nothing to show for it. Waste of a day, you know."

Jim shrugged. "So we spent a day looking at boxes. We've done worse. Could have been dead bodies."

Garth shuddered and set his boxes down. "What d-do you want me t-t-to do?"

"Help Nick go through the last few boxes. See if there's anything actually in them. If they were the ones buried back the farthest, maybe he hid something in them."

Jim looked at Nick and added, "Take your time. Go through them carefully."

Nick let out an exaggerated sigh. "I hear you, bossman. We'll be very, very thorough."

Nick put his arm around Garth's shoulders and led the younger man out of the room. "Come on, partner. We've got ashes to sort."

Jim waited until the two men disappeared out of the bedroom. He pulled out the bottom box Nick had nudged and looked at it. The front had an engraved figure of a Chesapeake Retriever on it. A knight chess piece had been burned into the bottom corner. The nameplate read, "Chessie." The date engraved indicated a time well before Collin had been born. Jim's eyes narrowed. Did it mean anything?

Jim glanced down the hallway to make sure no one saw him. He opened the box. A plastic bag with a notecard and a key sat under the pile of ash material. Jim picked the bag up. *"Timmon's Storage. Locker 15. Your family's legacy. Joy passed it to me to destroy after she died. I chose not to, but have kept it safe. Now I pass it to you to do with as you will. Handle it wisely. It assured my continuing presence in the family. Maybe it will do the same for you. Love, Grandfather Fenton."*

Russo slipped the bag into his pocket and closed the box. He heard a sound in the doorway and looked up.

Garth. The younger man stared at Jim, his eyes narrow and threatening. "What did you find?"

Jim shrugged. "Nothing."

"You put something in your pocket. Give it to me."

Garth had lost his stutter. And his innocence. "Hand it over."

"I don't think so. It belongs to Collin Walker. I'll give it to her."

Garth stepped into the room and pulled a knife from his pocket. "Give me the note."

Jim shook his head. "There's two of us, Garth. You can't take us both out."

"I locked your partner in the closet. He can't help you. And I can throw this faster than you can draw your gun. So hand it over."

"It won't work, Garth. Your father, his brothers…they can't kill every single person who might know their secret. The circle gets wider and wider with each body."

"Doesn't concern me. My job is to get the note."

Jim cocked his head. "How long have you been waiting here, Garth? When's the last time you heard from your father?"

Garth waved the knife at Jim. "Doesn't matter, either."

"It does. You don't know your dad and his brothers are in jail on murder and conspiracy to commit murder charges, do you?"

Garth's eyes narrowed further. "You lie."

"Nope. Truth. We arrested them this morning. Federal agents picked them up and are holding them. Seems contracting a hitman to kill someone across state lines is a federal offense." Jim smiled slightly. "Mert didn't know that when he made a deal to avoid state prosecution by giving names, dates, amounts. The state won't prosecute him, but the feds will."

Jim's voice hardened. "Walk away, Garth. Don't get swallowed by their past. I'm guessing your hands are still clean. Right?"

Garth looked less sure. The knife dropped a little in his hand, no longer directly threatening Jim. The younger man breathed hard. And breathed. And breathed. "No. This is the first thing I got told to do. No why, just do it." He lowered the knife altogether. "I don't even know what this is all about. Why do they hate her? What did she ever do to them?"

Jim stood and crossed the room to ask for the knife. Garth looked at it, much like he had looked at the gun. Jim prayed, *Be right, Lord.* He held out his hand…

Garth lurched forward to stab Jim. Jim caught the man's hand, twisted it. Garth fought against him, kicking and knocking Jim to the floor. Jim took Garth with him. The Winger youth drove his free elbow into Jim's middle. Jim caught the blow but deflected the impact to the side. The two men pitched and rolled and wrestled…

A gunshot sounded from the other room. Jim and Garth froze. Garth let go of the knife and stood, his eyes wide with fear. "The shot! It'll bring the others. We've got to get out of here."

Nick walked into the room, gun drawn, looking for revenge. "Lock me in a closet, kid? Are you serious?"

Russo climbed from the floor. He caught Garth's arm and ordered, "Come with us. Now." He looked at his partner. "Back-up is coming, and you called them with your shot. We need to clear out of here, fast."

Nick looked at the boxes in the room. "What about these? Won't they know—"

Jim shook his head. "Your gunshot told them all they needed to know. Move, now."

Russo shoved Garth ahead of him. The younger man raced with Jim and Nick down the stairs and out the front door to the car. Jim shoved Garth into the back seat, Nick jumped into the shotgun position as Jim slid behind the wheel.

Nick buckled his seatbelt. "Maybe now is the time for the county mounties."

Garth cleared his throat. "My dad…owns the sheriff."

Jim looked in the mirror at him. "Your dad what?"

"Um, owns the sheriff. Or the sheriff owes him big time for something. I don't know which. But the sheriff and my dad are very close."

Nick glared at Garth. "And you're telling us this why? Suddenly you're on our side?"

Garth glared back. "If they did plan on killing me, yeah, I'm on your side. I don't know what all this is about, and I never wanted to. What my dad and my uncles did never concerned me. I know they would meet behind closed doors a lot, but Gareth and I never knew why. And we didn't ask."

Jim jammed the car in drive and pulled around to the back of the house. Garth motioned with his chin. "There's an access road behind the shed. Don't know what it accessed. It winds around then stops. But you could hide a car back there, and no one would know you were around."

Jim's eyes narrowed. "Done it before?"

Garth shrugged. "Maybe once or twice. When I had to sleep off something before hitting Grandfather's door for reunions. Or gatherings. Or whatever they called them. Mostly they served to start a fight with someone. Not my favorite memories, you know?"

Nick snorted. "I'll bet."

Jim found the road Garth referred to. It looked untraveled, which would be a good thing. If his tire tracks didn't leave a trail to follow. He inched his way around stumps and dips and puddles. All the while, a clock counted in his head. *One minute to get the call. One to get a team together. Unless they're on call.* The car threatened to high-center on a particular rut. Jim risked gunning the motor to get over but grimaced at the noise. Were they still too far away to hear?

The road jackknifed and cutback and turned until it came to a stop. It stopped. Period. What could it possibly be for? Did it matter?

Jim left the motor running as he got out of the car to check the view. Garth climbed out as well. "You can't see this from the house. Or the road. Believe me. We're safe."

Jim nodded but withheld comment. The internal clock continued to tick. *Ten minutes from town if they are familiar with the roads. Should be coming over the hill about…*

Now. Two SUVs with lights and sirens came bouncing over the landscape. The cars were marked, but Jim couldn't tell whether they were Sheriff or Rent-a-Cop. He watched as the two vehicles screamed into the gravel driveway, effectively eliminating any tire treads which might have been there. *Score one for the good guys.* Guns drawn, four men ran into the house, not stopping to knock or announce their presence in any way. A fifth person sat in the car, seemingly ignored. *Calling it in?*

After several minutes, two of the "officers" emerged from the front doorway. They walked to the car, yanked the fifth figure out. His arms appeared to be pinned—or handcuffed—behind him. He did not go quietly. He kicked and struggled, dug in his heels, but to no avail. Two against one are not good odds. The officers dragged him over the porch and into the entrance.

Russo heard Garth inhale sharply beside him, holding his breath. Jim waited.

Waited.

Waited. A gunshot echoed from inside Fenton Mudd's residence. Garth turned to Jim, his eyes wide. "What?"

Jim motioned for the younger man to keep watching. Four men came out. Nick cursed under his breath. Garth's eyes grew round, filled with fear. Nick growled, "Always have a back-up plan." He added an unkind description of the men's heritage. Jim ignored him but looked to Garth. "Questions?"

Garth shook his head over and over. "No. No. We need to get out of here before they can find us." His voice cracked with panic.

Jim nodded. The quartet of "lawmen" huddled beside one of the cars. Two walked back to the house. One slid into the car. The fourth holstered his weapon and began talking on the phone.

"Back-up?" Nick looked at Jim for confirmation.

"Doubt it. Forensics. Or Sheriff, to let him know they're done."

"The poor sucker they killed. Wonder what he did?"

Jim shook his head. "Later." He turned on Garth. "You know a way out of here which doesn't involve driving back by the house.

Where is it?"

Garth swallowed hard. "Uh, yeah. Um…back about two turns. There's another access road. Gareth and I covered it with tree limbs and rubbish. We'd come in that way late at night."

"Let's go."

Jim, Garth, and Nick scrambled into the car. Jim idled the car as much as possible to reduce any tell-tale noise they might make. The wind appeared to be blowing toward the hill, further reducing any sounds that might give away their presence. He backed the car to the second turn, carefully negotiating every pothole and stump. He slowed at what looked like another turn. Garth tapped Jim's shoulder. "There. It's there. I'll clear the stuff away."

"Help him, Nick."

"Do I look like a Boy Scout who plays in the—"

"Do it!"

Nick muttered but got out and began helping Garth clear the camouflage from the path. An un-traveled but existent road appeared. Jim eased the car forward, past the point of the entrance. Garth tossed the covering brush back over the road. Nick lugged some fallen branches from the side of the trail to further disguise their passage. Nick and Garth jumped in the car, careful not to pull their doors fully shut. Not yet, anyhow.

Jim looked over his shoulder at Garth. "Where does this come out? What road?"

"It goes over the hill and comes out about a mile from the river."

"How far from the state line?"

"If you follow the road, about six miles."

Jim looked at Nick. Nick pulled out his phone. "On it." He studied the map. "If this is right about where we are, we can take this north another couple miles. It drops us off at Barton Bridge. May take us longer, but we'll stay out of sight. Providing this road exists and doesn't end like the last one did."

Jim looked at Garth. The younger man shook his head. "I don't know. We'll stand out more in the woods than on the main road. How are you going to explain what you're doing there?"

Jim looked at Nick. His partner ducked his head. "Good point. Go with what he said."

Garth settled back in the seat and seemed to breathe a little easier. Jim eased the car forward and began cautiously following the sometimes-delineated, sometimes not path through the trees. No one had to be told to keep an eye out for unwanted witnesses. Every tree trunk became suspicious. Every bush hid spying eyes. Jim forced himself to focus on the path instead of trying to detect and interpret anything which moved. He'd let his partner do that.

And he did it well. "What's that? Oh, wait…a sawed-off tree trunk."

"Did the shrub move? Never mind. It's the wind."

"Do you hear a siren? Guess not. Must be my imagination."

Jim's eyes narrowed, and his knuckles tightened on the steering wheel. "Nick! Knock it off! If you see something and you're sure it's something, tell me. Otherwise, shut up and let me drive."

"Touchy much? This trip wasn't my idea, you know."

"Yeah, yeah, yeah." Jim dodged the car around a particularly deep rut, straightened it out, went nose up over a short incline, nose down over a longer decline, and finally drove clear of the woods. A two-lane highway stretched in front of them. Nick gave an exaggerated exclamation of relief. Jim looked in the mirror to see Garth's face. The younger man looked relieved as well, if a little green around the gills. Jim motioned to the road in front of them. "Left or right? Head us toward the county line. Or the state, whichever is closest."

Garth nodded his head to the left. "That way. East. This is the river road, and you cross out of Ft. Newton county before you reach the Elton Bridge."

Jim pointed the scratched and clawed car east. He left mud tracks as he turned onto the asphalt. No help for it. If anyone wanted to backtrack their route, it would be easy enough. *Lord, blind their eyes.*

It took another ten minutes of driving to reach the turnoff for the bridge. Jim saw the barricades. Nick began cursing. County Sheriff cars effectively blocked any exit to the bridge. Jim let the fleeting thought of an orange and black Charger flying over the river move right on past him. No. He slowed the car to a stop, fifth in line to reach the barriers.

The occupant of the first car stood beside it. A uniformed deputy checked license and registration. Another looked through the car, had the driver pop the trunk. A quick look inside under any blankets or containers and the deputies motioned the driver to resume his journey.

Jim looked at Garth. "Any ideas?"

"I could talk to them. Most the county cops know me. Because of my dad."

Jim noted how quickly Garth had felt it necessary to add the last. Guilty conscience? Or guilty? Either way, Jim needed to make a decision. Now.

"We'll wait until it's our turn. We'll all get out, and we'll know what this is about."

Nick grimaced. "Yeah. It's about some kid being kidnapped by Oakton police. That'll play well in the papers."

Jim ignored his partner. The car directly in front of them cleared inspection and drove off. Jim eased the car forward until the deputy waved him to stop. He pulled up to the man and held out his police identification. He kept his voice friendly. "Hey. What's going on?"

The deputy looked at the ID. He looked in the car and smiled. "Hey, Garth! What are you doing, buddy?"

Garth climbed out of the car at the same time Jim did. The younger man stuttered, "Hey, R-r-ory. What's going on?"

"We locked the county, looking for a fugitive. Sheriff is convinced he's got her surrounded here. Nobody gets in or out without being searched."

Nick raised an eyebrow. "You have a warrant for a search like that?"

Jim overrode him. "Must be dangerous. You said 'she'? A woman?"

Rory nodded. "Yeah, it's what we've been told." He read the description. "Collin Walker. Twenty-six. Five-foot four. Brown hair. Medium build."

"What did she do?"

"Breaking and entering over at the Mudd place."

Nick scowled. "All this for breaking and entering? You must—"

Jim cut his partner off. "What did she take that calls for locking a county?"

Rory shook his head. "She murdered her partner in crime. Shot him in the back of the head. I don't have any love for burglars, but that's cold by any standard."

Jim nodded. "I see. Well, there's the car, and there's nothing in the trunk except a wooden box with the cremains of my dog, Chessie."

Rory's face screwed up, and he gave Jim a sidelong look. "Your what?"

"Cremains of my dog. Lost him a month ago. I like to take him out for a ride in the countryside every now and then."

Rory's eyes widened, and he took a slight step backward. "Uh…sure. Okay." He looked at Garth. "You okay, bro?"

Garth dipped his head to get the words out. "Yeah." He jerked his head toward Jim, lowered his voice. "Humor him. We do. C-c-cousins on my mom's side. Once r-r-emoved."

"Uh-huh. I see. Well, we'll not bother Chessie any more than we have to."

Jim smiled. "Thank you."

Rory continued to eye Jim sideways as the deputy walked around the car, looked in the trunk, pulled the blankets back, saw the box, threw the blanket back on top of Chessie. He returned to the front of the car. "You're good to go." He looked pointedly at Garth. "You take care, you hear?"

Garth smiled. "He's harmless. Thanks, R-r-ory."

Nick and Garth climbed back into the car. Jim took the time to walk to the trunk, carefully tuck the blanket around the box and pat it. He ignored the looks of ridicule and sympathy from the County Deputies, climbed into the driver's seat, closed his door, and said, "Thanks again, gentlemen."

The barricades were moved, and Jim turned right onto the Elton Bridge. Halfway across the river, they passed the sign welcoming them into Ohio. Only then did Nick let out his breath and begin laughing. He straightened to mimic Jim, "'I like to take him out in the countryside…' He nearly lost it there!"

Jim ducked his head. "Whatever works." He looked in the mirror at Garth. "Your stutter. You seem to pull it out at strategic times. What does the real Garth Winger sound like?"

Garth stared out the side window. "The now-Garth talks plain. As a kid, I stuttered. My dad wanted me to keep doing it. He said other people think kids who stutter are innocent or a little dumb. I'd have an advantage. I kept it to please him." Garth turned to look at Jim. "I worked hard to get over it. But it still comes in handy at times. Worked with you, right?"

Jim thought a moment. "Yes and no. I like to give people the benefit of the doubt. But I keep a close watch from then on."

Garth shrugged. "Whatever." He gazed out the side window again. "Where are we going after we get to Oakton? Am I under arrest or something?"

"Should you be?"

"No." Garth responded with defiance. He immediately tempered it. "I don't think so, anyhow. Other than threaten you and lock him in the closet, I haven't done anything wrong."

Nick growled. "Locking me in a closet is assault on an officer. That should get you some jail time."

Jim shook his head. "We were out of our jurisdiction. Let it go." He looked in the mirror at Garth. "I'm going to the hospital to check on Ms. Walker. Nick will escort you to see your father if you wish. He's in custody at the federal jail. Then, we'll arrange for you to get back to Ft. Newton."

"I don't want to see my dad. He's not going to like me helping you."

"Fine. You can come with us to the hospital. We'll make the arrangements from there."

* * *

Erin rolled his chair back and forth across the small hospital room, pacing after his own manner. Jeff wanted to join him but feared a collision would ensue. Better he sit and hold his worry inside. Roll it over to Jesus. Let the Lord carry it.

Erin drummed the arm of his chair with his fingers. "How long has it been now?"

"Five minutes longer than the last time you asked."

"What is taking them so long? How long does it take to do an MRI? If they had gotten it right on Tuesday and done it with contrast the way your uncle wanted, we wouldn't be wasting time repeating it. This is ridiculous." Erin threw his hands in the air.

Jeff agreed but only on the inside. "It depends on how thorough they need to be. How many angles and slices of the brain the doctor wants."

Erin whirled in the chair. "I could have dissected her whole brain by now."

"True, but would your patient be alive to tell about it?" The gowned figure of Dr. Rich McMannon followed his question into the room. "Collin will be back here in a few minutes. The procedure took a little longer than we anticipated."

Jeff tried to keep the snap out of his voice. "Why?"

McMannon settled into a chair. "She had one of her attacks while we were scanning. Had to stop what we were doing to help her."

Jeff's heart leaped into his throat. He swallowed hard. "Is she—"

"Alive? Of course. Okay? Yes." McMannon nodded. "This film gives us a better a roadmap for the surgery."

Jeff let out a breath he didn't know he held. "There is a tumor?"

"When Collin is back here and settled in comfortably, I will discuss it with her. If she chooses to allow the two of you in on the discussions will be up to her." He eyed Jeff. "Future fiancé or not, this still constitutes doctor-patient privilege."

Erin snapped, "I'm next of kin. I get to be in on it."

"Only if she allows it. She's an adult."

Collin's voice sounded from the hallway. "I wouldn't bet on it." A gurney rolled into the room accompanied by a nurse and an attendant pushing the bed with Collin riding in it. She looked pale, more pale than when she had left to go for the MRI. Her eyes drooped. Her lips were pursed.

The attendant and the nurse plugged the bed and Collin into all the necessary ports and places then left. Jeff leaned in and kissed Collin lightly on the top of her head. He waited for her "aim," but she didn't say it. *She's hurting bad. She must know something.*

Dr. McMannon leaned toward the bed and asked, "Are you up to talking about what we found?"

Jeff watched Collin take several deep breaths and let them out very slowly. "Sure, why not. I'm obviously not going anywhere until we do."

Jeff squeezed her hand. "I'm here, lady. We'll make it through this."

Erin moved as close as he could get to her side. "I'm here, too, Cane. We can do this."

Collin's eyes shone only a moment. She gave a tired chuckle. "Good. You two carry it. I'm done with this."

McMannon asked, "You want to allow these two in on the discussion?"

Collin looked from man to man. "I have the feeling they're going to play large parts in my life going forward, so yeah, they may as well hear it." She smiled at Jeff and Erin. "Since you're both so willing to carry it for me. You should know what it is."

Jeff lay his head on top of hers for a moment, then stood back to look at McMannon. Collin asked, "What did you find?"

McMannon pulled out a glossy paper with the image of the anatomy of a human brain. "Remember anything from biology class?"

"I remember it wasn't my favorite class. Or my favorite teacher."

McMannon took a marker and pointed to the brain. "This is your brain."

Collin quipped, "Always wondered where it went." Erin frowned at her.

McMannon ignored her. "These are the major arteries feeding blood to the brain."

"I remember those. But don't ask me to tell you the names."

Jeff scowled. "Collin…"

"Alright, alright. I'm listening."

"They are wrapped around the brain stem. The brain stem is the conduit through which most the electrical nerve signals pass to and from the brain."

Collin nodded. "Gotcha. So what's wrong with my brain?"

McMannon drew a mass of circles and squiggles around the stem. "The mass you have is tangled in and around the brain stem…and the arteries feeding it. Your 'attacks' happen when you move, and the mass puts pressure on the nerves in your spine."

Collin's face took on a determined look. Her eyes narrowed, returned to normal. She pursed her lips, relaxed them. She drew in a deep breath, let it out slowly. "I see. Well, that is a problem. But one you can fix, right? You do this for a living. It's why people pay you the big bucks." She smiled weakly.

McMannon's voice became soft. "Collin, the mass is putting pressure on the vertebral artery. It's essentially creating an aneurysm. Removing the mass without disturbing the aneurysm until we can address it will be difficult."

Erin jumped in. "Can you fix it, though? And she'll live? And be okay?"

McMannon looked at Collin, at Jeff. "Given enough time, yes. In a perfect world. Which is what I always anticipate. However, the hospital and my insurance prefer I give you the less-than-perfect outcomes. The first, of which is death."

Collin dropped her eyes. Jeff ached for her, longing to know what she thought, what she had running in her brain. *How many voices are screaming at you right now?*

McMannon went on. "There are the usual complications of a stroke, depending on how massive the bleed is, and how long it would take us to get it stopped. Your motor skills could be impaired." He looked closely at Collin, but she stared at a spot somewhere between the foot of the bed and the floor. At least it's where her eyes were pointed. What she focused on, Jeff had no idea.

McMannon reached out and touched Collin's arm. She did not look at him, even then. Her voice came out mechanical. "Go on."

The neurosurgeon looked at Jeff, his eyes questioning. Jeff nodded. The older man continued. "The imperfect outcomes are as varied as you like to imagine them. Anything and everything would be on the table." Again he touched Collin's arm. "The alternative is certain death. We can't fix the aneurysm without removing the mass. Left untreated, you will continue to have the attacks until the artery blows out for good."

Erin shook his head. "No. There's got to be something else you can do. What about radiation? Chemo? Something to shrink the tumor? Can't you start small and follow it with surgery? Won't it help?"

"If she had the time, it might. But you'd be playing a game I don't think you can win. My opinion is we go in, now, today. We remove the mass, we fix the aneurysm, and you live to be Mrs. Jeffery Farrell."

Collin still did not look at the doctor. McMannon looked at Jeff for support. Jeff put his hand on Collin's shoulder and squeezed it. He kept his voice low as he addressed the neurosurgeon. "Give her a few minutes. This is a lot to grasp."

McMannon stood and headed out. He looked back before leaving and said, "I'll assemble the team. We'll start as soon as you give me the okay."

He exited stage back. The door closed.

* * *

Collin drew in a deep breath, raised her head back toward the ceiling, and closed her eyes. She breathed slowly and carefully for several moments. She dropped her head back to level, looked at Jeff and Erin. "Well, that was fun."

She heard Jeff and Erin both give out audible sighs. She squeezed Jeff's hand, reached out to touch Erin's arm. "I'm okay, both of you. I needed time to absorb it. I didn't check out. I heard every word." *Every last word...*

Collin breathed in and out again. "Opinions?" She looked to her brother. "A-One?"

Erin snuck a quick look at Jeff. "I'm the interloper here. You need to decide this—"

"I didn't say decide for me. I asked your opinion." Collin tried to keep the frustration out of her voice. She partially succeeded. But only partially. She backed it down a notch. "If it were you. If you were in my position, would you have the surgery? First question. Second, if your wife-to-be or someone you cared about was in my place, what would you advise?"

Erin's eyes reflected deep pain. "Cane, you are in that place. I care very much about you. You know, right?"

Collin shook her head. "I'm sorry, A-One. I didn't think that one through. I know you love me." She closed her eyes, sucked on her bottom lip. "What would you advise me to do? Third question..."

Erin groaned. "I got interrogated last night by Detective Russo. Now you?"

Collin laughed. "No, I promise. Last question." She closed her eyes again. "What would you want me to do?" She opened her eyes, pursed her lips, and waited.

Erin looked at the floor. His voice softened. "Does he have to answer the same questions?"

Collin looked at Jeff. "Yes. I need to know."

"Let him go first."

Collin breathed in and out again. "It's not complicated. I want your opinions. Nothing says I'm going to follow them. But I want to hear them. Now." She looked at the door. "McMannon is waiting.

Jeff, go."

She watched him look up, look down, look up again… His voice cracked. "If it were me and I had people who loved me and wanted—"

Collin cut him off. "Forget the other people. You by yourself. What would you do?"

He paused a long time. "I'd have the surgery."

"Honest answer?"

He nodded. "Honest answer."

Collin turned to her brother. "A-One?"

He shook his head. "No. But only because I'm in this chair, and it's miserable as it is. For me, I'd take my chances. And hope it went fast."

Collin felt her throat tighten. She closed her eyes against the tears. "I'm sorry. I didn't think about that."

Erin shrugged. "Eh… I live with it." His voice hardened. "But would I advise you to have it? Absolutely. You and Jeff have your whole lives ahead of you."

Jeff offered quietly, "You're part of our lives, Erin. Or you will be. If you want."

Collin nodded to her brother. He ducked his head. Collin asked, "Last question?"

Erin stared her full in the face. "Have the surgery. That's what I want you to do."

Collin turned to Jeff. "You?"

"I would advise you to have the surgery. I am advising you to have the surgery. I want you to have the surgery." His voice shook. "I love you, Collin. I'm selfish. I want you with me here, not only in Heaven. I want us to grow old and fat and crotchety together. Please."

Collin nodded slowly. She stared at the ceiling. "What do You want me to do?"

No voice spoke. The ceiling didn't disappear and rainbows show instead. All there was, was peace. Overwhelming, all-surrounding, all whatever else she wanted to call it, peace. Collin nodded. She looked at Jeff, at her brother. "Call Dr. McMannon back in. I've got my decision."

Jeff's eyes held hers. "And?"

"And yes. I'll do it. I'll have the surgery, and you'll have the consequences."

Jeff leaned in and kissed her on the lips. Properly. He broke after a moment. "I'll go get Rich."

Collin sighed as Jeff left the room. Erin turned to Collin. "You got a good one, sis."

"Yeah. Better than I deserve."

Erin snapped at her. "Do not say that. Never. You hear me? You will not echo Robert Winger ever. Never again."

Collin's eyes widened in surprise. Erin continued, "I heard him all my life. I know you did, too. Well, he was wrong. He's still wrong. You're worth everything you get and more." Erin lost his fire and fumbled to explain his outburst. "I listened to Jeff for two months. He talked about you. He talked about God. He talked about…everything. He can talk." Collin smiled. Erin chuckled. "Yeah, I know. I can carry a conversation myself."

"Always could."

"Right. Back to Jeff. Anyhow, he talked about how the creator of something is the only one who gets to decide if a thing has value or not. If it's valuable to him, it's all that matters."

Collin nodded. Erin shifted around in his chair. "If God is the creator—our creator—then only God decides what we're worth. If God sent His Son to die for us, He must think we're worth something important."

Collin felt a sharp pain behind her right eye. She clamped her teeth together against the pain and nodded to Erin to continue. Her brother shifted around again, as if uncomfortable. Either the topic or the chair bothered him. Collin forced herself to keep her voice even and level. "Go on, A-One."

"That's it. I mean, Jeff had a lot of other things to say. And I'm not saying I buy it all, either. But he had some good points. He isn't going to argue me into believing what you two do. But the way he lives his life…" Erin trailed off, shook his head. "He's the real deal, Cane. I want to be like him when I grow up."

The pain escalated, shooting deep into her brain. Collin gasped, and her neck arched back with the agony. She could hear Erin's frantic questions, "Cane? Cane? What's happening? What's wrong?"

She couldn't answer. She focused all of her energy on her head not blowing apart. Deep inside, she knew it would be a losing battle.

A part of her heard Erin yelling, "Doctor! We need a doctor! Help her!" Another part didn't care. She'd waited too long. The darkness would come, and this time, there would be no light to follow. Collin felt herself falling…falling…falling… The darkness claimed her.

* * *

Jim Russo walked into the surgery waiting room. He saw Erin rolling back and forth, moving across as much of the floor as he could without running over anyone. Jeff sat by the doorway to the operating room, head down, his mouth moving with silent prayers. Beside him sat a young man, a teenager, Jim didn't recognize. He, too, had his head down. The elder Mr. and Mrs. Farrell sat together, holding hands, heads also bowed. Jim hesitated to enter, not wanting to intrude or disturb the prayers being offered. He stood at the entrance, unsure whether to stay or leave.

Erin decided for him. The younger man spun around. His eyes caught Jim's. He jerked his head to the side, motioning for Jim to come in. Erin moved to an area a little away from the Farrells. Jim walked softly over to Erin and sat in one of the more rigid chairs. Garth followed Jim, sitting as well.

Erin's eyes narrowed at the sight of Garth, but he said nothing to his cousin. He addressed Jim in low tones. "Did you find anything besides him?"

Jim nodded. "I did. It wasn't the cat. Fenton used the cat as a means to get Collin to the house where he hid the real clue."

Erin nodded. "Sounds like Grandfather. So did you find the real clue? Do you know what all this is about?"

Jim shook his head. "Yes and no. Yes, I found the real clue. It's another clue, but possibly the final one." Jim reached into his pocket and pulled out the key and the note. He handed the note to Erin.

The younger man read it, looked at Jim. His eyes darted back and forth as if trying to understand what it all meant. Finally, he nodded curtly. "So, this is where it all comes together, huh?"

"So the note says."

"Why didn't you go get whatever it is?"

Jim lowered his voice. "If keeping it hidden required the killing of multiple lives, I'm guessing it's something the police will want to know about. If I picked it up, I'd be obligated to obtain a warrant and turn it all over to the local authorities. I think Fenton wanted Collin to decide what to do with it. She could destroy it, she could turn it over to the authorities, or…"

Jim trailed off. Erin looked at him. He opened his hand and waved it. "Or what?"

"Or maybe Fenton wanted to give Collin the chance to use the evidence for her own benefit."

Erin cocked his head and looked at the floor. He looked back, his eyes widening. "Blackmail? Did he think Collin would blackmail her father?"

Jim shrugged. "I'm speculating. Maybe Fenton used the evidence to blackmail the Winger men into allowing him to remain as part of the family. Maybe it goes back even further... I don't know. And I may be totally off the mark." He opened his hands to indicate he didn't know anything for certain.

Erin rolled the key around in his hand, staring at it. "So, this is the answer to it all." He looked at Jim. "I'll go get it. Whatever it is. I don't want anything hanging over my sister's head anymore." He looked at the door to the operating room. His voice softened. "She's going to have a hard time of it as it is. She doesn't need this, too."

Jim hesitated. "Did something happen? This wasn't the scheduled surgery she planned?"

Erin looked at the floor. "No. Yes. But no. She…" Erin's voice caught. "She blew an artery before they were even ready." He looked at Jim. "Dr. McMannon doesn't know how much damage it did. They have to remove the mass to repair the artery…" Erin swallowed hard. "I'm next of kin. I signed the papers. She might not…"

Erin choked. He dropped his head. Jim saw the tears in the man's eyes. "If she makes it through the surgery, there might not be much…" Erin stopped. "She might not be..." He tossed his head in defiance. "She is going to make it through this. I know she will." He looked at Jim, his eyes glaring. "She will."

Jim nodded. "She's a fighter. She's come through a lot."

Erin lost his defiance. He sank back into his chair. "Yeah." He looked at Garth but addressed Jim. "Where did he come into the picture?"

"He was at the house when we got there. He helped us find the real clue." Jim left unsaid any other details. Erin didn't need to know. Not right now.

Erin's eyes scanned Garth up and down. Garth kept his eyes fixed on Erin's. At last, Erin nodded curtly. "Fine." He looked back at Jim. "Dr. McMannon said the surgery would take a long time. Six, seven hours or more. I'll go get whatever this is and bring it back." He looked at the Farrells and added softly, "At least they can pray for her." Erin motioned toward Jeff. "He needs to stay here."

Garth offered, "Can I g-g-o with you?"

Erin snarled. "Drop the stutter. I figured out your dodge years ago."

Garth straightened. He and Erin locked eyes. Jim watched the two cousins, knowing they would have to work this out between them.

At length, both men dropped their gaze. Erin looked at Jim. "I'll take him with me. Let Jeff know where I'm going, and I'll be back as soon as I can. Tell him to call me…if…if he hears anything."

"I'll tell him." Jim stuck out his hand. "You're a good man, Erin." He hesitated. "This has become a federal case, remember. If you decide to turn the evidence over to someone in Ft. Newton, I'd suggest you turn it over to the feds. Not to the sheriff."

Erin looked at Jim sideways. Jim nodded. Erin nodded in return. "Thanks. I'll…I'll let you know what I find. And what I decide to do with it."

"Do it first, then tell me." Jim hesitated. "I've got some friends in Ft. Newton. You might want to look them up. Or give them a call before you get there. Maybe they can help you with anything you might need."

Erin nodded. "I'll do it." He looked at Garth. "Come on, Winger. I've got to make some arrangements. Like, rent a car. Let's get out of here." The two younger men moved quietly out of the room. Jim took a seat in the corner, closed his eyes, and began lifting one more voice to plead for Collin's recovery. But only in His will. At the end of it all, ever and always His will be done.

* * *

Despite the rental company's prohibition of drivers under the age of 25, Erin let Garth drive the 90 miles back to Ft. Newton. It would give Erin time to think, to plan, to imagine, to worry… *Cancel that. No worrying. Jeff insists she's in God's hands. It has to mean something. God has to mean something, right?*

Erin didn't expect an answer to his musings. God was an abstract, a construct. Or so Erin believed. But… *Wouldn't it be good to have a God in your corner? Someone who would listen? And could do something for you?*

Erin looked at his GPS. "Don't take the cutoff. You have to head to downtown."

Garth grumbled. "It would be easier if you told me where we were going."

"If I trusted you, I would. But I don't. You get turn by turn instructions."

Garth glared at Erin. "Detective Russo trusted me. I helped him, remember? He said so."

"Of course. He likes to see the best in people. I don't. I'm a Winger. So are you. No trust until you prove it to me."

"What do you think I'm going to do? Steal the clue, take off with it. And what? Take it to my dad? He's in jail."

"So is mine. And Uncle Rupert. So that says something big happened. Something they want never to see the light of day. What would be bad enough you have people killed to hide it? And after 20, maybe 30 years."

Garth considered it a moment. "I don't know."

"Speculate. We've got time." Erin waited to see how his cousin would answer. And where his loyalties might lie.

Erin watched Garth's eyes. Feet and eyes. Those were the important things to watch. And Garth's were narrowing, pitching side to side, looking up, occasionally glancing at the road to make sure the car stayed between the white lines…

After five minutes, Garth looked at Erin. "You murder to cover a murder. That's the only thing I can come up with."

"All I came up with, too. And it had to involve all three of them. Otherwise, one ignores the code of silence and spills it to the cops to get out from under. And takes control of the family."

Garth's eyes narrowed again. "Makes sense. But none of them did. No one found out about it…"

"Someone did. Grandfather had the evidence. And Grandmother before him."

Erin stopped to consider the implications of his statement. He pulled the notecard out of his jacket pocket and read it again. *"Joy gave it to me to destroy…assured my continuing presence…"*

"What have you got?"

"Fenton's note to my sister." Erin mulled it over and over. "Maybe…but how…how did the police not get involved?" He looked at Garth. "County this small, how does a murder happen the sheriff doesn't know about?"

After a moment, Erin's cousin said, "My dad always said he owns the sheriff. He's paid enough for Sheriff Dalton over the years to have bought three sheriffs. Dalton has been in office since before I was born."

Erin snorted. "Yeah, I know. We campaign for him every time someone is fool enough to challenge him. Father loves to drag me out in the public eye so people can see how concerned the sheriff is for the weak and infirm." Erin's fists tightened. *No anger. Anger clouds your reason. Save it for revenge later. Wait. What…*

"Did you say your father owned the sheriff?"

"Sort of. I mean, if he's paid him all those years, he must own him, right?"

"Maybe. Or maybe they pay him because he has something on them. Like, he knows about the murder and has kept it covered in exchange for 'favors' and campaign 'contributions' and the like…"

Garth's eyes narrowed. "Could fit."

"Okay, so our fathers murdered someone. The sheriff knew about it. Their mother knew about it. And kept the incident…" Erin's eyes widened. "The evidence hidden. That must be what it is. Grandmother had the evidence. She wanted it destroyed when she died."

"Why didn't she destroy it herself?"

Erin's eyes narrowed. "How well do you know your father? Worse, my father? Power and money. How did Grandmother keep control of the family after Grandfather Jeremiah died? She had evidence of the crime her sons had committed. And most likely threatened to expose them if they made a move against her."

Garth's eyes jumped around in his head again. Erin interrupted his processing with a tap on his arm. "Take the next turnoff."

Garth obeyed. "Now, which way?"

"Left. Toward downtown. Turn right on Hedison."

Garth squinted at Erin. "Where is this place?"

"We're not taking a straight route. You'll know when we get there."

His cousin rolled his eyes but made the turns as Erin directed. As he did, he ventured a thought. "So Grandmother knew about this and kept it hidden. Grandfather Mudd took the box, and he blackmailed the family so he could stay part of it. Now he's giving it to Caitlin… Collin… so she can what, blackmail the family, too? Is that what they're afraid of, and why they've been trying to have her killed?"

"No. Yes. Yes, he gave it to my sister. No, they're not afraid she'll blackmail them. They're afraid she'll turn them in. Because they abandoned her, lied to her, shut her out…turned her into…"

Erin dropped his head as he imagined all the things his sister may have done to survive. Tears stung his eyes. He shook them off angrily. "You tell me. What if they'd done all that to you? Thrown you out when you were fourteen and left you basically to die? What would you do if you had the evidence?"

Garth fell silent. Erin motioned for a left turn, a right, another right…still nothing from his cousin. Erin waited. Garth shrugged. "I don't know. This is all guesswork. Maybe it's nothing. Maybe Dad and the others are innocent. Your sister could have crossed someone on her own. Maybe she cheated a dealer. Maybe she works for some syndicate…"

Erin cut him off, his voice dangerous. "My sister did nothing to bring this on herself."

"How do you know? You haven't seen her in twelve years."

"I know because your dad and my father and Uncle Rupert set me in Oakton to spy on her. They wanted to know where she lived, who she lived with. Where she worked. Who she hung out with. What she did on weekends. Her work schedule. The route she drove to the office. What her car looked like." Erin felt the fire burning in his gut. His hands shook. He made them into fists to keep them from shaking. "And I did everything they asked for. Except I wouldn't tell them where she was hiding after I found out about the third attempt on her life." He smiled without mirth. "For which I got beaten." He glared at Garth. "And I'm proud of it."

Garth looked down but kept his eyes on the road. "Still doesn't prove anything."

Erin nodded. "You're right, it doesn't. But whatever Grandfather Fenton is hiding may. We'll know in about ten minutes. Turn right at the next light. Go half a mile—three traffic lights—turn left. Pull over in front of the pawnshop."

Garth followed the directions without question. Erin let his cousin stew in his juices for the remainder of the trip. *Give him time to consider his options. And decide what he's going to do. We'll see which side he picks.*

Garth pulled the rental to a stop in front of the pawnshop as Erin directed. Erin had him pull out Erin's wheelchair and set it so Erin could transfer into it. Garth stepped back to give Erin room and took a quick survey around the street. He looked back at Erin. "So, where is this stuff or thing or whatever hidden? None of these look like they keep old junk. Except the pawnshop. And they don't keep things over thirty days, usually."

Erin debated a moment, motioned across the street. "Over there. The luggage store."

"Luggage?" Garth's voice rose in disbelief. "He hid stuff at a luggage store?"

"There are storage lockers in the back. Come on."

Erin checked for traffic, crossed the street. Garth did not try to assist him. *Good thing.*

Inside the store, at the front counter, a gentleman expressed his extreme displeasure with the establishment's return policy in no uncertain terms, at a volume sure to wake the dead. A red-faced woman stood slightly behind the man, wringing her hands and giving the beleaguered clerk an embarrassed look. Erin and Garth passed through the store with its tired, but well-kept aisles, past the valises and trunks and train cases, past vintage hard-shell suitcases big enough to hold a small child…

At the rear of the store, a door marked, "No admittance" stood open. Erin ignored the sign and went in. No alarms sounded. Garth hesitated, followed Erin in. Erin negotiated his way around jumbled stacks of boxes to reach yet another doorway marked, "No admittance." Erin took the key from his jacket pocket and slipped it into the doorway. It opened without protest. Erin drew in a deep breath and pushed inside.

Row upon row of lockers lined the walls. Erin searched for the one marked, "15." One of the larger ones, it sat on an upper shelf.

Great. Wonderful. Fantastic.

He quit the internal grumbling and looked at Garth. "This one. Open it, please. Don't take anything out. Open it. Stand back."

Garth took the key, tight-lipped. He unlocked the unit and stood back as he'd been told. Erin looked in the cabinet.

A cardboard box labeled "evidence," tightly wrapped in "evidence" tape. A signature written across it: *Sheriff Warren Dalton.* Written across it many times. On the side, an inventory transcribed in permanent marker: *Forensic Analysis: blood samples, hair fibers, fingerprints...*

Erin looked at the name listed as the case file. His whole being went still. Everything around him disappeared. Nothing was real except the name. The victim. The victim: *Jeremiah Winger.* His father's father. They killed their own father.

A small file folder lodged beside the box. Erin's hands trembled as he picked it up and opened it.

A note. Several notes. Erin touched each one gingerly as he scanned the contents. Three pages were inscribed with the same heading: *Confession.* Three different handwritings. A sheet of official County Sheriff letterhead with notes scrawled across it, and Sheriff Dalton's signature at the bottom. Stationary with an embellished "W" for a header. His grandmother's calligraphy.

Erin sat back and stared at the file. His eyes scanned the pages; his brain processed the symbols into words into sentences into comprehension. But nothing registered with his emotion. Nothing.

Jeremiah Winger. They killed their own father.

Jeremiah Winger. Erin stared at the name. He closed his eyes and bowed his head.

Garth cleared his throat. "What is it? What's in there?"

Erin's voice shattered. "Evidence. The evidence. Who they killed. It's all here."

"What do you mean? What evidence?" Garth snapped. "Who did they kill? How do they know?"

Erin spun on his cousin. "Their father. They killed their father."

Garth grabbed at the folder, but Erin stuffed it back into the locker. "No."

The younger man shoved Erin aside, grabbing his chair and throwing him to the ground. Erin grabbed at Garth's legs. Garth lashed out, hacking at Erin. He grabbed the box, pulled it from the locker.

"Freeze! Right there. Federal agents. Don't move."

Garth froze.

"Put the box back in the locker. Slowly."

The enraged customer from the front of the store held a gun leveled at Garth. The erstwhile embarrassed female customer stood behind the agent, her gun also out and leveled.

Garth slid the container back into its place. He put his hands shoulder high to show he wasn't armed. "What's wrong?"

"Move back." The female agent helped Erin back into his chair, dusting him off and straightening his jacket. "Are you okay?"

"I am so tired of being knocked around by thugs." Erin drew in a deep breath. "I think I'm fine." He hesitated. "My right foot hurts."

"You probably landed on it wrong."

"No, you don't understand. I'm paralyzed from the waist down. But my foot hurts." Erin looked at the woman, his eyes wide. "I shouldn't feel anything there. I shouldn't. Why am I feeling it?"

The officer shrugged. "I don't know. You should have a doctor check you out. In the meantime…" She turned to Garth.

Garth's eyes widened to appear innocent. "What's wrong? Did I do something?"

Erin snarled, "Drop it, Garth. They're not going to fall for it."

Garth switched tactics. He pleaded, "Please. Let me have the box. I have to have it. I have to give it to my dad." Desperation colored the younger man's entreaty. "You don't understand. My girlfriend…she's pregnant. Our baby. My dad has her hidden away. Somewhere. He won't tell me where until I bring him the box. Please. You can have it after I show it to him. I swear. But let me have it first. I swear. I swear."

Erin rolled his eyes, rolled his neck. Pain. Pain in his ankle. Pain seeping up his leg. Pain…pain he shouldn't be feeling. But he did. He wanted to laugh and shout and cry all at the same time. Except he had to deal with the police. And his cousin.

He gritted his teeth and nodded to the two federal agents. "Thank you. I appreciate you coming here." He looked at the box and the files. *Revenge. Retribution. Judgment.*

Mercy. Compassion. Forgiveness.

Erin struggled with the unfamiliar voice inside. *They deserve to die. What they did to Cane…and their own father… Cane would turn it over. I know she would.*

Yes, but not for revenge. For justice. And with forgiveness.

Forgiveness? After what they did to her?

"They?" Which "they?" The 'they' you were part of?

Erin hushed the internal debate. Not the time, not the place, for a discussion. First, Garth had to be dealt with.

Agent Ross asked, "What do you think of his story? Is there a pregnant girlfriend?"

Erin shook his head. "Never mentioned her before. Not once. My father never mentioned another person as part of any plan he had to recover the box."

Garth jumped in. "Your father didn't know everything. My dad wanted to keep it a secret, in case your father's ideas went south. Then he would use her for leverage against Collin to get control of the family finances. Collin would never let an innocent girl die, right? My dad would take control of the family finances. He hates your dad for taking over—"

Erin interrupted what would be a litany of grievances. "Yeah, yeah. They all hate each other. They're all jealous, and they're all money-hungry fatherless sons." Erin motioned to Agent Ross. "I don't believe him. He's never said a word about a girlfriend, especially a pregnant one. You decide what to do with him. I'm done with this family."

Agent Peters took hold of Garth's arm. Agent Ross nodded towards the locker. "You know you'll have to surrender it. All of it."

Erin sighed. "I know. I knew coming in here. Which is why I called you after Jim Russo gave me your names to set this up. I didn't know exactly what we would find, but I had a suspicion it would go bad; however, it played out." Erin fingered the folder with the letters and confessions. "You think we could get copies of these? So we know why?"

Ross and Peters put their heads together for a moment. Ross nodded. "Timmons has a copier. I'll burn them off for you. We keep the originals."

"Thanks." Erin's foot throbbed. Welcome as any sensation might be, the pain continued to radiate up his leg. He breathed slow, breathed again, breathed again... He looked to Agent Peters. "Ma'am, I'm ready to get back to Oakton. My sister is still in surgery. I should be there when...when she...wakes up." No other possibility. She would wake up. Period. She would. *Please? If you're there, if you're real, if you love her the way Jeff says, please make her okay. I'd promise you everything, anything, if I thought it would make a difference. But what do you offer a god?*

No answer came. Erin watched as the agents removed the box from the locker. He signed a custody statement indicating he was the legal owner of the box or the owner's designated representative, and he voluntarily surrendered it to Agents Ross and Peters. Any contents of the box not directly related to the murder of Jeremiah Winger would be returned after the trial, when and if one were brought.

Agent Ross made copies of the papers in the folder. He made sure to handle the pages with gloves so as not to contaminate any evidence which might remain. Erin folded the copies, stuffed them in his jacket pocket. They would make interesting reading on the way home. Given the option, he asked for a driver to return him and his rental car to Oakton and "his own" physician to look after his ankle. Erin swore he would make a statement to the Feds in Ohio after his sister got out of surgery. The agents agreed and graciously supplied.

Erin rode in the back seat so he could read the documents without anyone watching. Or asking questions. No one did. No one interrupted. No one took him out of his thoughts. No one rescued him from the nightmare reality of having proof his father and his uncles plotted and executed their father's murder. His grandmother knew about it. Condoned it. Encouraged it, even.

Why?

Because Jeremiah Winger planned on dissolving the family business. Giving the money to charity. Leading a simple life. He'd found Jesus. He wanted to obey the Lord, sell all he had, and follow Him. A new start. His family would be happy. No more fights over who had control, and of how much. No, they would live in harmony at last. So he believed, and so he died. Murdered in his bed by his sons.

Erin shuddered. *You knew all this, didn't you, God? You knew this would happen, and you let it. What kind of God does that?*

Arrangements were made with Sheriff Dalton to keep the affair private. Arrangements which involved a great deal of money and influence being pledged to future election plans. The funeral director would be told only the case would be investigated, but could never be discussed. More money changed hands.

Grandmother Joy insisted her sons write everything. Confessions. Lest they think she, too, would prove to be a detriment to their futures, Sheriff Dalton collected evidence as if for an actual case. Joy promised to have the evidence destroyed at her demise…

Erin sat back in the seat. He stared out the window without seeing the countryside. *Why, God? Why didn't you stop it? If Grandfather Jeremiah wanted to follow you, why let his sons get away with murder? It makes no sense.*

Jeff always told Trey you seldom got an answer to the "why" question. God knew. Man didn't. Why some things happen aren't as important as, "what are you going to do about it?" In Jeff's world, you either trust God, or you don't. *How do you trust a god who lets murderers get away with it?*

Did they? Did they get away with it?

Erin turned from the window. He looked at the floor of the car to continue his musings. *Depends on what 'getting away with it' means, I guess. They stayed with Grandmother their whole lives so they could get the money. Which they still don't have. They're always looking over their shoulders, wondering who will crack and tell the truth, or if they'll be found out. I bet they were relieved when Grandmother Joy died.*

Except…

Except Fenton didn't destroy the box. He kept it. Used it to keep control of things. And kept it hidden so if he met an untimely demise, it would be turned over to the police, right?

Erin nodded to himself. *Yeah, I see how it would make someone bitter and hard and always on edge. Like Father.*

Would you have been born if Jeremiah had lived?

Humm. That hadn't occurred to him. Erin tapped his hand on the door armrest. *Fine, I'll give you one. We probably wouldn't be having this discussion if things were different. So why isn't the question. Maybe I can see how you used this…some good came from it. Cane and me. Are we enough good to make it cost a man's life? Exchange one life for another?*

Jeff's words echoed in Erin's head. *"Jesus gave His life in exchange for ours. He died so we could have life. New life, free from guilt, from fear, from death…free. It cost Him everything. And we give Him everything in return."*

Erin drew in a deep breath. Ah, yes, the *"what do you offer a god in exchange for someone's life"* question. What does he want?

Everything. Heart, mind, soul, strength. All of it.

Erin went still. Silent. *Is that the exchange? Not death, but living for you like Jeff does?*

He mused a moment. Another. Another.

Death would be easier. Can we do it that way?

Silence.

So you hold Cane's life over my head to make me obey you? That's blackmail.

Except I'm the one trying to make the bargain, aren't I?

Erin sat back in the seat. *But what good is my life to you? What do you expect me to do?*

Jeff's words again. *Trust me, He doesn't need us. He doesn't need anything. He offers us life and love and freedom and peace. It's not we* have *to serve Him. We* get *to serve Him. You give Him your life, and He gives it back to you clean. Which is where the joy comes from. And why I talk about Him all the time. He loves me, and He saved me from myself. There's not one regret. None.*

Erin looked out the window but didn't see the landscape. He saw himself. What had his life meant so far? What would it look like in the future? "More of the same." He shook his head. "More of the same. Nothing changes. Nothing matters."

But it could. And it does. Life. Light. Joy. Peace. Hope. Love. It's all here.

Erin closed his eyes. *What do I do?*

Trust. And wait.

* * *

Erin rolled into the surgical waiting room. The same players were in evidence as when he left: Harmon and Lacey Farrell, Jeff, the youth Erin didn't know, Detective Russo… Another man, maybe in his early twenties, maybe earlier, sat next to Jeff and the kid. Erin's eyes narrowed as he studied the younger man. *Maybe…could be. Rob. The one Cane took to Camp Grace. Yeah. That would figure. But who is the other guy?*

Detective Russo looked from his prayers as Erin entered the

room. Erin caught the man's eye and motioned for Jim to meet him across the room. Jim got up without fanfare and moved over to sit beside Erin. The detective's eyes played over Erin's newest bruises and cuts.

"Can't say out of trouble, can you?"

Erin shrugged. "Some secrets don't go without a fight."

"But you managed to solve the case, right?"

Erin looked at the floor. "Oh, yeah. All the evidence is now in the hands of the federal agents in Ft. Newton. Thanks for the hook-up, too. I needed it in the end."

Jim shrugged. "No problem." He eyed Erin in question, "You want to tell me?"

Erin drew in a deep breath. "It's what we figured. Those fatherless sons became fatherless by choice. They murdered their own father. For the money. Grandmother knew about it and covered for them."

Jim's voice softened. "I'm sorry, Erin. Not the sort of legacy a son wants to find out about his father."

Erin shook his head. "No, but in my case, I'm not surprised by it. Well, surprised by who, but not what." He motioned to the door to the surgical suite. "What's the word?"

"One of the team comes out every hour or so to let them know she's still alive, and how she's doing. Last report we got said they'd be another half hour or so and Dr. McMannon would come out and talk to the Farrells."

"How long ago?"

Jim looked at his watch. "An hour ago."

Erin's eyes widened. "You think something's wrong? Something happened?"

Jim waved a hand to indicate he didn't know. "All we can do is wait and trust."

Erin's head snapped. "What? What did you say?"

"Wait and trust." Jim cocked his head. "Is there a problem?"

Erin breathed out hard. "No. No. It's all I've wrestled with the past hour and a half on the way back from Ft. Newton. Trust. And wait. I'm not good at either."

Jim squeezed Erin's shoulder. "None of us are. It's an acquired skill." His eyes filled with sympathy as he added, "Acquired through having to do exactly that over and over and over."

Erin grumbled. "Which I'm beginning to figure out."

The door leading to surgery opened. A tall man walked out, his mask laying partially untied on his chest, his gown clean and without spot. *Guess the days of parading around in someone's blood are over, huh?*

Jeff and his parents looked up as the man entered. Jeff stood. His voice tightened but remained under control. "Is it over? The surgery, I mean."

The man nodded. "Dr. McMannon will be in shortly to give you the full report. They will be moving her to ICU after she gets out of recovery. You should be able to see her there."

Erin asked, "So it all went according to plan? The mass is gone and she's going to be alright?"

The man looked at Erin with some degree of suspicion in his eyes. Jeff waved at Erin. "He's family. Her brother. Next of kin, in fact."

The gowned figure nodded. "I see. I'll let Dr. McMannon give you all the details of how the surgery went. He can explain all we did."

A cold feeling swept through Erin. "But she's okay, right? She's fine. Tell me that much."

The man shook his head. "I'll let Dr. McMannon tell you…"

Erin grabbed a handful of hospital surgical scrubs at the man's chest and jerked himself to his feet. "No. You tell me. You tell me exactly what it is…"

He looked. *Standing. I'm standing. I'm standing up. I'm…*

The injured ankle gave way beneath him, and Erin collapsed back into his chair. He gritted his teeth and refused to express the pain shooting through him like an electrical charge. Up one side of his body. Across his chest. Down the other side. Like he had hold of two ends of a live wire and couldn't release them. His head arched back. He became vaguely aware of someone talking to him, someone else calling for a gurney, someone else calling for something—he had no idea what and didn't care… *I stood. I stood. I stood…*

As the attendants wheeled Erin off to wherever they were taking him, two words repeated in his head. Over and over. All he needed to hear.

Trust.

Wait.

* * *

Jeff watched the nurses take Erin from the room. *He stood. How? How did he stand?*

A familiar voice broke his thoughts. "I'll look in on his case as soon as they get him settled somewhere."

Jeff turned to face Dr. McMannon. Concern for Erin fled his mind. "How is she? Is she alive? Is she going to be okay? What happened?"

Rich took a seat on the arm of a couch. He looked at the floor, looked to meet Jeff's eyes. "We were able to remove the mass. Got it all; will have it tested, but I'm certain it's not malignant."

Jeff stared at his godparent. "And?"

Rich drew in a deep breath. "And before we could remove all of the mass she blew the aneurysm. The mass kept it contained. But once we pulled the vein free, it had nothing to hold it together."

Trust. Wait. Trust. Wait. Jeff's voice shook slightly. "And?"

Rich tossed his shoulders. "She bled a lot before we could get in to fix it." He looked at Jeff, put a hand on his shoulder. "I don't know what her condition will be until she wakes from the surgery." Rich squeezed Jeff's arm. "She might wake and be perfectly fine. She might not wake at all. It's up to God." He looked at Harmon, Lacey, and the others in the room. "I'm sure you've all been talking to Him about it the past few hours. He'll make His decision known one way or another."

Jeff went still. He felt frozen. His mind circled around and around the words, "might not wake …" *Might not wake. Might not wake. Might not…*

Jeff nodded and sat in the chair. He stared at the carpet but saw nothing outside his head. *Might not wake. Might not…*

No! Everything in him rebelled against the notion. *No! This is not how it's supposed to be. You promised! You said she was the one. I know You did. You promised. You can't change Your mind. You can't. God, please. Please. You promised…*

He heard his father's voice asking Rich, "Can we see her now before she's moved? It might be more private."

Jeff jerked out of his internal battle to look at Rich. "I want to see her now. Please." He stood and faced the surgeon. "I won't get in the way. But I need to see her. Now."

Rich chewed the inside of his cheek. "I'll take you back to recovery." The man looked at Harmon and Lacey. "You'll have to wait until she gets moved to ICU. Then I can let you in."

"Of course." Harmon nodded.

Rich motioned for Jeff to move through the door to the surgical suite. They passed by several closed but occupied rooms before coming to an open bay. Curtains separated the room into private recovery areas for up to ten people. Four were full. The occupants were in various stages of waking from anesthesia. Attendants could be heard asking, "Can you hear me? Do you know where you are? What level is the pain?"

Jeff blocked out all the voices.

Wait.

Trust.

Rich pulled back the curtain to the last area at the back of the room. Jeff stepped beside the bed.

Collin lay still before him. The IVs and monitors and tubes shouldn't have bothered him. He saw them all the time. He'd started more IVs than he could count. Monitors beeped and buzzed and recorded every vital sign requested. Pulse. Blood pressure. Oxygen levels. Respirations per minute. It shouldn't have bothered him.

But it did.

This was Collin. Collin, the love of his life. Xena, warrior princess. Street smart. Tough. Not stopping for anything Collin.

Wait. Trust.

Jeff moved to the head of the bed and stroked her cheek. She breathed steadily on her own. Slow breaths. Deep breaths. Life-giving breaths…

He knelt beside her and whispered, "It's okay, milady. It's over. You did great. Rich got the mass. It won't bother you again. And he fixed the aneurysm. You made it through. Now wake and show him what strong looks like. We've all been praying for you. Mom and Dad and Rob and Mano. Even Detective Russo stayed and prayed with us."

Jeff stroked her cheek again. "He said he was off duty." Jeff hesitated. "Erin went after what your grandfather left you. I haven't been able to talk to him about it, but I saw him and Jim Russo talking before Rich came in to tell us you were out of surgery."

Breath in. Breath out. Breath in. Breath out.

Jeff hung his head. "You have to wake, lady. We have a wedding to plan. I can't do it all by myself. I need you to…" His voice caught. Fear of loss, anguish over a future without Collin, overwhelming sorrow all cascaded down, shattering his defensive walls. Jeff closed his eyes against the pain. Tears ran down his face. "You have to wake, Collin. You have to. I need you. I love you. Wake up, milady. Please. Oh, God, let her wake up."

Sobs wracked his frame. "God, please. Please."

Rich's voice broke through Jeff's internal agony. "Come on, son. They need to move her. You can see her again in ICU. Let them do their job."

Jeff climbed to his feet. He leaned over and kissed Collin's lips. No response. He whispered, "I'll see you later, lady. I love you." He turned and followed Rich out of recovery.

* * *

TEN DAYS LATER

How many times does a heart beat in ten days? How many breaths do lungs take? How many times have I said, "I love you," and she still doesn't wake?

Jeff knelt beside the bed. His whole body ached with exhaustion. His shoulders drooped, his head rested against the bed Collin occupied in the hospital room. He forced himself to move into the chair next to her side so he could speak directly to her. Jeff held her hand in his, stroking her cheek with the other. "Lady, they want to move you to another facility. I'd bring you home. I would. But Rich is against it. He says I would wear myself and you out." Jeff snorted. "What does he know? I'd never get tired of taking care of you. I wouldn't."

Would there ever be an end to the tears which continued to choke him? Jeff tossed his head back, looked at the ceiling, looked at the floor. He cleared his throat. "Erin wants to take you to a private facility where you both can get the care you need. He's almost walking."

Jeff smiled, but even Erin's triumph wasn't enough to kill the pain. "Rich says when Garth knocked Erin over, he must have jarred loose something which compressed Erin's spinal column. Whatever. Erin calls it a miracle." Jeff shook his head. "He's got a long way to go to make up for all the time he's been in the chair, but he'll do it. He says he's doing it for you. He wants you to see him walk again. He's planning on walking you down the aisle when we get married."

Jeff stroked her cheek again. "Can't be a wedding if you don't wake up, milady. I know you're in there. I know you are. I know you're going to beat this thing. You have to. Rob needs you. Mano says you have to make it back. Says you owe him free throw lessons. Leesa wants to know where you are and why you're not coming over to the house anymore."

He closed his eyes tight against the tears. "I love you, Collin. They're going to throw me out of here soon. I've been banned from spending the night here. Seems I snore or something ." He squeezed her hand.

The curtains to the bay opened, and Erin entered in his wheelchair.

Jeff's eyebrows raised in question. "Where's the walker?"

Erin grimaced. "I got worn out at rehab. I wanted to come and tell Cane goodnight. And give her the latest news about what remains of the Winger family."

Jeff cocked his head. "New news?"

"Patrick is off the hook. He may have tried to help Robert deceive Cane into thinking her memories were faulty, but he had nothing to do with trying to have her killed. Or so he insists, and the prosecutor agrees with him. No charges."

Jeff wasn't sure how to respond so didn't. Erin continued, "Same thing with Richard's wife." Erin's voice darkened. "There's no proof she had anything to do with Cane or knew about the murder of Jeremiah Winger. I'm not as convinced as the investigators are. They may visit the charges again, in the case evidence does show."

"Garth and Gareth?"

Erin shook his head. "Yeah, they didn't know about it. Or so Richard tells the story. Maybe the one honorable thing he's done in his life, to not implicate his wife and kids. Little late in coming."

Jeff considered well. "Are you going to make them all move out? Take possession of the houses? I know legally they belong to Collin, but you think that's what she would want? "

Erin slipped beside his sister and took her free hand. He intertwined his fingers with hers. "I'm starting to understand more of what my sister would want and why. Not sure I agree with it all yet, but I understand where it comes from." He gave a self-conscious grin. "I told you I accepted the Lord, didn't I?"

Jeff smiled his first genuine smile for the day. "Yeah, I think you mentioned something about it. Once or twice. Or more."

Erin's grin faded as he looked back at his sister. "I thought I made this grand bargain, my life for hers. I forgot what you said about He already holds us all." His eyes softened as he looked at Collin. "This isn't what I meant by letting her live." He looked at Jeff, his mouth in a set line. "But He keeps telling me to wait. To trust and wait." He squeezed Collin's hand. "I didn't know it would be this long."

Jeff hated himself but knew he had to ask. For Erin's sake had to ask. "You sorry you made the deal?"

"No. Never." Erin shook his head. "Okay, so maybe it was stupid thinking I could bargain God into something. I mean, who am I? But He took my offer. I'm learning how little it actually amounts to…what I had to offer, I mean. He doesn't need me. Doesn't need anything I do. Still gave me my sister back. What kind of God does that?"

"One Who loves you more than you love yourself."

Erin lay Collin's hand down and patted it. "She's going to make it through, Jeff. I know she is. God isn't keeping her around so I'll keep my side of the bargain. He has plans for her. And for you. I know He does. It's why He keeps saying, 'Trust. Wait.' I know it."

You have to. It's all you've got, isn't it Erin? Jeff nodded. "Yeah." He tried to put conviction in his voice, but he and Erin both knew he didn't feel it. Not after ten days. And her heart stopping for a full minute…twice. The nurses hadn't tried to revive her, either. Collin had a standing DNR order. Jeff wanted to rail and argue her order hadn't applied to *this* situation. But no one listened. And all he got from above was *Wait. Trust.*

So hard, Lord. So hard. I know You're there. I know You care. Why so long? Why no answers?

Why are you asking why?

Because I hurt. And I'm scared. Scared what You think is best won't be what I want. And I don't know if I can handle it.

Wait. Trust.

Trust You? Or trust myself to handle it with You? Lord, please.

Erin half-whispered something. Jeff looked at him sharply. "What? I missed what you said."

Erin shrugged slightly. "If you had to choose…one or the other…could you?"

Jeff glared at Erin and snapped, "What kind of stupid question is that?"

Erin dropped his head. "You've walked with Him a long time.

You've only known my sister a couple of months. I guess it is a stupid question. I'm sorry."

Jeff's insides turned cold. He stared at Collin's face; still, silent, drooling a little on one side. He reached up and wiped the drops from her mouth. All the sounds of the hospital died away. Erin's question hung in the air. But he'd asked the wrong question. Not could he. Would he? Who did he love more? Who had first place in Jeff Farrell's heart? God? Or Collin?

Jeff felt his guts being ripped apart. *Don't ask, Lord. Don't ask me. You already know the answer before I say it. Don't make me choose. I don't want to face it. Face You. Face her.*

But God wouldn't let up. *Who? Who do you choose?*

Why? You know.

Because you need to know. You need to speak the truth to yourself and Me. Because I do already know.

Erin cleared his throat. "I'm sorry, Jeff. I'll leave you two alone. I can see her in the morning."

Jeff waved Erin's goodbye off. "No. Wait." He drew in a long shaking breath, stood, and leaned over Collin. *You, Lord. I love her. But I love You more. If You need to…want to…take her, I will understand. And I will thank You and praise You and love You even then.*

Jeff brushed his lips against Collin's forehead. "I love you, lady."

Collin exhaled. A long, slow exhale Jeff would have sworn made a sound. His face froze in fear. "Collin? Collin did you…did you…"

She exhaled again. "Aaaaa…" Barely audible. "Aaaaa…" A long a sound.

Erin shook Jeff's arm. "What is it, man? What's happening?"

Jeff cut Erin's inquiry off sharply. "Wait. Shh." He looked back at Collin. "Say it again, lady. Try. Try again."

"Aaaaaaaa…mmmm"

Erin stared at Jeff in confusion. "What's she saying?

Jeff's mouth fell open. He threw his head back and laughed, gathered Collin into his arms, and hugged her as hard as she could stand. "Oh, lady! You're in there! I knew you would be. I knew it." Jeff let the tears of joy flow. Nothing could stop him.

A nurse came running in, disapproval on her face. "What is the meaning of this? You can't be carrying on like this."

Jeff continued to laugh. "I can. Oh, yes I can. Go tell Dr. McMannon Collin is alive and well. He'll want to know how wrong he's been. Call him."

The nurse gave Erin a sidelong look, but exited the room. Jeff hugged Collin a second time. "Oh, Collin, I love you! I love you!" He raised his head to Heaven and wept. "Thank You. Thank You."

Erin grabbed Jeff's arm. "What is it, man? What did she say?"

Jeff shook the tears off his face. "She said, 'aim.' That's what she said. Aim."

And he did.

246

* * *

If you enjoyed *Inheritance*, sign up for Colleen Snyder's newsletter to stay up with new books and new projects. It will also give you a place to talk to the author directly!

Emails will NOT be sold, shared, or used for any other purpose. Promise!

Go to: colleensnyderauthor.com and leave your email to sign up.

Did you miss the first book in the Collin Walker series?

<u>Verdict at the River's Edge</u>

What terrifies you?

In the dark recess of your soul, what is it that you've managed to avoid, to hide, to bury deep, never to be faced? And what if the Lord asked you to face that fear for no other reason than, "Because I'm asking?" What would you do?

Welcome to Collin Walker's world.

Collin Walker, a social worker from the inner city of Oakton, Ohio comes to Camp Grace for what is billed as "an extreme sports camp." Her single purpose: to show her ward, Rob Sider, that there is more to life than the streets "...show you can be strong and still love, win without cheating, and succeed in life without all the bells and whistles…" Collin has no way of knowing that God has other plans for her week: facing a lifelong terror of rushing rivers, and perhaps her greatest fear of all, the possibility of real love.

Available now on Amazon: <u>Verdict at the River's Edge</u>.
And here is a sneak look at the opening of the third and final installment in the Collin Walker series:

FRIDAY AFTERNOON

In the dark, Erin strained to hear. Hearing was the only sense they left him. Unable to move, he'd been bound in a fetal position with his knees buried to his chest, his arms wrapped around his feet. He lay on his side on a hard, unyielding surface. Mouth and eyes taped shut. *Thank You, Lord, I'm not a mouth breather like Cane.*

Where am I? What happened? The woman by the side of the road...two small children beside her. A car with the hood up. I stopped. The battery, maybe? Infant in the backseat. I looked under the hood.

That's it. That's all I remember.

Erin's world jolted. He felt the sensation of falling, of being dropped. The sudden stop at the bottom jarred his bones. Voices. He heard muffled voices. Near him? Above him?

"Can't happen. No pink slip. No registration. I can't crush a car without something to prove who it belonged to."

Crush? Car? Erin's eyes would have widened in fear if he could have opened them at all.

"I got five Benjamins that say I own this car, and I want it smashed."

"I don't care if you've got ten Benjamins. I can't crush a car without the proper paperwork. Not while the boss is here."

Silence.

"What time does your boss leave?"

"Come back around six with the Benjamins. Ten of them. I'll crush your car. You can leave it where it is for now. I'll tell the big man that you went to get the title."

"You got a deal. I'll see you tonight."

"What's so important about this car? It's a sweet roadster. I'd almost pay to take it off your hands."

"I have instructions to stay and watch this car be crushed. Then I load it on a flatbed and drive it to Oakton. Supposed to drop it off at some house. My boss wants pictures. I wouldn't sell it to you for any price. It's not worth crossing my boss."

"Suit yourself. See you tonight."

Footsteps walked away. A diesel motor came to life. Drove away. Someone banged the trunk of the car that served as Erin's prison. "Shame. She is a sweet ride. Wonder who he made mad?"

Footsteps walked away. Silence again.

Crushed?

Also by Colleen Snyder:

Finding Freedom, a novella, part of the *A Hero's Heart* Kindle Set...

FINDING FREEDOM

The stakes couldn't be higher.

Thirty-six years of marriage. Two children. Two granddaughters, the lights of her life.

Her home. Her friends. Her church. Her God?

Will she throw it all away for freedom? Freedom from abuse? From neglect? Subjection?

And what if he comes after her?

For Sheridan (Dash) Warren, the options have never been more clear. Stay, keep the status quo and watch her life descend further and further into the soul-stealing denial of all that is Dash Warren, all that is life and light and joy and peace…

Or abandon it all in a desperate flight to save what little of her true self she has left. If God is for her, who can be against her? But is God for her? Is He leading her out, or is it her own voice she's listening to?

And what will her husband, Roy, do if she does run? He's been violent before. Will he come after her? What if he catches her? What will her future look like? Will she even have a future?

Dash must make the decision of her life. Can she make the right one?
<u>Finding Freedom</u> available in paperback and Kindle.

ABOUT THE AUTHOR

Colleen K. Snyder has always had a passion for writing. She authored two previously published books: *Journey to Amanah: The Beginning* and *Return to Tebel-Ayr: The Journey Continues* (B&H Publishing). She lives on a "ranchette" in California and is the juniorest ranch hand. She serves on her church prayer team, writes the weekly prayer letter, facilitates a women's Bible Study and exercises a ministry of intercessory prayer. She has worked as a factory line worker, pharmacy technician, USAF missile systems analyst, janitor, nanny, teacher, accounting manager and anything else the Lord required. Her son, Bear and his wife Krystal, their two daughters, Mara and Kaylynn, and her daughter Katie all live in Ohio.

Colleen's story is for His glory, always.

Connect with her on Facebook at Colleen K. Snyder, Author and on her website colleensnyderauthor.com.